THE BOOK OF OTTO AND LIAM

PAUL GRINER

SARABANDE BOOKS
Louisville, KY

THE

BOOK

OF

OTTO

AND

LIAM

Library of Congress Cataloging-in-Publication Data

Names: Griner, Paul, author.
Title: The book of Otto and Liam / a novel by Paul Griner.
Description: Louisville, KY : Sarabande Books, 2021
Identifiers: LCCN 2020016775 (print) | LCCN 2020016776 (e-book)
ISBN 9781946448767 (paperback) | ISBN 9781946448774 (e-book)
Classification: LCC PS3557.R5314 B66 2021 (print)
LCC PS3557.R5314 (e-book) | DDC 813/.54–dc23
LC record available at https://lccn.loc.gov/2020016775
LC e-book record available at https://lccn.loc.gov/2020016776

Cover and interior design by Alban Fischer.
Illustrations on pages 16, 45, 82, 105, 148, 264, 271, 291, and 355 by Cassidy Meurer.
Illustrations on pages 30 and 31 by Laura Hill.
Illustrations on pages 69, 179, 248, and 352 by Paul Griner.
Printed in Canada.
This book is printed on acid-free paper.
Sarabande Books is a nonprofit literary organization.

This project is supported in part by an award from the National
Endowment for the Arts. The Kentucky Arts Council, the state arts
agency, supports Sarabande Books with state tax dollars and
federal funding from the National Endowment for the Arts.

Third Anniversary—Leather

OCTOBER 10, 2018

I drive my usual three loops around the high school parking lot, windshields flashing in the sun, cars baking in the surprising October heat, on my final pass five late boys slow-walking their way up the massive granite steps toward the stone columns and big white doors. Freshmen, probably, thirteen or fourteen, their bodies still all angles and flat planes. Younger, they'd run, but they're old enough now to be abashed. One in a blood-red shirt laughs.

When I was a boy, my school looked just like this, brick and stately, and the doors were wooden and always unlocked, but now if you arrive after the start of school you have to be buzzed in and they're made of steel. Behind them a row of metal detectors.

Two patrol cars in the lot, which is usual, one parked, the other circling, which is not. I pass the second, heading in the opposite direction, nod at the driver, eyes invisible behind his blue-lensed Oakleys, drive on. Birdsong, from the cluster of maples where the leaves are beginning to orange—a late fall this year, as it was then—the muddy scent of the creek, high from the recent rains, and the long thin shadow of the flagpole and the broader rippling one of the flag, the flag at half-staff.

When I'm done with my final circumnavigation, the second cop rolls up behind me, following me the last fifty yards past the long brick front of the school and out the tree-lined drive to the stoplight. I turn right, past the Wendy's, where the shooter got a drive-through coffee after circling the high school parking lot three times, spooked by a single parked cop, before changing his plan and heading to the elementary school.

The coffee they found in his cupholder, still warm, next to two

Remington 870 Wingmaster pump-action shotguns. He brought a third one with him, along with two Glock G17 Gen4 MOS's and an AR-15, this one sawed-off, stuffed into a blue duffel bag. The two shotguns in the car were propped up on the passenger side, beside ten boxes of red shells, low-bottomed brass and with a tendency to jam; some had spilled onto the floor.

At the next light I flip on my blinker, turn. Behind me blue and white lights flash on, though the cop doesn't sound his siren, and I pull into the post office parking lot, nose in, to show I won't flee. Car angled in behind me, so it would be hard for me to get away, he makes me wait, the giant flag's undulating shadow passing over the car again and again. Full staff, here.

I lower my window to the smell of baking pavement. He puts on his hat like he's crowning a Pope, steps out, shuts his door and approaches in my sideview mirror, backlit by the early morning sun. He rests his hand on the butt of his pistol as he walks, and it surprises me when he kneels behind the car for a few seconds, before standing and coming around to the driver's side.

Hello, sir, he says, his voice unexpectedly high. He squares his shoulders as if he knows that, making himself taller, and his leather holster creaks under the pressure of his hand; pink grips on the handle of his Glock, cancer in the gene pool.

He says, Do you know why I stopped you?

No sir, I say. I don't.

That school? We like to know who comes and goes. Keep everybody safe.

That's good, sir. I understand.

Do you have any business there?

Not really.

I see. And are you in the habit of driving around school parking lots?

Some of them, sir. On certain dates.

Today, for instance, he says. It's not a question, more an expression of disdain, which I understand. Most of the cops around the school I know or have met; not him.

Yes sir, I say. Today for instance.

And is there any reason you'd cover up your license plate before doing so?

I'm sorry?

Your license plate. He nods toward the back of the car. It's covered by a red rag. That's usually a sign of gang activity.

Hoaxers, I say. Assholes.

Excuse me?

Sorry, sir. Never mind. I grab the door handle to get out and check but, alarmed, voice raised, he tells me to stay where I am and clamps his left hand to the door frame, the right one gripping the butt of his gun, his knuckles white. He leans closer, his shadow passing over me, and goes rigid when I shiver, wondering what's got me spooked, his glance darting from me to the seat beside me to the art supplies piled in the back, for work I'm supposed to get done today but won't. A new urgency to his voice when he speaks next. Do you have any weapons, sir?

He's got reason to be afraid; a cop is shot to death every six days. No sir, I say. I don't like guns.

I see. And so why is today the day you drove by this high school?

Because today is the anniversary.

Of the shooting, he says. But not there.

No sir. That school doesn't exist anymore.

That's right, he says. They tore it down. And do you know why?

Oh yes, I say. I do know why.

For a long time he doesn't speak, and I swear he's developed a five o'clock shadow since he stopped me, his beard like dark splinters under the skin. That hyper-masculinity of so many police, which I've never liked, though I've come to respect. Three cops lay on the ground in their uniforms that day after seeing the classrooms, overcome; they might have passed for dead, except for the lack of blood. Still, as he stares at me with that hard cop look, I think, *What do cops know?*

Other cars go by, drivers turning their heads, wondering. At last he nods, straightens up, his breath whistling through his nose, which appears to have been broken and poorly set. Listen, he says. It's kind of ghoulish, this disaster tourism. Before I can respond he says, I went in to that school that day. You should really let all of this go. He sounds older than my father, older than time, and now his body is generating terrific heat. A wave of it passes over me.

I say, I was there that day too. His forehead contracts as he tries to place me. That morning, I say. To drop off my son. He was wounded in the shooting.

Oh, he says, a small sound, but it's like a big hole in a tiny balloon; he deflates all at once, his entire posture changing. I'm sorry, sir, he says, his hand coming off the gun. What's your name?

He'd know if he'd been able to run the plates, though even then I might have made him forget, my new superpower: with a few words, I wipe out memories, though never my own, or my spooky, unsettling thoughts. *If I pulled a pistol, I could pop two in your chest before you ever saw it coming.* The strangest thing; despite my hatred of guns, I think about them almost daily, and often in the weirdest ways.

Otto, I say. Otto Barnes. Liam's father.

He takes off his hat and puts it on his fist, turns it with his other hand, thinking of something to say. A white tan line cuts straight across his forehead, and his dark cropped hair glistens with sweat. Twice, he opens his mouth to speak, twice he closes it again and remains silent. His forearm twitches when he puts the hat back on.

Officer? I say. I'm sorry you had to see those things, and I'm sorry my visit brought them back.

Which is true, I'm sorry, though it's also true I'm not, two contradictory truths, both parallel and in opposition, as far as the east is from the west: I don't really want his pain, but I want my own pain even less. The fundamental paradox of my current life.

No, he says, his voice thick now, like he's speaking through a mouthful of molasses. He tries to say something else, can't, shakes his head instead. A tear trickles from under his blue sunglasses. He puts one hand on my shoulder, squeezes, and walks away.

Back in his car, he tosses his hat on the dash and turns to look out the passenger window. Traffic streaming by, drivers who don't notice him still speeding, others who catch a glimpse of the squad car at the last second tapping their brakes. I put my car in gear and make my way toward the exit, sure he isn't seeing a single present-day thing.

I'm not either, and end up back outside my new apartment without remembering the drive back, how I got there at all, if I even completed my normal route: high school, Wendy's for a coffee I will not drink, two winding miles to the elementary school, or rather, the patch of landscaped park where it used to stand. I want to understand and doubt I ever will.

I have a handful of mail, which means I'd gone back to the post office and checked my box. I have no memory of that, either, or of ripping off the red rag and tossing it aside, my building fury at the hoaxers. Most of the mail will be trolls or junk, some of it might be important, but I throw it all away and text Lamont.

Bring the bourbon, I tap out, knowing he will.

Interim 1

Number of school shootings in the three years since: 142
Number of school children killed: 217

Incoming

May was at her desk when the call came, deep into a manufactur-ability analysis for a laser-surgery prototype, work she loved—work she got to *engineer up*, as Otto said—meticulous and specific. She ignored the ringing phone at first, but the light kept blinking and they wouldn't leave a message, so at last she picked up; she didn't catch the detective's name, just his words about Liam.

Liam's been shot, he said. I'm not a doctor, but I think he's going to make it.

She stood so fast her chair fell over. What about the damn apples? she said.

Zhao, cubicled beside her, knew something was wrong. He was torn: Leave to give May privacy, or stay in case she needed him? Who could turn away from it? He should, though he wouldn't. Before he judged himself, he reached over and saved their shared work on her computer with a couple of keystrokes and was glad she didn't notice. He didn't want to miss this. What an awful person he was, sitting still so he wouldn't miss a thing. He swallowed. He would never admit this to anyone.

The detective was used to people saying odd things. He said his name again and May seemed not to hear him. Who are you? she said. How do you know?

Call me Nash, he said. I know because I'm at the school.

Is Liam there? Can I speak to him? I want to say I'm sorry about the apples.

Nash said, He's on his way to the emergency room. St. Luke's, I think.

It was the first piece of misinformation she received, though far from the last.

What's your cell phone number? Nash asked.

What? Why do you need that?

Was he about to ask her for a date? Her heart was pounding its way through her ribs and the phone turned slippery in her hand, as if she was gripping a fish.

Follow-up information, he said. I was going to call so you'd have my number.

She gave it to him and he called as they were talking. Got it? he said.

She did. She was already throwing her silver thermos into her bag and Zhao had stacked the articles she'd been reading in case she needed them, which she didn't notice either. It shamed him that he wished she did.

Liam had wanted to decorate her thermos, but she liked its austere look. Why hadn't she let him? What kind of mother denied her kid that? It had been a small thing and she'd had a hard time explaining it, that though she loved every cell in his miraculous body, she also wanted a little separation, a little something that was just her. Her old self, still present in the eight-year-old reality of *him*. Now, tearing out of her office, she saw that that was not only wrong, but an impossibility. There was no blood-brain barrier with your child, your molecules were indistinguishable.

She stood a long time sweating beside her car in the unusual heat, perplexed by her key ring. Which key opened the door? She couldn't decipher it. Then she remembered the car key was in her purse and had an automatic unlock button and that she didn't need it anyway because she left her car unlocked while at work.

She had to use both hands on the gearshift, her hands shook

so badly. She put it in reverse and glanced in the mirrors and said, Don't cry. Your vision will blur and you won't be able to see the road.

That worked. She didn't cry the entire way.

Mystery Woman

I knew I'd find the woman in the videos, with her stunning face and soothing arguments, her honey tongue and heart of gall. Kate, who in one video denies Liam's existence, in another denies mine, and in all of them denies that the school shooting happened or that our pain was real, inspiring hoaxers to seek me out, to confront me, to finally break me and make me swear the shooting never happened.

I hadn't cared that much about her at first, only later. Then I made it my business to find her, though I didn't know it would take so long. Years.

She became my obsession.

The Full Catastrophe

OCTOBER 2011

Liam at four in the back seat, singing.

Christopher Lombus
he sailed the ocean bloom
and found a continary
in 1492.

A deer bounds up the hill at the sound of our approaching car, his black tracks crossing grass silver with dew, and May smiles at me. A sunny midweek October day, the crisp air warming, the three of us on our way to pick apples.

After I'd dressed him for preschool, while I searched among my drawings and billing statements for my keys, the front door opened and Liam hurried out; he wasn't supposed to leave without us. I found him standing in the driveway. Green Crocs, blue shorts, blond head tilted back, looking up at the big cumulous clouds speeding by, like a child's drawing of how the world should be.

What are you looking at? I asked.

He said, Clouds, flying away.

His eyes were like two fresh buds. We'd play hooky, I decided, though at first May told me I was setting a bad precedent and asked to be dropped at work—the engineering gene—then called in to take a personal day, yet seemed to regret it, fiddling with her phone while glancing out the window at the fall colors.

Hey, I said. You can go to work if you want to. No harm, no foul.

No, she said, and dropped her phone in her purse and her purse to the floor and settled back and stretched her legs like a cat. This is good for me. She put one hand back between the seats for Liam to squeeze. Good for us, she said.

11

It is, I said, and she leaned over to kiss me. We were on the Cherry Valley Turnpike, her favorite route to O'Neill's, past rolling fields of corn stubble glinting in the sun and the dark shiny earth, a sinuous line of yellowing weeping willows that traced a stream. After a long curve a small white wooden church came into view on a hill, with a single thin stained-glass window, the deepest blue. Navy on some days, sapphire on others, today it looked Egyptian. I'd driven this route because she loved it and I loved to hear her say what she did each time we passed it.

If I was a painter, she said, I'd paint that church in this light.

She put her window down to take in the scented air: sun-warmed earth, leaf decay, burning corn stubble.

Liam stood on one of the round-runged wooden ladders picking apples; I held his waist through his fleece so he wouldn't fall. Already our bags were heavy with Jonamac and the tiny Gala, with Honeycrisp and Macoun, now we were on our favorites: Northern Spy. May didn't cook much, but she made the best apple pies. Overhead, skeins of southbound geese surged past, sounding their mournful cry; Liam watched them, an apple clutched in each hand. When he climbed back down, I made a quick sketch so I could draw or paint it later.

Later still we had May's tuna salad, inedibly salty, and then from the store kitchen warm apple fritters, so hot from cooking we passed them back and forth between our hands to cool them. Fresh cider pressed as we watched. After, we picked more, the apples warm from the sun, May with her fineboned hands.

When May was up on the ladder, I held her waist too, and pinched her ass through her jeans.

You stop that, she said, not meaning it; she thrust out her shapely ass and shook it. Mister, she said, you're not putting that one in your sketchbook.

It was so good to have her relaxed. I said, I'll make it apple-shaped. Liam said, You guys.

He sat under a freighted tree eating an apple, the dropped Macs around him like a red blanket. The clouds all gone now, a clear turquoise sky and the shadows lengthening across the tall, uncut bent grass, the ghost of winter on the cool breeze.

Liam slept on the ride back and we were silently happy. Home, I started a fire as Liam and May peeled apples. A blackbird with its sleek head tilted up and its yellow beak open for a pie chimney; Liam put it in after he helped her pick up the long peels spilling off the newspaper-covered table onto the floor.

After we cleaned up the pie-making mess and the pie was well started, I cooked dinner. My homemade red sauce, Liam's favorite. The scent of sautéing oregano and onions competing with baking cinnamon and apple, the fire crackling, May tapping on her laptop, the scratch of colored pencils on construction paper.

May liked Rao's sauce more than mine, a small bone of contention, but Liam had sided with me, which pleased me, though I was careful not to show it; marriage teaches you the respectful limits of celebration. I hummed as I cooked, but quietly, stirring in the garlic, which grew fragrant on the heat, and added minced carrots for sweetness and the tomatoes and some of the cooking water from the pasta to thin the sauce. I overheard Liam show May what he'd drawn.

Oh, good, it's a kitty, May said.

It's not a kitty, he said, it's a horse. Everyone knows that.

Oh yes, she said. Sometimes I mix up my animals. *Moo.*

Giggles from the other room.

———

When we were done eating, Liam rocked in his chair and collected his silverware and stacked his plates and aligned his rectangular glass with the seam of the table leaf. May's genes. We waited.

At last he said, Otto? He often called us by our first names, which made most of our friends laugh. You know I love your pasta, right?

Yes, Liam?

He picked up the last piece of crust on his plate and smelled it like a fine cigar and ate it. After he swallowed, he said, Well, I do and I always will, but some night, could we have May's pie for dinner *and* dessert?

May's huge smile was nine-tenths triumph.

After Liam's bath we read, *Owl Moon* and *Go, Dog. Go!*, my childhood favorite. Chilly air leaked in around the windows, so we added another down comforter to Liam's bed. We loved the big drafty house with its tiger maple floors and leaded glass windows, though they needed replacing and the heating bills were sometimes $500 a month. I'd replastered walls and painted inside and out and May had rejiggered the steel poles holding up the massive basement beams and first floor joists, and in the meantime it was ours.

When we were done, Liam said, Can I have *another* story? *The Snowy Day*, he said. It was one of my favorites too, the way Keats used simple blocks of color to illustrate the story—I'd learned a lot from it. But though it *was* a perfect day, it had to end, so we said no.

May did, actually. She's always been better about routines and schedules. Liam looked at her and said, Please, and she said, No, again and bent to kiss his high warm forehead.

He turned toward the wall before she could and said with his back to her, I hope you get a loose tooth.

———

Later, in front of the fire, shades drawn, we kissed. I had May's blouse off, but not her bra, and began sucking her taut nipple through the blue lace, which made her arch toward me, my hands on her back, each finger to a rib like piano keys. She tugged my hair and whispered in my ear. *Suck it really hard. So hard you get a mouthful of loose teeth.*

We both laughed about it, mouths against each other's necks to stifle the sound, but not too loudly. Liam came equipped with an inborn erection detection system, and we didn't want to wake him.

Radio Static While Picnicking beneath a Clear Blue Sky, Two Years Before It Happens

OCTOBER 2013

Detective Sawyer took the phone call at his messy desk, wrote notes on a yellow pad with faded circular coffee stains as he asked questions. A teenaged boy a neighbor was concerned about, threatening to shoot up his school.

She'd overheard him talking with another boy, and no, she couldn't identify the second one. They were outside her garage leaning against the wall, smoking. She'd thought of shooing them away, but remembered her own teen years, the urgent business of trying to grow up free from parental supervision.

They kept talking, now and then a tennis ball bonking against the shingles. She'd been sorting gardening tools and hadn't really listened until their casual conversation turned to shooting other kids, which scared her so much she hadn't moved, afraid they'd hear and hurt her. The whole time she was on the verge of sneezing because of the dusty grass-seed bag, so she'd pinched her nose. Now it looked bruised.

But this boy? the detective said, refocusing her. You saw him?

No, but I know his voice. He's a neighbor. I know his laugh. I heard his name.

Now Sawyer asked the important questions. Were his plans detailed? Did he have a specific date in mind? Did he talk about a specific weapon?

No, she said. He just said he wanted to kill a bunch of people at his school.

Anyone in particular?

She fell silent. Sawyer put his pen down and squeezed his purple stress ball. No, she said at last. Just the idiots who always gave him a hard time.

Idiots?

Well, not that word. Assholes, I think it was. Sorry.

It's okay, Detective Sawyer said, and put down the stress ball and took up the pen again. After a few more questions he thanked her and said he'd look into it.

Can you do me one favor? she said. He'd asked her to spell her name. Everyone said African Americans had crazy names but he hadn't heard this one before. Venny Bosc. Venny said, Can you not tell them I was the one who called?

Her fear worried him. She'd been scared when she overheard them talking, which was natural. The irregular rhythm of the tennis ball hitting the wall had come to terrify her, and when the boys moved away she found she'd been clutching a garden spade that she hadn't even remembered picking up, but she was still scared now, an hour or so later, even though she'd debated whether or not to call.

Everything else was general. Teenaged boys were trying to figure out how to become men and they blew off steam all the time, and even if he was a little off, counseling would be better than incarceration. But why was she still so afraid? When he leaned on his elbow he winced; he would have to get that looked at. Ms. Bosc? he said. Has he ever threatened you, or hurt anyone else? An animal?

Oh, no, Venny said. He's always been a good boy. Though lately he's been setting off a lot of fireworks. The back of my garage has scorch marks.

Okay, he said. Thank you. I'll make sure your name is left out of it.

He wondered if he could.

Kate

He never existed, your boy; she says in one video, addressing me directly in her educated east-coast voice. *You shouldn't fake pain, Otto. If that's your real name. It convinces people, and it's cruel.*

For a long time that video was one of only two clues I had to her, that and an earlier video that she'd made about 9/11, walking in lower Manhattan as taxis passed her, incurious crowds. In it, she raised question after question about the hijackers. I'd watched that years before the shooting, and remembered how reasonable she sounded. The way she made me think.

But at first I didn't even connect them. Thirteen years between the videos, after all; she'd aged. Later, it took some effort, but I put all the videos I ever found of her together in a loop on iMovie and as you watch them, you see her age. Just like me.

It was her necklace that finally did it, visible at the base of her throat, because her blouse was partially unbuttoned. A small silver horseshoe on a beaded turquoise chain. I'd watched both videos so many times and for some reason the connection finally clicked, and once it did, I couldn't stop noticing it.

Remember that necklace. Turns out I'm not the only one who noticed it, and it ends up being important.

Letters

Hey, how's it going today?

I wonder sometimes what days are hardest for you, weekdays, when all the kids are back in school, or weekends, when you have more time to think about it all?

I just wanted to let you know that we are here for you.

We will always be here for you.

Watching, waiting.

And sooner or later, everyone will realize you began lying the second you opened your mouth about your "son."

And then we will take you out.

Hands-On Learning

The train horn sounded and we whooshed by a line of stopped traffic on a narrow road between high rows of ripe corn. Pickup trucks and sedans, the crossing bars down and lights flashing and the corn bending in the wind, and then it was back to the click-clicking of the wheels over the rails, the car swaying into turns.

It was the first fall for Liam in his new school and we were on a field trip to DC, me as his chaperone because May couldn't take the time off from work.

I haven't been in my job a full year yet, she'd said. I have presentations.

I was supposed to have client meetings, but I rescheduled and said nothing about it. Not just altruism, I thought, feeling the humming train in my bones. There was a *lot* of altruism, I wanted her to do well at work she loved, but I also knew that at some point I'd need to say it was my turn. In even the best of marriages—which ours was—you had chits.

Cornfields spread out to the west, glowing in the slanting afternoon light, telephone lines dipped and rose and dipped beside the tracks, and I wondered if Liam would remember this train ride, if I would, or if for both of us it would fall into that vast black hole of memory. Into eternity.

Lamont shifted on the seat beside me. I didn't know him but our boys played together all the time and had asked to stay together, so we were sharing a room. The boys were across from us, Latrell towering over Liam, who wasn't short, lost in a game of *Lego City Undercover*.

Man, that school is funny, Lamont said, putting away his phone.

We were facing backward on the train and I had only half a seat because Lamont was so big; he'd played football in college.

How's that?

Being so sure they don't want the kids to be snobs.

Well, I said. I think that's a good thing.

I didn't want to argue since we were staying together, but I also didn't want to be quiet. To set an example for Liam; kids were always watching. Our hotel was slightly downscale, kitchenettes to save money, blocky furniture in the online pictures, which some parents weren't happy about; they were used to staying in better places. I thought Lamont might be among them.

Oh no, Lamont said, and slapped both his knees with their big purple scars. I agree. Sorry. Didn't mean that. Just that around our town you usually have to pay big money to find bias against snobs. You have to go to private schools for that.

I laughed. I've always been able to tell pretty fast if I'd be friends with someone. It made me happy to be going off to DC with him and our boys. I didn't really have friends in town yet and it was something to look forward to.

Lamont said, We should switch seats. He ran his hand over the two small gray circles in his hair, which looked as if he'd leaned against a chalkboard. The boys should be facing backward, he said. In case the train derails, they'll be safer.

Okay, I said. Hadn't thought of that.

I don't like trains, he said. I like to be in control.

So we switched with the boys. Now I could see where we were heading and I liked that more. I'd only sat next to Lamont facing backwards so Liam and Latrell could sit together. For a few more miles we watched the farmland and small towns racing toward us, a stand of cattails beside a copper-colored river bending in the wind from the passing train, before the river disappeared and the landscape became more densely populated suburban sprawl as the train picked up speed.

No, Lamont said. Sorry, and slapped my leg. Gotta switch again. If the train derails, we'll be missiles headed at our kids. Not good. They wouldn't survive that.

I knew the feeling of trying to love your boy into safety, but I couldn't resist teasing him after we switched back to our old seats. You played college football, right? I said. Tight end? Receiver?

Look at me. He spread his hands over his girth. Offensive lineman.

Should have been obvious, I realized. The fat girdling his midsection. Too bad, I said. If we derail, I was thinking maybe you could catch the boys.

You're a grief artist, aren't you?

He had such a stern face I thought, *Uh-oh.* You never knew if someone liked being teased until you did it, and by then it was too late.

He held that face so long I started to apologize, until he grinned and said, Nah, and tapped me with one forearm, hard enough to rock me. Just ragging you.

Right away in the hotel room with its two sets of bunk beds and chunky dark wooden bureaus, the boys started roughhousing.

Lamont and I were unpacking, putting folded shirts in the sticking drawers, and Lamont said, You boys stop that. Someone's bound to get hurt. He punched the drawer closed with the side of his fist.

The boys didn't listen and Liam's head hit the corner of the bed, hard.

I told you boys, Lamont said.

Yes sir, you did, Latrell said.

He said, Yes sir, and, No sir, a lot, and I felt momentarily inadequate, that I'd been lax, until I realized that Latrell hadn't listened to his father any more than Liam had me. Liam knelt on the rug and rubbed his head over and over. Lamont stepped over him to put his suitcase away. Seeing he wasn't getting much sympathy, Liam said, I don't know whether or not I have a concussion, but I can tell you this, I don't remember much about yesterday.

Don't worry, Latrell told him. I didn't hit my head and I can't remember much of yesterday either.

What do you know? Liam said. You're just a big hunk of fuck.

Uncle Sam Smackdown

OCTOBER 1, 2015

Nine days before the shooting, the Navy notified the shooter that they'd rejected his application.

Home Visit Checklist,
Two Years Before It Happens

OCTOBER 2013

Two days after Venny Bosc's call, Detective Sawyer sat for ten minutes looking out the rain-speckled window at the trees all black with rain and finished his coffee while he turned the events over in his mind; it was good to shape things. Then he typed up his report, including his visit to the boy's house. Venny Bosc's name appeared in the report, it had to, but it would never come out.

Both parents home, both attentive and polite, the schoolteacher mother clearly distraught, the father, a former Air Force officer, short and wiry and contained. On his office wall hung a small, framed medal; the commendation said it was for meritorious service in Niger.

Sawyer had a dim notion where that was. The father straightened the citation's plain wooden frame with his thumb and said, We moved around a lot when he was younger, but we've been here since I got out. Four years now. He'd become a commercial pilot, but left that for the private security business.

No signs of trouble in the house then, which nonetheless troubled Sawyer. More school shooters came from two-parent homes than not, each time there was another one the profiles were updated, but the truth was there wasn't a profile.

Some were bullied, some were bullies, some were both bullied and bullies. Some had loving parents and others parents who beat them. Churchgoers and atheists, strict or lax, moving a lot or stable, popular or loners or jocks or somewhere in between, no more pattern than rain. Some made detailed plans and some seemed impulsive and some were psychotic, though they did always tell. Sometime, somewhere, somehow, they all let their plans slip.

A cry for help maybe, or the thrill of teasing, the rush of power, you never knew. So many teen boys were awed by violence, they talked about all kinds of things. As a boy, Sawyer had filled his father's old cologne bottles with gasoline and turpentine, thinking they might make bombs, and tucked them behind berms and lit fuses for them and waited. Maybe this was that, but you had to check.

This boy, once he knew a detective was there, looked sad and scared, not guilty. Not angry. And apologized right away. Freckles and skinny arms and a baggy mustard-colored tee shirt with a famous skateboarder's face. Sawyer's own boys had that shirt. So much Axe body spray it was a wonder the walls still had paint.

No TV in his room, unusual in this neighborhood, steroidal houses and multiple late-model cars and nearly all white. Nearly all school shooters were white, so that was something to look out for, but no TV meant that in here, at least, he wasn't playing violent video games. Yet that wasn't a clue either, really. Girls played violent video games and they never shot up schools, so what was up with that?

Sawyer asked if there were guns in the house and the parents said no and the boy did too. The irony of a Black man asking about guns in a white household, he never said a thing about it. A joke might lighten the mood, but sometimes a little tension was a useful tool.

You don't mind if I search your room then? That would be okay?

The slightest hesitation before the boy nodded, it could have been anything.

So Sawyer searched. Under the mattress, in each drawer, his backpack, the closet. Some porn under his sweaters, that was probably what had caused him to hesitate, which surprised Sawyer. Most boys found porn on the internet these days, his sons did. Hell, he did from time to time, but the magazines were old-school. He tried to make sure the parents didn't see the magazines when he lifted the sweaters; they each sat on one arm of a stuffed chair, still as statues. No guns, no bombs, no fireworks; maybe the other boy was the one supplying them.

Sawyer hadn't asked about the other boy and didn't think he would. Doing so might tell this one it was his neighbor Venny Bosc who'd made the call, and besides, this was the boy who'd unnerved her.

From a bedside table drawer Sawyer took a leather-bound journal and read through it page-by-page, long enough to see that nothing in it indicated planning. Frustration, grandiosity mixed with searing self-criticism, anger at being cut from the baseball team. Each of those Sawyer remembered from his own teen years, markers of depression, he knew now, but also markers of standard teen mileposts. Which way would they send him? That, you never knew.

Also, mad love for a girl the boy hadn't yet had the courage to talk to, Barb Brown. Her daily schedule, the way her brown hair hung halfway down her back, the warmth he felt when she turned her smile on him. Her freckles. The room was so quiet then. The boy and the boy's parents waiting and watching as he made his slow way through the book, their slow breathing, the crinkling of the turning pages.

It had a lot of pen-and-ink drawings. He studied those too, and took pictures of a few with his phone. Some of them were really good, none violent. Some were of birds or animals, a few he guessed were of the girl and some were of heavily muscled men, perhaps the man this awkward skinny boy hoped to turn into.

You know, he said to the boy, I always wished I could draw. Still do. That ibis you did? And the ones of the rafting trip? He tapped the notebook. You're good. Keep at it. You have a gift.

He put it back in the drawer and closed the drawer with his

fingertips and tapped it, twice. If there were problems, and there were always problems, even the smoothest-looking life had them, you always wanted to point them toward a way out. Ways, if you could. But the drawing would do. Really, I mean that, he said. You could have a career in front of you.

Typing up his visit notes, Sawyer wondered why he'd said that, if it wasn't too much. What kid believed a detective had a good eye for drawing talent? He laughed at himself. Well, he'd tried. He'd wanted to ask the boy why he used pen and ink to draw instead of pencil, and perhaps he should have, the start of a conversation. Maybe if he had, the kid would come to him some day about whatever was troubling him, but he doubted it. He'd find others to talk to first.

Sawyer put the report in the system just in case, including the bit about the drawing. If another call ever came in or if the boy got caught stealing or vandalizing a store or a car or a neighbor's house, it would be another red flag, the slow but steady movement from stray talk to tough talk to criminal behavior. Something to watch for, to raise the alert level, a pattern. But his gut told him that wouldn't happen here, not with this boy. Though you never knew. He trusted his gut, but sometimes his gut didn't deliver.

White Ibis
Corkscrew Swamp Sanctuary
Naples Fl
Jan 5 2013

In the Beginning

OCTOBER 10, 2015

Liam lay on his back in the hospital bed in a recovery room, strapped to various beeping machines, one shoulder huge with gauze, much of the rest of him covered in blood. His face, his hair, what was left of his clothes, not his pale chest or hands. The nurse said they'd cleaned him up as best they could but he had numerous facial fractures and they worried about hurting him, so they hadn't yet cleaned his face. It looked like someone had dumped a vat of purple Kool-Aid on him.

He'd already had one operation and they thought there might be more. I wanted to hold him, but I couldn't, and even if I could, I wasn't sure where I could touch him that wouldn't hurt. *Come back!* I thought, but was too shy to say aloud. Later, social constraints would disappear for me, but just then they still held.

Why the facial fractures? I asked. The nurse had told me her name, but I'd forgotten it. Or it was another nurse? Time crawled and then sprinted, a slug and a cheetah, and amid all the confusion, faces blurred together. Police milled in the hallway, radios squawking. A man shouted, *She's coming! It's a mother! Cover her up! It's a mother!*

Was he shot in the face? I asked.

I remembered coming into the kitchen once to find Liam standing before the open fridge wearing his swim goggles and a snorkel.

Oh no, she said. Shoulder. We don't know about the facial fractures, how they happened.

Orbital bone, palatine bone, cheekbone, nose, jaw. She listed them off matter-of-factly. On the underside of his wrist was a smeared map of the world in fine black ink; I'd drawn it on him

32

that morning. South America and the US had been rubbed off, Canada was half-bloody. He'd been disappointed that we couldn't play hooky and go apple picking again—to make it a tradition, to do here in his new town what we'd done in our old one—and the drawing had been a small consolation. It looked like a temporary tattoo. Show Latrell, I'd said. He'll be impressed.

I'd wanted to go apple picking too, had suggested it, but May nixed the idea. Rigidity had returned and Liam wasn't the only one who was disappointed, though he'd overcome his more easily than I had mine, drawing a flower in the ten minutes after breakfast before leaving for school, a red tulip, May's favorite. I'd sat and sulked. Did I regret it? Not yet. There was a before and an after, but I still wasn't fully in the after. I kept thinking I'd find a reset button to end the nightmare.

From the hallway came raised voices and a shriek of agony, and my heart flatlined. It sounded like a hawk, but I knew it was the mother, another parent, getting the final news. I thought, *They can't all die.* She shrieked again so loudly it seemed as if her spine was being ripped out. I supposed it was.

Pull harder, I thought, to the hawk-god destroying her. With his bloody beak and sharp claws busy elsewhere, maybe we could slip away unnoticed, though my own spine tingled with superstition and shame.

Can I touch his foot? I asked the nurse.

Yes, she said, typing notes on her iPad. That would be okay. His feet are fine, I've taken his toe temperature.

A long time later, I learned about toe temperature gradient, that the nurse was worried he'd die right there before me, but just then, all that vocabulary was still ahead of me.

In the hallway, someone shouted. *It's another mother!*

Liam was warm, warm. I was holding too tightly but I wanted

to feel his pulse. Later, the police would wonder about the bruise circling his ankle that developed over the next days, but I never told them where it came from, not even after I got to know Nash, the lead detective on the case. Pride and embarrassment, I guess, and the desire to have something with Liam that was just us, that had nothing to do with the criminal case he'd become part of.

Over the woman's sobs from the hallway, I heard May's voice. Where is he? she said. Where *is* he? Let me *through*!

She'd been to three emergency rooms, part of a group of parents rushing from one hospital to the next, most sent on to another, an odyssey with dozens of Ulysses. Nearly all ended with terrible news.

I'd been working with my phone turned off, but even so I made it to the hospital before her, which filled me with an obscure and shameful sense of power, as if my shock and fear were somehow purer because I came to them first. What was wrong with me? Dread, I supposed, or terror, terror and anger and trepidation and confusion. Latrell was dead, I knew that, though not much else, and I lost my breath from surging grief. A cop had pounded on the door to get me. He had a face, I'm sure, but I don't think I even saw it.

Kate

Sometimes I dream about her. Meeting her, confronting her, once about living with her. In that one, we had four boys and a rambling country house set amid golden wheat fields rising and falling over the surrounding low rolling hills. She wore a crisp white blouse with a stiff collar and black pants and black flats and a silver cuff on her left wrist that beaded with water as she rinsed the dishes and looked out at the cloud shadows passing over the rippling wheat.

The most recent dream was hyperviolent, a drill being pushed through her ear into her brain. I don't know who held it, someone else perhaps, or maybe me.

What can I say?

You don't control your dreams.

Escaping Education's Death Valley

OCTOBER 2, 2015

At dawn in the hotel room, dim yellow light leaked around the heavy curtains. They looked burgundy in that light, which was better than by day; then, they didn't appear to have been cleaned since they'd been installed. I pushed them aside to a view of metal roofs and air-conditioning units, ladders to other buildings, black roofs and white roofs, patterns and forms.

We had a full day ahead of us. The Smithsonian and the Newseum and the Spy Museum, the boys were looking forward to that one. I thought the Smithsonian might have things I'd want to sketch but wondered if I'd get time to. Lamont said he wanted to look through their drafting manuals; his medical sales job had an engineering component, and I decided he and May would be good friends. He took a long time to get upright in bed.

Coffee? I asked. May can't get up without it.

That would be nice. Thanks. Though it probably tastes like mud.

Lucky for me I rarely drink it, I said, pouring in the water.

You a Mormon?

I laughed. No. Hate the taste but love the smell. I pushed the buttons and the machine hummed and gurgled.

When I brought Lamont the mug he was rubbing both his knees, so hard it looked as though he was trying to raise a genie.

Bad today?

Bad every day, he said. His voice wasn't angry; it was just a fact.

How do you take your coffee?

Just like me, he said. Black as hell.

I laughed and let him drink in silence while the boys used the bathroom. May never liked to talk much before she'd had a cup or two either. I sketched the room and what I remembered of the hotel lobby from the night before, the big old-fashioned crystal chandelier that had once been elegant.

You're not sketching me, are you? Lamont asked.

No, I said. Though that tiger tattoo is something special.

It arced across his chest. Army, he said, and slapped it twice. Got it after my first parachute jump. Remind me to tell you about the crabs.

Crabs?

He nodded but didn't go on. From the bathroom came the sound of snapping towels and a howl of pain and the door opened and Latrell emerged grinning through a cloud of steam. He fetched Lamont his pants and Lamont leaned back and pulled them on over his feet and shins and knees and thighs and put his feet on the ground and arched his pelvis to get them up the last bit. He lifted his feet off the floor and lay still for another minute, the pants unzipped and unbuttoned, before he sat up and put his feet on the ground.

Latrell knelt to put on his socks and shoes. It looked practiced.

Lamont said, Thank you. When you're done, you need to change that shirt.

Latrell didn't look up. Nana packed it, he said. Lamont picked up one foot and Latrell worked on his sneaker.

Not that shirt, Lamont said. The undershirt. He put his foot down and wiggled it into the sneaker and lifted his other foot.

Mama packed it.

Because you asked. We talked about it. Sleep in that shirt, but boys don't wear pink by day.

Yes sir, Latrell said. He tied and retied both sneakers until his father was satisfied they were tight enough.

I thought about Liam's pink blanket, which he'd brought with him to sleep with, and wondered what Lamont thought of that.

Latrell didn't have a blanket, which had impressed me, and now I guessed his shirt served the same purpose. I thought of saying something, but people got to raise their own kids. Eventually, Lamont got out of bed. It took half an hour, from start to finish.

Is it like that every day? I asked. From football? I said.

Yeah.

The price you paid, I said.

It shocked me. He was a young man. All to be part of a team in the world's most violent sport, a game I loved.

I know, he said. And I wasn't even at a major program. I wonder all the time about those guys, what they must be feeling.

Would you do it again, knowing that now? I asked.

In a flash, he said. The army? Those guys I served with? They'll be my brothers forever. But football? Nothing like it. Eleven boys all working as one. Men. When it goes right, it's a thing of beauty. Nothing else in life has ever equaled it.

Letters

Who seeded your town with new families, including yours, in the years leading up to the "shooting"? And why were so many black and silver (Government-type) cars in place around the school before the event? How far back in time did you and your government handlers begin planning this?

I guess that's what disgusts me the most, all the time and effort and money that goes into these things. Think what a use you could be to society if all that was for good purposes. But I guess cockroaches like you don't have hearts, so it doesn't bother you a bit.

Know this though. Boots are coming, by the thousands, to squash you and yours.

The Bakery

She had been a prostitute. Silver. That was the name she'd gone by. They'd all been prostitutes and they'd all had one name. She used the name now as a badge.

We were like rock stars, you know? Silver said, sliding scissors into a drawer, a soft southern burr to her voice. Tennessee, I thought, and wondered about the chain of events that had brought her this far north for that kind of work.

Celebrities, she said. It was how we made it through our work. It wasn't us.

Wide cheekbones and startling green eyes. Not Paris or jungle; jade, I decided.

Talk to me about the bakery, I said

A sketchy neighborhood, which realtors called up-and-coming; I'd walked to it from my new apartment. Cars with mismatched hoods and doors, deferred-maintenance shotgun houses, closed businesses with plywood windows, the open ones with metal safety grills. Adults came around on Halloween, without kids, and it was patriotic and poor: flags and flowers out all along the street in honor of Veterans Day, its streets and squares named for the fallen.

I put my thoughts aside and listened to Silver. Products and goals we'd gone over at the start, competitors, target clients, the job schedule and project deadlines, but it was useful to have clients talk. It gave me time to sketch and sometimes they would say things that weren't in the corporate bios or on websites. You had to be there to hear it, and you had to connect your hand to your ear so that most of your brains and all your imagination were in the tip of your pencil as you drew.

So I sketched as she talked, just a few quick strokes, her face full on at first, though that didn't seem to work. It would be better in three-quarter profile, highlighting those jade eyes. If we ended up working together, she'd grow used to me sketching in every meeting, ideas that would come to me as she talked.

Okay, Silver said. So, we're trying to give these women useful skills. Mine was baking. It led me out, and I decided to use it for others. She dusted flour from her thighs. We were sitting at a small table with a computer and receipts and inspirational slogans push-pinned to a corkboard. Fifty-pound bags of flour stacked like grass seed in a hardware store, the smells of cinnamon and baking bread.

She kept talking, and I listened to her words but also to the space behind them, to what the way she spoke meant. Focused and exact showed she had clear expectations for the work, and wouldn't likely have an endless list of changes. I was drawing a thumbnail, but this first meeting was a thumbnail too; all the things that happened in it would likely happen again as we worked together, good and bad.

Silver said, We have volunteers from the culinary school and yoga instructors who also volunteer. And teachers who provide daycare while the mothers are in classes. And accountants who teach them how to balance checkbooks, also for free.

For a while there was silence, other than the sounds of my pencil scratching over my sketch pad and of the heavy metal oven doors clanking open and of the women sliding trays from the hot ovens onto cooling racks. Rolls baking, an exhaust fan blowing. Then I realized Silver was waiting for me to speak. In my head I replayed what she'd been saying and said, So, you have a lot of pro bono work.

Everyone, she said. Well, almost. She looked over my shoulder at the women working behind me. We pay the girls an hourly wage so they can transition from their former lives. Above her head was a big gray square time clock.

I nodded. I had the composition now: Silver kneeling in a garden planting small seeds that bloomed into cupcakes, stills and animated GIFs for a website. Okay, I said. And you're looking for another.

Another? Silver said. She shifted in her creaking wooden chair and the light changed on the planes of her face but it didn't matter, I had it down. The hum of a big industrial mixer switched on, its huge paddle swirling around the giant bowl.

Yes, I said. Another person working for free.

Oh, yes, she said, and looked right at me, unafraid to ask. She wasn't going to say another word, I knew. The power of silence. I admired Silver for that. How many times must she have used it to help her workers? Two were behind her with their strong tattooed arms in vats of dough up to their shoulders, punching it down. One, Silver told me, had become a prostitute at thirteen to pay their mother's hospital bills. It was probably true, but it might also be embellished. I'd read about that very person in one of the articles, and maybe it was her, or maybe she was the most recent incarnation of her; it wouldn't be any less true just because she wasn't the one. Essential truths remained true, even if they arrived in counterfeit packaging.

Pro bono was a judgment call. I liked her, and thought I could do it. I still had money from the Victims' Compensation Fund and other jobs were coming my way, so I turned my sketchbook around to show her. Lines appeared on her forehead as she looked, and she traced the design with her finger, intrigued. If she hadn't been, I'd have stood, shaken her hand and left, no point in going farther; I never charged for the first visit. But because she liked it, I shook her warm hand across the table and said, Yes. I can do that. Two things, though. First, I can only do pro bono initially. Planning out the campaign and generating the first materials. Anything after that, which will be a lot less expensive, I have to bill for.

She nodded, diamond studs flashing. And the second? she said.

I get to use the finished product in my portfolio.

I wouldn't keep you from doing that, she said. We all have to make a living.

Her fingertips had picked up a silvery sheen from the underside of my hand; pencil-lead residue. Silver on Silver, I said, and she laughed.

Such a clear sound, as untroubled as a church bell. Remarkable, I thought, given all she'd come through. She'd said that as a girl she'd been a storm with a skin.

One more thing, I said. Won't change my answer, but I wondered how you came across my work.

Oh, she said. Her smile showed beautiful teeth. *Business Insider.*

Our local business paper; they'd run an article on me. It didn't mention Liam. They wanted to, but I refused to profit from my son's shooting, and it kept awkward questions at bay. The article did say that I was quirky and always prompt. I put my sketchbook away and gathered my papers and stood and told Silver I'd call in a few days with a detailed timeline and she thanked me and returned to her other work.

The one who might have been a prostitute at thirteen was transitioning. They stopped me on my way out. A cheek tattooed with blue stars and a black smock over a white service uniform with straws lining one front pocket. Thin forearms. *Must be new,* I thought. Here, they said. The deepest voice, eyelashes like bird wings, a *them fatale.* They gave me a chocolate cupcake with orange frosting. For Halloween, they said. For free! Oddly, they also gave me a straw. *What a smile,* I thought, and knew I'd use that somehow too. I was glad they'd come through to the other side.

I walked back to my apartment eating the cupcake, which

made it hard to look like I shouldn't be messed with as I passed a methadone clinic, wondering what their home life had been like. Not good, I imagined, mourning a past I knew nothing about, because after all they must have loved their mother to do what they did. But it was a difficult past, and some with difficult pasts became prostitutes while some with difficult pasts became school shooters. Which wasn't a fair leap; kids with loving pasts did too. Really I was mourning other irreplaceable things, wayward pasts and possible futures.

Because I wouldn't see Liam today, I ate the entire cupcake. When he was seven, he turned contrary. Later, we decided it had to do with the upcoming move. He'd ridden his bike to Aiden's house, even after we told him he couldn't, and when he came back, he told May he was going to be a detective when he grew up.

May said, The way you've been acting recently, you're more likely to end up on the other side of the bars.

That night when she put him to bed he said, I know I've been bad recently. I'll be better. And there's one thing you'll never have to worry about.

What's that? she said, and stroked his cheek.

I'll never nail somebody to a cross like they did to Jesus.

Interim 2

Number of school shootings since:	143
Number of school children killed:	223

Boo Humbug

SEPTEMBER 30, 2015

A month before Halloween, Liam hadn't decided on his costume. In a secondhand bookstore, I found a book on Egyptian beliefs that I thought he'd like, maybe use as a guide. We'd always made his costumes together and usually he planned two months ahead but so far he hadn't said a thing about it. He was eight, it was a new neighborhood, but there was no way the romance had worn off, so I wanted to nudge him.

He was practicing cursive when I gave him the book, small looping letters in pencil on lined paper. He put it aside to finish his letters and then leafed through the book slowly, without a word. Finally he closed it and put it aside and said, I don't think it's very nice, people being mummies for Halloween. It's not like being a witch.

Why's that?

It's kind of like making fun of someone's religion.

Not for the first time, I wondered at how his mind worked. You create these little beings, who grow up to amaze and enrage you, to fill you with love and wonder, and, after, when they get hurt, with cruelty toward others.

Whatever darkness hides inside you? Their pain brings it out. I didn't know Kate yet, but she was on my horizon.

The Kindness of Strangers

OCTOBER 12, 2016

I sat in the faux-wood-paneled reception area of Safeway 6 Trucking, flipping through mock-ups. New truck logos, for advertising in *Overdrive* and *LandLine*, the biggest trucking mags. Safeway 6 wanted to be placed alongside upcoming stories on employee drug testing and counterfeit parts; big readership, evidently. Not a glamor client, but it would pay bills, and, a year out, I was rebuilding my freelance client list, ready to work again. Money, peace of mind.

Beside me sat another freelancer in a too-small blue suit, watching the TV bolted to the wall, a morning talk show about teenaged parents and questionable paternity. He listened to the girl and addressed her. He does what he do, he said, shaking his head, and that's on him, but, dang, girl, close your legs and open a book.

His drawings looked to be dashed off by a reluctant child, and when he noticed me checking them out he introduced himself. Bill Scott, he said.

Otto Barnes. We shook. His soft hand felt like he'd never done a day's work. I'm the 9:00, I said. What time are you?

9:30.

I glanced up at the clock over the secretary's head. She was on the phone, running a pick through her hair and ignoring us. Half an hour each.

Yeah, Scott said, and smoothed his retro sideburns with both hands. Nothing worse than when you run out of time, he said. You just always got to be ready, Mr. Barnes. You just never know what's coming. He spoke with his hands, which flashed light and dark, like leaves and their pale undersides in a high wind, and his eyes vibrated with the intensity of a Bible salesman, but freelancers tended to be a motley crew, so I didn't really think much of it; I did give an interior shout of triumph, though. *The competition!*

Right at nine the secretary hung up. Evelyn had pictures of two school-age children taped to her computer monitor and her coffee was a flat white from Starbucks; she wore a lot of very floral perfume. Helpful to notice small things. I kept a notebook with entries for every place I went; if you got on the good side of secretaries, it could make all the difference.

Evelyn said, Mr. Barnes? Mr. Swanson will see you now.

I thanked her and said good-bye to Mr. Scott, who stood and shook my hand with both of his this time and said, Kate says, Good luck.

I was so startled I couldn't respond, but my mind was awhirl as I went into Mr. Swanson's office. Tall and with a long shoebox-shaped head and wire-rim glasses, in another faux-wood-paneled room, this one smelling of pipe tobacco. His voice sound garbled when he asked what he could do for me.

Was he having a stroke? I thought that maybe I'd misheard him, flustered by Scott, so I reminded Mr. Swanson that he'd reached out to me for some possible freelance work as I shook his hand. His face was so pale it looked as though he'd never left this room, but now it grew even paler.

I'm sorry, he said, frowning and running a hand over his crew-cut gray hair, so flat you could run on it. There must be some mistake, he said.

When I came back out, Scott had gone. Evelyn thought he was with me, a partner, to help with a cold call.

They thought I'd initiated the contact—they showed me the email chain, a Yahoo account that I'd never opened, with replies from a dummy account in their name. To prove I wasn't delusional, I explained about the hoaxers, how they sent me unwanted gifts and messages, had damaged my car, forced me to move. Spread rumors about me that showed up on the internet.

Mr. Swanson was solicitous and sorry, turning his meerschaum pipe over and over in his hands. I don't actually have any freelance work I can send your way, he said, but let me take your cell phone number in case at some future point I do. Hand on my elbow, he said, I'll call the police, tell them about this. Awful!

No, I said, and searched the parking lot for anyone who might follow me. Cloudy, which made it easier to see into cars. Scott wouldn't be hanging around, but sometimes they worked in pairs. I added, They already have a thick file on these people. I'm just sorry you were dragged into it. And they want you to call the police, to waste their time. They think it's a way to undermine the conspiracy.

The wind buffeted the door as I pushed it, and Evelyn said, Wait, and came around her desk to slip me a small New Testament, with worn green edges. Her personal copy, Psalms and Proverbs. There are a lot of evil people in the world, she said. But some good ones too. I read this whenever the bad ones make me doubt that.

There was nothing to say but thank you, so I did, and went out to find a note clamped under a wiper blade on my windshield, flapping in the rising wind.

Kate was right about your evil ways. No one whose child had been shot would be back to work so quickly. Your new address is 607 Whitebirch Road, Apartment #7. I'm going to post it now. Expect a lot of company in the coming days.

I looked him up on the internet, but no Bill Scott, freelance artist, existed. I sketched him while sitting in my car, took a picture of it with my phone, and sent it to Nash. *Kate, again,* I texted. *That woman is insidious.*

Driving home, I doubled back, waited at green lights until they changed, hoping I was followed. My fantasy was to ram him, to pin his car against a guardrail, to watch horror spread across his face as I got out and approached with my Louisville Slugger. On 12th and Eastover I couldn't believe my luck when I saw him—or that shiny blue suit—and sped up to get beside him, both of us approaching a yellow light. He wasn't going to stop, I knew, so I kept my foot on the gas until nearly the last moment, when the hood of his car dipped and I had to slam on the brakes, rear-end fishtailing and bumping against his. I grabbed the door handle to get out, only it wasn't Scott, just some teenager, eyes agog at my craziness.

Impossible to explain, so I punted, shutting my door and turning my face away and staring resolutely ahead as if nothing had happened. *Just one more crazy white man out for a drive.* When the light changed, I turned right and drove off slowly, another normal citizen obeying traffic laws.

After five more minutes of backtracking and sudden stops, I pulled into a gas station to check for GPS tracking devices. Under the hood, in the wheel wells, beneath the bumpers. It started to rain, a whipping cold rain, so I didn't get on the ground to check under the running boards, but they must have had one. How else had they found my apartment so swiftly? I darted into the store to buy a coffee and the clerk noticed my shaking hands when I paid. So tall and thin, I wondered if he'd even cast a shadow.

Long night, he asked, or starting early?

Long life, I said, and I started years ago.

I sat in the car, clothes and coffee steaming, flipping through Evelyn's Bible until the adrenaline left my system. The pages were heavily underlined, mostly in black, but here and there in red, the red passages about anger. The two I liked the most were from Proverbs, though I doubted for the reasons she had. *Anger slays the foolish man, and jealousy kills the simple,* and *Pressing milk produces curds, pressing the nose produces blood, and pressing anger produces strife.* I wasn't simple, and the foolish one was Scott, or would be, if I got hold of him, when I would press his nose with the bat. A peculiar pleasure, enhancing my anger where others sought to master it, but one I was happy to indulge. I thought more and more about Kate.

At last I charted the information in my incident log, though I didn't think it would change anything, and surfed the web, searching for another apartment, thinking, *Heads up, Liam. They're still out there.*

Interim 3

Number of school shootings since: 144
Number of school children killed: 223

Ball Breaker

OCTOBER 7, 2015

Leaves were blowing, brown and brittle. I had to rake, to muck out gutters, I had undone freelance work, our household budget was two pounds of nails in a one-pound bag. And there was the recently defiant Liam. We'd asked him to clean his room and instead he'd played computer games, and when I found out I sent him up to do it again while I drew. I heard a ball bouncing and breaking glass.

He was standing against his bed with his arms folded when I came in.

What the hell are you doing?

Surprised by my tone, he said, Nothing. The window broke.

Liam. You threw the ball in the house, which you're not supposed to do.

I did, he said, and smiled, which angered me.

All right, I said. You can't go to Latrell's house for a week.

He shrugged. Okay. I'll just have him here.

No, I said, you won't. You won't have anyone here.

Then I'll play games with him online.

Nope. You've lost computer privileges for a week. TV too.

A losing proposition, ratcheting up the punishments in response to each new act of defiance, but I wanted him to stop. Sunlight flashed on the jagged glass.

That's not fair, he said.

It's not fair that you don't do what you're asked, and now I have to replace a window when I need to work.

I'll stay after school and play with him there.

I'll be picking you up. You'll be coming home right on time.

I might get detention and have to stay after. You'll probably have meetings and won't be able to get me. Then Mum will but she can't leave work either.

Fine, Liam, take the bus. I pocketed the tennis ball. But no art at home. In the morning, you just get up and go to school.

Good, he said. I was going to stop anyway. That erasure book was your idea.

It hadn't been, but I didn't bother arguing. Go get the broom and dustpan, I said. And a couple of brown paper bags. We're going to tackle the window first.

He stomped down the stairs while I tried to figure out what was going on, with him, with me, and took a picture of the broken window to remind him of what he'd done if he started complaining about a week without privileges. I began jimmying the shards of broken glass from the frame, carelessly, it turned out, and cut my hand, which I was rinsing when he clomped back upstairs holding the broom.

You cut yourself? he said, noting the bloody trail. Good. I hope you bleed a lot.

I am, I said, angry that a bandage would throw off my control of pencils. Take the glass out now, I said. And if you cut yourself, you're on your own.

May heard Liam's version first and told me I had to apologize. For what? I said. A poor decision? I lined up my pencils to show I wasn't angry.

May said, A poor decision is spreading mayonnaise on a brownie. This was glass. He's eight. He could have cut himself, badly.

Yes, he could. And it would have been a useful lesson about consequences.

Well, these consequences have could have been disastrous. So I've restored his computer privileges.

No, you didn't.

She turned to go. Yes, I did.

I followed her out. And I suppose you want him to have a party with all his friends now too? I said to her back. *That* would certainly teach him a valuable lesson.

Don't be foolish, Otto. She sorted through her purse and refused to look at me, because she knew that made me angry and that, angry, I argued poorly. The grounding is fine, she said. Deserved. But you went far too far and you know it.

Peanut butter and jelly sandwiches for dinner, all of us silent around the table; my night to cook but I refused to. Liam drank his glass of milk in a single long swallow. We all had milk mustaches. Normally I'd have pointed it out and we all would have laughed but instead I listened to the hum of the old electric clock on the wall, which May and I found in a tumbledown store on our honeymoon. Liam had sliced one of the pages in the erasure book, which he and I had been working on together. Where had all his anger come from? Perhaps he needed comfort.

I read to him at bedtime, his warm body curled against mine, though that didn't mollify May, nor did I want it to. I'd been wrong, though I wasn't ready to admit it. When she came to bed she organized her bedside drawer—pens, glasses and vitamins had to be in their places—then turned out her light and said, You shouldn't be on the computer either, for a week. You're acting just like a child.

And like a child, I rolled over and went to sleep without a word.

Crash Course in Anatomy and Physiology

OCTOBER 11, 2015

On the second morning we sat in high-backed stools in the café window and looked out through our reflections on the dark glass at the passing trains while May stirred five sugars into her coffee though she usually drank it black, the spoon clink-clinking against the thick white ceramic mug. She made a face when she tasted it and pushed it aside with her thumb. We waited as long as we could for visiting hours to begin and when we couldn't wait any longer we left our coffees unfinished on the counter and stood leaning together into the wind waiting for the train to pass, even though we were still an hour early, and when the final graffitied boxcar shuddered past we crossed the tracks to the hospital as the train clicked away down the rails.

The sky blued with the first light of dawn and turned yellow during our walk down the long echoing hallways. Beeping monitors in other rooms, otherwise the hospital hushed like a church; the officer on duty outside Liam's room didn't even check her watch. Liam's face was swollen, the skin stretched so tightly it shone. Go away! May said, and banged on the window to shoo away a pigeon on the ledge.

What's that about? I asked. She wouldn't say. The doctor arrived.

Tell me why that's happening, May said. His face?

I understood May's peremptory tone. Efficiency was the way she interacted with the world, and a mask; all the emotions could come later. Would the doctor?

It's normal, the doctor said. Swelling will be worst today and tomorrow. Then it will go down. She flicked through charts on her iPad and seemed distracted.

The nurse said, But you should prepare yourself. It will discolor badly.

May and the doctor frowned. The doctor said, Yes, best to be prepared.

How long will it last? I asked, looking from one to the other. I still didn't know anyone's names. I'd seen these two multiple times but their names wouldn't stick, something about processing. Their names were on pins but I couldn't make them out without my glasses and so I didn't look, not wanting to seem as if I was staring at their breasts. Better to be thought rude than a perv. A couple of days? I said.

No, the doctor said, and pushed her weave back over her shoulder. It'll be a lot longer. Purple at first and over a week or so fading to yellow. But it won't mean anything except that the body is healing. This will be a long process. Probably best if you accept that. She straightened her red weave again.

Okay, May said. She didn't seem turned off by the doctor's lecturing tone, though I was. But how did it happen? May asked. All those broken bones?

The nurse had short electric-blue hair that stood up in tufts like meringue, thick with a faintly rose-scented product. She glanced at the doctor.

What? May said. Her face paled. Tell us.

It might be from the fall down the stairs.

What else might it be? I said.

The doctor sighed and said, Or the shooter might have struck your boy with the butt of the shotgun or his pistol. The injuries are consistent with that.

The gurgling noise from May's throat was half-sorrowful, half-angry.

The door opened and a short elderly orderly with a prosthetic arm came in with Liam's breakfast. He won't need that, the nurse said. She bustled over and took the tray and seemed glad to have something to do.

First Texts from a Stranger

As a mum myself, your wife is proof that the "massacre" never happened. I saw pictures of her at Latrell's "funeral."

A lovely skirt and jacket in earth tones.

The first reaction to grief is ALWAYS guilt, even though it's irrational. In the pictures she's wearing lipstick and a beautiful pair of matched earrings.

If one of my babies had been shot, I'd feel so guilty that I hadn't protected them (even though there was no way I could have!) that there's no way I could put on lipstick or would think to reach for earrings. Let alone those EXPENSIVE GORGEOUS clothes.

Putting yourself together JUST after having your child SHOT would NOT be possible

Liam at Three

After a lunch of grilled cheese and my own tomato soup I'd barely eaten, with Liam napping and May watching him, I draw an alphabet, playing with letters; a local dry cleaner's wants something unusual, something different. The look I've chosen, the pictures, the graphics, the logo, they love it all. *Love* it. Except maybe the font. Somehow, that's a little off. Six times so far, and each version is great, but . . .

This will be my last try. If this one doesn't work, I'll thank them, bill them for my time, and write them off; it happens. Frustrating, but I'm okay with it, though I want to get it right. The struggle is part of what I love about the work, the breakthrough, when it comes. Instead Liam walks into my office with his pink blanket over his head, holding half the grilled cheese I didn't finish.

Do you don't like the grilled cheese? he asks, and takes a bite.

What's with the blanket? I ask, thinking he must be cold in the drafty house.

He chews and swallows before he answers. I'm a nuns.

I pull him up on my lap and he leans forward and before I can stop him puts one buttery finger on the letter *M*, smudging it.

Look, he says. *M*. That's May's letter.

It is, and it's slightly different now, better. Perfect. *Liam's font*, I think, and know I'll use it. After I get him settled in bed, the plush red comforter with blue foxes and green dogs tucked under his chin, I create it. Cleaners who clean things up, dirt disappearing from a stained shirt, the smudged font changing to a clear one.

Kate

Kate's good. I'll give her that. She's at her best about Liam. The hoaxers who confront me, and the number of letters I get because she's so convincing. And because Alex Jones picked up one of her videos and ran with it.

The letters are always forwarded, no matter how many times I move; you'd be surprised at the number of people who still take the time to write them. Dozens a week, usually, though it varies. Anniversaries are big, of course, but beyond that it seems random. Some are filled with invective, nearly all are filled with questions.

The local trauma helicopter company says they were ready to go within minutes of hearing about the "shooting," but were never called. Everyone knows that trauma helicopters are the swiftest way to transport victims. If so many people were shot, why were no trauma helicopters ever summoned to the school? And why weren't paramedics and EMT's allowed in to try and save lives?

Kate was so right about you. I wish I'd listened earlier. I wish we all had. Hearken to her voice, and give ears to her.

The Fishermen of Souls

The echo fades, but the first school shooting after Liam's was dire, a day with a freak early snow and a bitter wind. May came early to the hospital from work but didn't stay long; neither did I. Improving, playful, Liam joked with us both and the doctors said he could use the extra rest. 100/59. Perfect BP, his nurse said.

Home, May unplugged the house phone and turned off her cell and shut all the shades and took two sleeping pills and kicked off her Ferragamos and went to bed fully clothed. No TV, she said. Please. Not a word about Paramount Springs.

She was shaking and I lay down beside her and held her, face pressed against her silk blouse. She didn't still, even after she fell asleep, her body hot as a griddle, and I wondered if that was a medical condition but found nothing about it on the internet. When I checked on her after an hour, she was cooler and had stopped shaking, though her scent was a mixture of sweat and perfume.

I unclasped her silver necklace and brushed her hair back from her pale forehead and kissed her and left to warm up a Lean Cuisine and with the volume down flipped between channels, inhaling news reports, avid for the smallest detail, adrenaline surging when a new casualty number appeared or a reporter speculated on how old the shooter was. Narrow and tense, I leaned forward like a carrion bird every time I switched channels to find a slightly different version of the same story, twitching as I waited for something to stir; the thrill of doom. I zeroed in on the first survivors and their affectless voices. Two teachers.

Liam's shooter's mother was a teacher. I wished she'd been in that school, forced to live through it, physically unscathed if mentally and emotionally wrecked, but I knew that she was wrecked and, not wanting to feel sympathy for her, I snapped off the TV and made a series of violent drawings and burned them all. I didn't want them and I didn't want them to affect whether Liam lived or died.

Irrational, I knew, but I burned them anyway and scattered the ashes on the new-fallen snow in the cold dark, a cold so sharp it froze my lungs. That way they'd be gone in the morning, covered, as if nothing had happened. I scrubbed the ash from my hands and threw out books and expired cans of food from the pantry and dozens of letters, which changed nothing. Nothing.

Voices echoed on the street. No one was outside the window, no group of boisterous drunken friends, no couple quietly conversing, no dog walker on her phone, and the streetlight showed that no footsteps other than mine had disturbed the freshly fallen snow in any direction. I shivered and thought of Liam, his soft voice.

At six, the story of Samson was his favorite. He loved it, asking to hear it night after night. Once, after listening, eyes glowing from the hallway light, he said, God is everywhere. Like at night and you're sleeping and you hear voices out on the street and you think it's ghosts, it isn't. It's God. So you shouldn't be afraid.

Everybody loves their kids. How many want them to be prophets?

Letters

Dear Mr. Barnes,

We, the Carmelite Sisters of the Most Sacred Heart of San Diego, are writing you with profound wishes for a blessed Thanksgiving. The world is inflamed with hatred, from which you and your family have so grievously suffered. But God's love also exists, and in the end will triumph, though in the solemn hours of the night, it must often seem otherwise. For us, the way to that path is to raise ourselves to Christ, who is our heaven, while our shadows fall in charity upon earth, trying to do good to all people.

We pray for your union with God, we pray with deep love for Jesus, we pray with devotion, we pray for your soul to find peace. We pray that the meaning of this season—that even as we speed toward the darkest night, we have harvested joys to buttress our strength—will help you find it. And we pray day by day that those who torment you will come to witness God's love and be altered.

We believe in apostolic works as well as prayer, so we write letters on your behalf as well. To them, to all we can find who doubt what you have endured. This is a mission of the heart, a labor of love. You do not know us, but you have been entrusted to our care.

Limbo of the Infants

OCTOBER 14, 2015

Hunched over in the waiting room, I sorted through illustrations, freelance work I was supposed to have done, a big contract and a real break for me, the first since we moved. Holiday sales. It seemed foolish, almost immoral: thinking of money as my son lay in a hospital bed—so I found it difficult to concentrate.

I sketched a swan on my phone for Liam in red ink, something he'd be able to complete or correct. I'd begun drawing for him, sending texts and pictures to make him laugh, things he would stumble across in the future while he recovered, which was my superstitious way of making sure he did. Someone entered and walked across the floor and stood over me. A national reporter, I decided; his boldness, and the shoes. Polished but old, with turned-up toe boxes; you had to run a lot as a reporter, and loafers wouldn't do the trick. He could go fuck himself.

One reporter had pretended to be Latrell's mother; her pictures from the morgue were splashed all over the news. A few reporters were kind and thoughtful, but it hadn't taken long for most of them to become the enemy, so for longer than necessary I just looked down at those black sensible shoes, making the reporter wait.

When he said my name, I shivered in recognition; Nash, the detective. It didn't make any sense but I thought, *Bad news,* and stood so abruptly that I bumped into him. *Please don't let it be May.*

Nash smiled and touched my arm. Hey, he said, it's okay. I breathed deeply to relax, and smelled coffee and cigarette smoke, seemingly a police force requirement.

Nash said, The father gave him the guns, but because no one else was involved, and because the father bought the guns legally, giving them to his son is the only illegal thing. Well, he said, and flicked his jacket aside and put his hands on his hips so that his gun showed. That is, he said, aside from the shooting.

He didn't have to tell me why they wouldn't be leveling charges against the father. The shooter killed him first.

And the mother? I asked. What about her? She must have known too.

No. He looked disappointed and rubbed one elbow with the other hand, a gesture I'd already grown used to. Some aberrant random pain, or a self-comforting gesture. Liam's was to suck three fingers at once, even now.

Nash said, His parents are separated. Were. Just in the last couple of years. She didn't know about the guns. Thought they were stolen from neighbors.

I so wanted her to be arrested. For her to feel her life being crushed around her like a Dixie Cup. Lust for her destruction surged through my body; I snapped my pencil and had to still my breathing.

Nash seemed to realize my attention needed to be redirected. He pointed out my sketch pad. Ever give lessons? he asked. Always wanted to learn to draw.

Sometimes, I said. Usually kids. Maybe later, I said, and waved the broken pencil at the TV with its healthy eating infomercials.

I'd changed the channel before I started working. A segment on American soldiers killed in Niger. I hadn't wanted to watch it, because we were all in the waiting room for bad reasons, and I didn't want anyone to be sadder, including me.

I said, Do you know where Niger is?

Nash blinked in surprise. Nee-zher? he said. Why?

He was coiled now, paying attention. Did he think I was losing it? I mentioned the soldiers who'd died, why I'd changed the channel.

Oh, he said, shoulders relaxing. Yes, I do know where it is. South of Libya and Algeria, north of Nigeria. Mostly desert.

No wonder he's a detective, I thought. He knew things I hadn't a clue to.

So, he said, shifting the conversation again. Drawing lessons?

I looked around at the other patients' waiting relatives and friends, nearly all with coffee and magazines or playing games on their phones. Except one, who I latched onto. Good Samaritans, May's sisters and a few friends rotated in and out as life demanded, one of May's quiet nerdy colleagues from work, Zhao, who'd brought food and sodas, but this guy had brought nothing, though twice I caught him staring at me. He didn't seem to be waiting for a patient; he never looked up when nurses entered the room, hopeful and afraid, and he was watching us now, with his linen sport coat over the back of the seat beside him, taking up an extra chair.

Tall and thin with the thinnest blond hair, like it had been transplanted from a doll. He spooked me and I was about to say something to Nash but thought better of it. He'd already seemed troubled by my random mention of Niger. Besides, hoaxers were already a thing, only a few days after the shooting. It had never happened, we were all crisis actors, part of a vast government conspiracy; he was probably one of them. I only learned his name later. Dexter Fenchwood.

So I said, Lessons? Sure, maybe. Why not? Maybe after all of this is behind us.

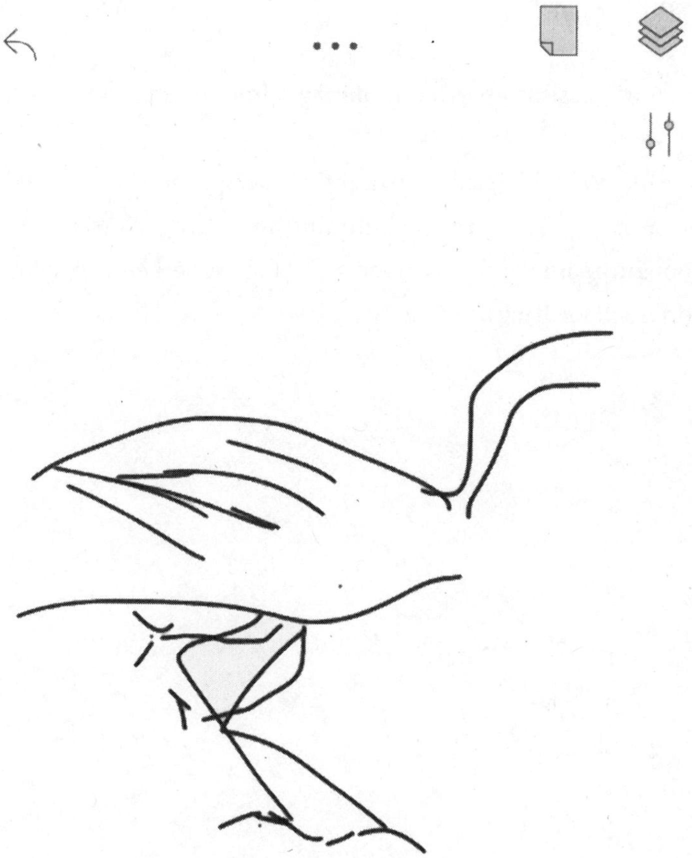

Note to Self, after My Most Recent Move:
OCTOBER 22, 2018

Check out possible apartments *during* school hours, and *around* Halloween.

Too many laughing children near this one, spilling from the rear doors over the field at recess, bumping and racing, glowing like balloons in a summer sky, too many ghosts and superheroes ringing the doorbell for Trick or Treat.

Retain the Covenant of Light

OCTOBER 2015

The service? Closed, though with an open casket, Beanie Babies tucked in beside him. It sickened me, but I understood. He was buried in an unmarked grave.

The minister quoted Bible verses, then people talked: the shooter's mother, his brothers, some cousins. A neighbor, who'd been cooking for her and shooing away reporters. Telling stories about him, things that made them laugh or smile, restoring him to childhood, before the violence. I hated them, but I understood.

Parents were appalled. The minister urged people to grasp the glowing metal ingot of forgiveness, both brutal and necessary, a requirement. *Judge not, lest ye be judged; forgive, and ye shall be forgiven.* Lamont told me he was going to seek him out, but I urged him not to and hoped he would. If I'd known about the service, I could have done anything, gone inside and glared at them, tipped over his coffin, barred the doors and burned the church. In some versions of that fantasy, I'm on the outside, watching, but in others I start the fire with me inside and inhale the superheated smoke.

Some parishioners left after hearing what he'd done; others stayed, and still others began attending. I understood those who fled and those who flocked.

Funeral of a killer. I drew one version with a knife plunged through his eye. Too much, even for me. My work was what I imagined his drawings were like.

Wanting to be a god, so far above him I didn't deign to notice him, I erased it.

His sins were manifest, mine hidden, yet for all that, no less original.

Boo Humbug

OCTOBER 31, 2015

The town council debated canceling Halloween in the days after the shooting. The first hoaxer showed up, asking about the school surveillance cameras, whether he could see footage from the day in question. At the time, people thought he was an odd townsman, someone who lived in a Unabomber shack with a bedraggled dog.

In the end, the town decided not to cancel Halloween. May and I were glad, some of the other parents angry, Lamont furious.

He said, You think I want little ghosts coming to my door? I won't be answering it, that's for damn sure. And if they try any mischief, they'll be sorry.

I wasn't sure how that would come to pass, and I didn't want to ask. May and I were up at the hospital so it didn't really affect us, and there, the Halloween decorations lifted people's spirits. Chains of miniature lighted pumpkins strung across hallways, witches flying into walls. No ghosts, though.

May took apart a malfunctioning table lamp in the waiting room while I went out and bought two dozen Halloween cookies. When I came back, the lamp was fixed, May sitting beneath it reading journal articles, and I handed out a cookie to everyone and put the leftovers on the communal table. Because I wanted to brighten the wait for my fellow travelers, and because I thought that even the smallest acts of kindness might be entered into a cosmic ledger, and because I wanted to be a good man. Though if I wasn't, if I couldn't be, I hoped the appearance might be enough to fool whoever was watching. A single cookie might tip the scale.

Kate

I kept asking myself: *Why did she do it?* Was it just for money, or did she believe these things? A cult, I decided, a cult of disbelievers in the truth, and she their figurehead.

In one video she sits in a high-backed wicker chair on a sunny porch wearing a pink-and-white flower-print dress, discussing the impossibility of the so-called police response to the school shooting (only four police cars for the first half hour, she claimed). I originally found it on Metabunk. Soon after, it went viral, which meant tracking it grew harder. Still, I traced it as far as I could, over the course of several days; the coding skills I'd learned from May came in handy.

Coverups and Illuminati, false flag and 9/11, political manipulation, Infowars and David Icke, a string of others. But the trail ended with an anonymous poster, who wouldn't respond to my comments or answer my email and had no other contact info. A dead end, like so many of my searches for Kate over the years.

But I persisted.

I had pictures of her, a name—even if it was fake—and eventually, through the Wayback Machine, I learned that some of her videos were produced in Phoenix. Bit by bit, by asking questions, I built up a file on her. The public places she was shown in, the people she referred to, her clothes. Facebook was a goldmine, their Graph Search. The hoaxers kept finding out where I was, but eventually, I knew I'd discover where *she* was, the face of the entire movement. And wouldn't she be sorry then.

Wine on the Lees

Karlene divorced Lamont after Latrell's funeral, a homegoing that featured a choir, witnessing and weeping, and that startled and reassured me and left me drained. She showed up at his Thursday night bowling league with the papers.

He'd been looking forward to a couple of hours with the Elbow Benders, leaving his awful personal life behind, and yet there she was. He ignored her. If he got up somehow it would all be true but if he sat there and drank beer it would all go away. Someone else had to take his turn and the guys on the other team—the asshole sticklers from E-Bowl-A, who never let *anything* slide—didn't say a thing.

With his beer done and no one getting him another, Lamont said, After my second ball. He went through his preshot routine. Right shoe four inches back from the left one and in line with the second arrow, ball tucked to his left side, one step, the ball going back, two steps holding it, three steps with his arm arcing forward.

For the first time in his life, he stepped beyond the line as he released his ball and went airborne. Splatted flat on his back and Karlene came and stood over him waving the papers. It was a long time coming, she said.

It didn't have to be, he said.

When she didn't answer, he grabbed the papers from her and signed them like that though it took a while; the pens she gave him didn't write upside down.

Yet it worked out in the end. Two teammates were engineers and they had specialized pens. She didn't seem any happier as she strode off, but it was done.

First Date

Sautéing garlic and the spicy vanilla scent of Palmer Skutch's perfume competed on the cool breeze. We stood on the crumbling sidewalk in front of my latest apartment, near the exhaust fan of a red-sauce Italian restaurant. Inside the new apartment the same clothes, the same drawing materials, the same eternal hope that a new place would be better, that the hoaxers wouldn't find me.

I like your pin, I said to her. Lamont had set us up. *She's alladat!*

I'd told her we'd meet outside because I'd just moved in and the place was a mess, which was true, though it would always be a mess. The things I kept, the things I didn't, the last thing brought from each previous apartment and the first into each new one: a plastic bag of Liam's clothes, taken from the hospital.

This pin? she said. A peacock with a ruby eye and glittering jewels arcing down its long blue tail. This is from my ex, Palmer said, levering the peacock with her thumb, so it flashed in the light. He was an asshole but he had nice taste.

Yes, I said. But what kind of asshole?

A smile, followed by a frown. My friend said it best. He was deficient. God gave him a penis and a brain, but not enough blood to run both at the same time.

I laughed, which she seemed to like, but her eyes narrowed. He was the cheating kind. Lamont told me you were married before. Were you that kind?

No.

She waited, but when I did not go on she said, Was she?

No. She's an engineer. She lusts after electronics. I realized that might have sounded odd, but I didn't want to explain I hadn't meant sex toys, so I didn't.

Okay, she said, and we headed toward her car. Such an interesting face. The long arc of her cheekbone, the elliptical starburst of her iris, the gorgeous full lips. She indicated the passenger side for me with her mauve clutch. A nice walk, one foot swinging in front of the other as if traveling along a tightrope, and she looked good in her skinny jeans. I said, Lamont told me you were shy as a Lenten rose.

A loud guffaw. He told you no such thing. But you get points for trying.

Her Lincoln smelled seductively new. I was glad we'd taken her car and not the mess of mine. So, I said, and slapped my thighs after I buckled in, stiff in my linen pants and sport coat. Where to? She'd told me she'd pick me up when we set up the date, and that where we were going would be a surprise; my guess was lunch or a gallery. That it started at eleven a.m. felt odd, that it was my first date since my divorce felt even odder, but I said nothing. Why scare her off prematurely?

Stones, she said. I have a garden. I'm busy with sales and don't pay enough attention to it, so today we're looking at edging stones. After, maybe we can lunch.

Oh, I said, a twofer. The date *and* the stones.

I liked her laugh, which mattered. May and I used to play a game, *Dealbreaker.* Back hair topped her list, a donkey laugh mine.

Familiar streets. We passed by Sweet Surrender Bakery and I studied its windows. Want something sweet? Palmer asked. Maybe a good place for lunch?

No, but thanks. I did some work for them recently. Just checking for signs of it.

And they were there in the window above the clustered croissants and stacked baguettes, the brightly colored posters I'd designed. It felt like a good omen.

She slowed and looked. You did those posters? How beautiful. The way the cupcakes bloom from the ground, become flowers. And the colors. They're so vibrant I want to eat them. Maybe someday you'll draw something beautiful for me.

I'd love that, I said, and it was the first really nice thing I'd wanted in a while.

We made our way through the standard questions while in an unfamiliar part of the city, light industry, low sprawling apartment complexes, the gold dome of an Orthodox church. She asked first and I liked her voice; it wasn't guarded. Childhood, jobs, how long I'd been divorced and etc.; her turn revealed Pennsylvania, Amish country, and that she'd worked on farms as a girl and decided she wanted nothing to do with them. She asked if I had kids.

No, I said, looking out the window at billboard after billboard for personal injury lawyers. Did people in this part of town get hurt more? No, I lied. No kids.

Me either, she said, and cut in front of a car without using her blinker. And I don't plan to, she said, over the noise of the car horn.

So if you ask me to marry you at the end of the date, I'll keep that in mind.

She laughed again, a little less convincingly; she'd gone cold. I'd done something wrong and didn't know what. *Don't ever play poker,* I thought.

The entire place smelled of stone dust, and I hadn't known there were so many kinds of gravel, small patches set out one next to the other and separated by bricks: moonstone crushed stone #411 crushed stone #57 quarry process pea gravel yellow gravel. We were standing by them, Palmer's feet by the pea gravel and mine by the moonstone. She squatted and got her hands right into it. I admired that about her, and her thighs, and wondered again what I'd done to tank the outing. Perhaps I'd find out from Lamont, in the gossipy after-report.

I thought it would be this, she said, letting a scoop of pea gravel sift through her fingers to clack against the rest of it. But it's the moonstone, she said. The larger size and the blacks and browns and whites. I like that mix.

I do too, I said. The colors work together to keep the eye moving.

But? she asked.

I liked that she picked up on my hesitation. Maybe her mood had nothing to do with me, maybe the outing could be saved. Well, I said. I'd have to see where it was *going* to be sure.

A little early to invite yourself to my place, she said, and clapped her hands clean on those beautiful thighs and stood.

Oh, I said, surprised by the wave of sadness that washed over me. Had I thought she liked me? That she might come to? I hadn't realized I was so lonely.

I didn't mean that, I said. Just that I need context. I'm a visual person.

I see, she said. Okay. Right. Red blotches bloomed on her throat.

I had the odd thought that maybe everything would be all right if I started to dance among the stones, just a few steps and a pirouette. If I took her hand and invited her to join me. Where it came from I had no idea, and I held on until it passed.

The wind turned, colder now, and Palmer shivered. I'll be back shortly, she said, and wandered toward the office door, while I headed over to the bays.

———

Beyond the last one was a nursery. A boy of about ten or eleven sat on a stack of pea-green plastic chairs, swinging his blue sneakers. They didn't have much stock this late in the season, mostly mums whose autumnal smell I'd never liked, though some very pretty small sprays with blue iris in them. I asked the salesgirl what they were. With a slight lisp around her pink braces she said, For the cemetery. St. Olaf's.

All the other customers were coupled off, hopeful people, planning to plant things to make their houses or apartments and maybe their lives better. Things that would live a short while and die. I wandered back to the gravel office. Palmer was just coming out, a big yellow receipt in her hand.

All set, she said, waving at me. Her smile didn't last long enough for her to fold the receipt and put it in her clutch. Shall we go? she said.

Ha! I said, pointing out the car window at two teddy bears hanging from a light pole outside a strip mall. Look at that, I said. Lynching stuffed animals now.

She turned her blinker on and said, Someone died. It's a memorial.

A mass of flowers bunched at the base of it; I saw them as soon as she spoke.

Must have been a kid, she said. Accident.

We came to a light and stopped, to take a left. The cars zooming past us rocked her car, as big as it was.

Above us were two billboards, one for a nearby rosary factory, the other advertising direct flights to Phoenix. So many people looking for relief, I said.

Palmer said, I'd take some desert heat, any time. Love Arizona. And I didn't mean to imply you were an asshole, earlier, at the start of our date, when I was talking about my ex. I do that sometimes. It's just I never thought he would be like that.

It's okay, I said. I understand.

The light changed. We crossed through the intersection and she said, Can I ask you something? Why didn't you tell me about Liam being shot?

A weighted silence between us. In no time she was up to fifty, the telephone poles flicking by close to my window. The speed limit was thirty-five; she wanted this morning over, fast.

You knew? I said at last. Lamont told you? Did he tell you his kid died?

That felt mean, and I was sorry, but didn't say so.

I Googled you. Lamont told me you were friendly and funny and a great artist. I wanted to see your work. I hated all the secrets my ex kept.

So that's what I'd done, I realized. I should have listened to her, to hear not the words themselves but what they were really saying. A lesson I needed to learn again and again.

Where is he now? she asked.

With May.

Was it that you didn't like me? she said. Is that why you didn't tell me?

I was still looking out the window at the telephone poles passing through my reflected face. No, I said. No, I liked you immediately. That's why I didn't tell you.

That doesn't make sense.

Yes it does, I said. I didn't want to be pitied.

You liked me but you didn't trust me.

No, it's not that either. You ask, Any kids, and I answer, One, and you ask, Boy or girl, and I say Boy, and you say, What's the most interesting thing about him, and I say, He got shot. How does a date go on from there?

I see, she said. Yes. When she lifted her hands from the leather steering wheel to check her speed they made a tearing sound, like Velcroed tabs being pulled apart. She said, Maybe it goes on from compassion? From trust?

At last I looked over at her, her lovely, lonely face. I felt terrible that the date had gone wrong and that I couldn't reach out from my loneliness into hers, to bring her relief. It reminded me of a time I saw a sad-looking woman turning into a Burger King at dinnertime months before. She would eat alone and I would too. Why couldn't I say to her, Hey, let's go in and sit at a table and eat together? We can eat and talk and not be lonely for a bit, even if after we part our loneliness returns like a shadow. But of course, I didn't. People would think me mad.

Now I said to Palmer, Thank you.

For a date at a stone-seller's that didn't go well?

For being kind. For thinking about how to raise difficult questions. I should have been more open from the start. *I even liked your soft chin,* I thought, though was smart enough not to say.

Thanks, she said. But don't beat yourself up. It wouldn't have worked anyway. Her mouth turned down. It never does, she said. It's like that song. I'm bad at love.

Which is all we said, until we pulled up outside my apartment and she let me out and drove off.

Palmer in the Morning—Before She
Dressed and Before I Made Her Sad

Pluses and Minuses

NOVEMBER 2016

Foraging in an old sketchbook, I find May's yellowed *Pluses and minuses* list about a possible move tucked inside: *a better job, a promotion, a raise, warmer winters, earlier springs, better schools, new friends for us and Liam* vs: *the loss of older friends, Otto's need to re-establish his freelance business, more expensive housing.*

Her notes appear in perfect outline form, unlike my messy scribblings, and I'm surprised she'd begun contemplating a move without even mentioning it, but suspect her initial silence had to do with kindness; why bring something up that might never happen? More surprising still is Liam's list, a later addition, penciled in blue beside hers after we'd moved: North Clarendon Rutland Center Rutland Proctor Pittsford (+ in winter) Florence.

We took only two days to decide to move—the new job was simply too good an opportunity for May to pass up—but Liam's list is a record of homesickness, detailing in differently sized lettering the whistles for outbound trains he'd hear from his Vermont bedroom at night that used to help him sleep, each a little farther away and a little quieter than the last. Church bells in our new place, but no train whistles, and only from the closest one, and those startled rather than soothed him.

I keep matchbooks and leaves, acorn caps and marbles, shells and smooth stones, bits of poetry and hand-painted postcards for my work, to contemplate, to draw, to train and retrain my hand and eye. I tuck the double list back in the sketchbook, planning to use it in the erasure book, but I won't draw it. The minus side is missing the possibility that Liam will be shot.

Letters

There were Port-A-Potties on the scene of the supposed-school shooting within three hours. Who predicted their necessity and who requested them and why is there a higher priority for toilets than for paramedics if it was all true? And why, when I called the Port-A-Potty company to ask about this, did they say the information was classified? Classified! Classified toilets! The next day the police called and told me not to harass the company any more or I'd be arrested. A homicide detective. A Detective Sawyer! Why would a homicide *detective waste his time about someone supposedly harassing a Port-A-Potty company if he had actual deaths to investigate?*

Liam at Five

FALL 2012

He plucked a small black feather with white polka dots from a blazing red Mexican burning bush in the back yard, the size of a large peanut. I pulled a bird book down from my reference shelf and he stood beside me looking over the pages as I flipped through them.

Too many black birds to figure out now, buddy, I said after a few minutes, and snapped the book closed and put the feather in the top desk drawer. I had to get back to work so I said, I'll take it to have it identified by someone who knows these things.

He nodded solemnly, a covenant. Instead I forgot about it, for years, one of the many things May tasks me for, my inattentiveness to the things she thinks matter the most.

You're disorganized, she says. And it spills into your emotional life.

How do you organize your emotions? I want to ask her, but it's a fight I can't win, so I don't.

Burger King

I texted Lamont. *You set me up with a blonde but I like brunettes.* A diversion, before I texted the truth. *Made a mess of it.* I hadn't eaten and it was cold and dark, so I walked up to the Burger King past people huddled in the bus shelter. No lonely-looking women sitting in a booth by themselves to tempt me into asking to eat with them, men either. Halfway through my second burger, Lamont texted back.

Attaboy! A drink soon to celebrate the end of celibacy! Successful date=audition for sex passed! It was good that he joked; he'd grown so angry recently he could have an argument in an empty house. I gripped my coffee in both hands for warmth.

Home, I sorted through my Kate video collection. That was her name in the first one, about 9/11. In later ones she went by different names, Phoebe and Amanda, but I always thought of her as Kate. The first thing I'd noticed was her throat. The crisp white blouse with the stiff collar, unbuttoned three or four buttons, no cleavage, a small chest, and the thin braided turquoise beaded necklace with its silver horseshoe shining against her smooth skin. It had made me want to meet her. Irrational, but so was everything then, and a quest I wasn't about to abandon.

In this first one, the one on 9/11, and in all that followed, I liked her voice. East coast or mid-Atlantic, educated, with a little bourbony huskiness and no voice fry, and what she said about architects and engineers, demolition experts, sounded reasonable. In between shots of Kate walking around lower Manhattan, she detailed the buildings' odd collapses. She didn't say there were no planes, she didn't say they were dummy planes, she didn't say the government was behind it. She *did* say that buildings didn't fall that way, and never had, unless rigged with explosives to make them implode, and that I should be open to new possibilities. Superbly, she called into question the official story, which set me to doing some research on my own.

And I'd found inconsistencies and suspicious threads. The high number of Saudis involved in the hijackings, indicating that the royal family must have been involved, that a plane took off with dozens of Saudis for Riyadh the day after the attack, from Lexington, Kentucky, when supposedly all across the US all planes were grounded, that for years the government denied the flight ever happened until the pilot and copilot testified that it had. I sat. Outside it was growing dark.

Once again, Kate had lured me in, that easy inherent sexiness of her first video; they knew what they were doing when they cast her. And it was Kate I tried to follow, long after I'd given up on being a 9/11 Truther, which was long after May had grown tired of me talking about it. Not that I believed it, but I found a scintilla of it plausible, which, later, I came to realize was all hoaxers needed. I shut the computer off. Then I turned it on again and watched her walk in lower Manhattan once more. She was nice to listen to; for a few minutes in the otherwise quiet apartment, I forget how angry I'd grown at her, until the video where she denied the school shooting ever happened, that Liam was real.

If the government lied about 9/11, she said, *why wouldn't it lie about a school shooting? I can prove that "Liam" is a hoax, if you'll listen.* Such smooth cruel words, spoken in her lovely voice I'd grown to hate, that I wanted to silence.

Thursday

Ninety-six Americans will be killed with guns today; seven will be children or teens. Forty other children will be shot. Mostly male, mostly young, many unarmed.

Tatts, Temporary and Everlasting

FALL 2013

I piled up the dusty books on photographers and landscapes and birds. Old typefaces, graphics, fonts, I might use them for customers who wanted a retro look, or find images I could steal or alter. The things themselves, but also the pleasant quiet mindless poking in an antique store, as good as scrubbing floors for generating ideas. Nothing had clicked yet but I had faith it would and held up an old pale green rocks glass to the light to admire its weight and faceted shape. A woman stopped beside me, blinking through her bangs.

I said, I'll be careful with it.

She said, Oh no, I was just noticing the rainbow. It arced across the other glasses from the one I was holding. You seem to have magic hands. Light-giving, she added, and blushed, as if she'd realized that sounded flirtatious.

She had a rich southern accent, so I said, Not local, are you?

A wry smile as she tucked her dark hair behind an ear with five silver studs climbing it. You could tell?

I smiled back. Shops like these were my métier and we had just moved to Rutland for May's new job so I would be here often and it paid to make friends with the owners. I said, I'm semismart, in bursts. How'd you end up here?

The door to the back of the shop stuck as it opened and a tall thin man with a single silver streak shot through his black hair emerged after he put his shoulder to it. The woman looked at him as he and his wrinkled chambray shirt made their way behind the counter to ring up someone's purchase and she was still looking at him when she said, I like to think by mistake. I didn't have to ask more, but I wondered if once he hadn't seemed to her like a man going over the top of a hill, singing.

The floors creaked. It had been an old schoolhouse and here and there on the walls children had carved their names into the dark wood. In among the fake antique Tiffany lamps and real faience bowls was a baseball book from the 1940s, my grandfather's time. I leafed through it on the white marble top of an old tiger maple dresser. Some of the pages were foxed and it smelled of mold but I liked the pictures. The crowds of men dressed in suits for the ballgames, the outfield walls with their painted advertisements and the players' old dark small leather gloves and baggy pants and shirts; it was a wonder they could even run. Inside, someone had tucked a sleeve of temporary tattoos. When I brought them home to Liam, he was sure they were as ancient as the book.

I let him believe it, thinking that plenty of mysteries would disappear for him soon enough. Together, we picked out two tattoos for him. A small flock of birds in flight across the underside of one forearm, wings up on some, down on others, and, on the underside of his other forearm, a heart rhythm with the end of the rhythm turning into the words *C'est la vie*. In school, his kindergarten teacher was reading *Owl Moon* to them in French.

On mine, I put an outlined map of the world, and Liam and I trooped upstairs to May's office to show her. He ran ahead he was so excited, long hair flying.

May turned from her desk and held each of his arms in her hands in turn and studied them. She said, They look foolish, and turned back to the computer. Two windows open: an online jewelry site and a vintage Heathkit electronics site.

Liam said, Why do you ruin everything? He turned to trudge downstairs.

Her face stoic in the glow of the computer screen.

When I heard him in the kitchen getting out a bowl and cereal, I asked the same thing. That she'd crushed his happiness shocked me. For the first time, her nose looked too narrow for her face and I made a mental note to sketch it after.

May said, I don't like the temporary tattoos because I don't like permanent ones. She scrolled through the displayed necklaces. By shopping and not looking at me she was saying *You're so wrong I don't even need to think about it.*

She said, You apply those fake tattoos now? It'll just encourage him to get real ones when he grows up. She ordered a simple silver necklace and closed the screen and tapped a few keys and the Heathkit fine print enlarged to 200 percent.

She knew I hadn't left, but she didn't want to talk about it anymore. I did.

And what would be so bad about that? I said.

She leaned forward, pretending she needed to squint at something on the screen, and, satisfied, sat back and continued scrolling without looking at me, electronic kit after electronic kit.

I decided to outwait her but it didn't take long. He came out of me as perfect as an egg, she said, fingers tapping the keys. The way we're all created. I don't want that ruined. And I don't want you planting that idea in his head.

Three Knocks on the Window

NOVEMBER 1, 2015

Beside me in the hospital cafeteria, an older man wearing strategically unbuttoned blue coveralls topped his friends' stories when he said his sister had lost her leg to infection after being bit by a mule. He scratched his pale smooth chest with his long fingernails and handed caramels to everyone and said, I want to buy a smaller walker. One with a tripod foot.

No response at first, as they fumbled with the crinkly wrappers, but at last one of the women said, Oh, you can get Mary's. She put both hands under one heavy thigh in its bright pink tights and shifted it to the next chair and added, They're selling it, now she's dead.

Superstitious, I didn't want to hear more, so I went to buy a coffee. Is the coffee fresh? I asked the server. The softest skin, her dark hair pulled back into a bun, a perfectly round bindi between her luminous brown eyes.

Her fingernails clicked on the touch screen. So fresh it'll talk back to you, she said. I laughed, went for a walk. Liam's second surgery wasn't for a couple of hours and May was with him. On the street the smell of freshly baked bread, the smell of a dryer, the smell of cigar smoke drifting out open windows.

The weather had turned awful in the first days after the shooting— early snow, ice, sleeting rain—but today it was sixty and cloudy and sunny and half the city seemed to realize it was time to get outside, because it wouldn't last.

Bicyclists, dog walkers and older couples moving slowly, mothers pushing baby carriages. One jogger with a pen through the ponytail sticking out the back of her baseball cap that swished back and forth like a wiper. I thought I might sketch her later, a good sign; I was entering the world again. I drank the coffee as I walked and some spilled onto my hand but I didn't have a handkerchief or a napkin so when no one was looking I wiped my hand on a brick wall, scraping my knuckle.

On the next block, a man stood polishing the roof of his car with milk.

I asked, Does that work?

Don't know, he said, elbow working as he pushed the rag in wide circles over the dull black paint. That's what I'm trying to find out.

I went up a hill past a fifties brick apartment building and down the other side next to a field, empty except for a huge flock of star-lings. At the sound of my footsteps, the birds rose a foot off the ground and settled in a wave, like a giant shaken iridescent blanket. When would I ever see anything like that again? It seemed a sign; Liam would be fine. I could draw that in several panels and turn it into a GIF for him, or a flipbook. My phone buzzed, May.

How soon will you be here?

I turned around. *Fifteen minutes.* The sun came out and created shadows of trees and cars and the sun dipped behind a cloud and the shadows faded away.

Don't worry, I told myself. They'd said Liam was out of trouble. He'd been in the hospital a couple weeks and the facial fractures were healing on their own; this surgery was to set a broken arm. He'd begun talking to us, though he had no memory of the shoot-ing. But I dropped the coffee in a trashcan so I could hurry and sucked at my bloody knuckle. *Don't worry don't worry don't worry,* I thought, making sure not to step on cracks as the world lighted and faded and lighted and faded.

Halfway there, two businessmen in matching blue suits stood

looking at a construction fence, one standing behind the other on a bench. As I got closer he said, Hey, slow down. Hawk. You have to stand here to see it, and got down so I could.

My phone buzzed in my pocket, May's tone. I didn't want to have to explain so I stood on the bench and looked and sure enough there was a sleek falcon, perched on the flat tin roof of a construction trailer. Brown-and-white checked feathers and black eyes in a black hooded head, so still he might have been cast, a fierce raptor. An ill omen.

You don't ever see those in this part of the city, the guy said.

The other said, Totally worth it. I don't care if we're late for the meeting. To me he said, Your finger is bleeding.

My phone buzzed again and I hopped down and hurried off, sucking my knuckle again, the taste of old pennies in my mouth. When the phone began buzzing constantly, I started to run, not caring what I looked like or who was in my way or that blood was dripping down my finger, and when I got closer I mistook the rumble of an idling parked truck for that of an approaching train and I sprinted so I could beat the train to the crossing.

You won't make it, I thought, and didn't stop, even after I realized my mistake.

Kate

I wondered why she stopped making hoaxer videos. Moved on to another cause? A possibility. Guilt? Because she'd achieved her goal, of getting people to doubt the truth? Or was she just an actor, not a true nonbeliever, now replaced by others?

I wanted to ask her all those questions and more, but to ask her, I had to find her. I would, I told myself, especially nights I lay awake filled with bourbon, and refined my search, during my relentless scrolling through hoaxer websites.

The length of her hair (shoulder), its color (brunette), her body type (thin/athletic), approximate height (5'8"), weight (130), and age (close to mine), her blue eyes. The name was certainly fake, but I had several images of her, screen grabs from the videos, and when I uploaded those to TinEye, I found a lot more.

Some were ads, some were for causes. People liked her voice; that came up again and again in the comments. That and requests for her name and contact info, always unanswered.

Through The Years

OBGYN to pregnant May: Will you breastfeed?

 May to OBGYN: No. I don't like mixing business and pleasure.

Liam (6) to May: Tell me about breastfeeding. They talked about it in school.

 Always straightforward about biology, May explained it.

 Liam (after thinking it over): Did you ever breastfeed me?

 May: No, honey. I didn't.

 Liam: Then how about you lift your shirt now and I'll take a drink?

Our divorce final, May came by my apartment—the first one I'd had by myself since college—and said, Liam doesn't want us to be apart.

 I'd moved in months before, but with all my stuff still stacked in boxes in the rooms behind me, I didn't let her in, though the visit wasn't a surprise; my lawyer had told me to expect it. Not because he knew much of May, but because it happened often.

 I know Liam doesn't, I said.

 No, she said, and reached through the open door and circled my wrist with her fingers, which had grown so thin, I wondered if she was even eating. I know we can't be together, she said. But Liam wants us to talk. Let's do dinner once a month.

 Her face was hollowed, her arms sticks, her breasts gone. I said yes.

During this month's dinner, May mentioned attending two town council meetings with Nash, which was unusual. White tablecloths and heavy silver in a converted barn, ancient adz marks shiny on the thick beams, a cold clear night with few stars and no moon. She had a new peach-colored wallet. A gift from Nash? Bit by bit she was becoming a stranger, though she never would be. I tracked back through conversations and memories, picking out Nash references.

She picked up on my retreat and switched topics to people she worked with.

Do you remember Carol? she asked, and fiddled with her silverware.

I must have looked blank. A short busboy cleared my salad plate, a man no bigger than a boy.

My co-worker? Her husband bought her a new pair of breasts for Christmas?

Yes, I said and laughed. The busboy hoisted the tub and left, plates clanking.

She used them to meet Zac Efron at some event. She had him autograph them. Now they've begun an affair.

It'll end, I said. Everybody comes to Jesus at some point.

It will, she said. But I hope not until she's had some fun.

She picked up on my surprise. What? she said, and drained her wine. If her husband hadn't told her she wasn't good enough with the fake tits, maybe she wouldn't have been looking around.

I thought of May and Nash. Why was *she* looking around? But of course, why shouldn't she be? Was she happy? She was, her figure fuller, she was eating, I was glad. Glad and jealous. I had no right to jealousy, but since when did right and wrong ever get in the way of emotions? I ordered another bottle of wine.

Faulty Memories

The Birds in my Back Yard

The birds in my backyard
fly so neatly the little
birds sing so sweetly
the little birds in my
back yard rol in a heap
Liam pottreey (age 3)

May thinks *rol* should be read *roll*, but I know it's *are all*. That's Liam's reading. Unreasonable, I know, but it infuriates me that she won't change her opinion; on this one, at least, there shouldn't be two truths.

Letters

Want to know how I know it isn't true?

In America, we file lawsuits. Every parent who had a child wounded or die at Columbine sued. You haven't. Not one of the other parents of kids "wounded" or "dead" has either.

That's un-American.

No. I don't think you're foreign agents.

I just know you're a liar. The lot of yous.

My Benbow Hurts

More texts were coming from May as I got to Liam's room. May's blotchy worried face, and flowers stacked on the windowsill, shading the light, Liam restless in the bed. Hi, Otto, he said. My benbow hurts.

Your elbow?

That's what I said.

May smoothed his hair from his forehead, which still hadn't been washed, her fingers quick and dexterous as she tried to groom it, as if she was picking pearls from seaweed. Her face hovered next to his. We'd just hired someone to come wash it.

Is May? Liam said.

That startled me and drew a moan from May; it was how he'd asked where people were when he was two. It startled me all the more because his facial swelling had gone down and he'd been talking regularly, asking us about his friends. We hadn't told him yet, no one had, his room didn't have a TV, but he didn't seem to mind and he was getting better swiftly, so what was this?

She's right next to you, Liam, I said. Tell me about your elbow. I took his good hand but he yanked it away.

My benbow hurts so much. How come?

He was having trouble getting his breath and his glance darted around the room and he began to thrash. I'd become good at reading his bedside monitor; his respiration was down to four or five a minute and his O_2 levels were low, the numbers dropping, his skin as pale as his twisted sheets, which looked like a shroud.

It hurts, Daddy, he said. He only ever called me Daddy when he was in real pain so I knew it did, and he said again, My benbow.

He began making odd sounds, vowels and consonants strung together in weird patterns, like bad computer speech. Was his tongue getting thicker? He seemed to swallow it and his chin tilted up and he arched his body from his bed and now his mouth was open, his throat straining, but even sound had deserted him. His respiration rate was down to one a minute, the green number flashing.

When it hit zero his eyes rolled back and his body became deathly still. Alarms went off on his flatlining monitors and doctors and nurses rushed into the room and shoved us aside, shouting Liam's name, working on him, opening his gown and rolling his bed as they did, May and I trailing along behind, terrified. He was going, my body shrank, the air grew chilled.

Is he going to die? I asked.

A nurse pushed the bed by the rails. She said, He must have a brain injury, they must have missed it. I worked in the Neuro-ICU for years. I think you'll get him back, but it'll be a long process. Nurse Ernie, she said, and gave me her card.

They were taking him for X-rays and possibly surgery; we hurried through bright hallway after bright hallway past doctors and nurses and patients pushing up against the walls to let us through until we came to Radiology, where we had to wait behind the doors after they swung closed with a concussive, conclusive click. May and I leaned against one another for support, our throats closing.

Cheese

NOVEMBER 2018

I'd stayed up until three a.m. tracking Kate, which meant that the cheese wasn't going well: flat, boring sketches of cows, of farmers and farms, which Cora and Henry wanted, which most cheeses advertised with.

I'd interviewed them at their farm, seen their fields of cattle and sheep and goats and how they made their cheeses, watched the goats run from their pen in the back of the house through its central hallway to their pen in the front. The craziest thing, I thought, as they bumped passed me in the narrow passage. You forget how strong they are.

During my brand immersion, I'd sketched, taken extensive notes, and made sure I understood the differences between sheep, goat and cow cheeses, about which Henry had been voluble, talking for an entire two minutes, when normally words came out of him as if he paid for each with a rib. After, he'd been so upset that he'd had to walk away, his entire body vibrating.

I had everything I needed but nothing clicked, no matter how many times I rearranged looks and logos, which was usually a sign. Rearranging once was fine, multiple times meant something was off, something fundamental. But it might have been Nash; I'd ignored his call. If he had information, I'd hear it from May, unless it concerned hoaxers arriving in town; then, he called me directly. Or maybe he wanted to tell me why he was taking May to those meetings. I didn't want to know.

It wasn't just incipient jealousy. I don't know why I'd grown weary of his calls, of calls from any cops, though they'd become less frequent over the years. Self-protection, my therapists would probably say, since some cops called to express their sorrow, which only increased mine. To some therapists, that was a good thing, to some it was self-defeating, and I listened to each and moved on to the next, but no longer. If I was going to get better, it wouldn't be while sitting across a desk from them in a comfortable chair, though they tried to help. And perhaps had.

I pushed aside the work for Meron Farms and sorted through Liam's collages and drawings and flipbooks, our erasure book, which I kept nearby. *New School Composition*, by Swinton, part of the Harper's Language Series, 1881 edition.

We started that one together, after finding it on one of our outings. Short—only 113 pages—with beautiful handwriting on the flyleaf. Underlinings and parenthetical interpolations, some by its various owners over the years, some his, and small images of mine that he cut and pasted into the first and last pages. Two birds, a duck and a partridge, a horse and chariot, a cutout of a colonial-era soldier. All bright and somewhat smudged, as by time and erasure. And one of the first pages cut jaggedly, so that only part of the title page showed when you opened the cover.

Another of his contributions to the book, when he was angry at being punished for breaking his bedroom window. It made him sad at first, and always made me feel guilty, and then he came to like it, after which he wrote in some of May's engineering jokes—*What do you call a nerd in 20 years? Boss!*—and cut paragraphs from a 1921 book of conundrums to paste in the flyleaf.

3 *Why is the letter T like an island?*

4 *What is that which occurs twice in a moment, once in a minute, and not once in a thousand years?*

He liked the erasure book because it had been printed exactly a hundred years before I was born. I liked it because he'd chosen it and because we worked on it together each morning before school, deciding which words to erase from one page at time, to make the book new, to make the book ours. Adding drawings, clippings, doodles, Liam diligent and playful. May and I in his genes, how could it be otherwise?

Cora and Henry were the least playful adults I'd met. I tried to imagine them in their teens or twenties. Every time, they looked the same. And that was the issue, I understood: *sameness*. The logos I was drawing, the campaign, they looked like every other cheese brand, and people tended to buy brands they grew up with. I had to break out of that, get people to want to try their cheeses, the sharp creamy cheddar, a smoked Gouda served with apple chutney, a fruity Manchego paired with thinly sliced prosciutto.

In Liam's flipbooks, hotdogs were being plated, dressed, picked up and eaten; a weird droopy-faced woman tried to walk; a balloon inflated only to be pierced by an arrow that sank into a bull's-eye on the far edge of the pages. Movement and timing and spacing, the crucial elements of animation.

What if Cora and Henry *didn't* change, though everything around them did? What if they had the same faces as kids that they did as adults, became the cheese masters they were? What if all that made people laugh, or smile, remember their product? Better than everything I'd so far done, I thought, and took out a new sketch pad and began again.

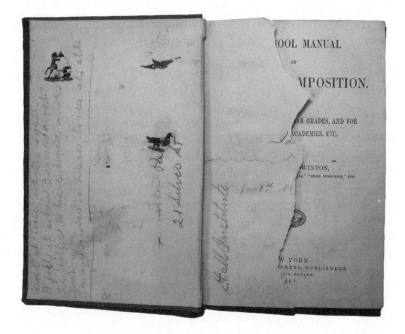

OOL MANUAL

OF

MPOSITION.

AR GRADES, AND FOR
ACADEMIES, ETC.

WINTON,
.," "BIBLE WORD-BOOK," ETC.

W YORK·
THERS, PUBLISHERS,
IN SQUARE.
881

Walk On By

NOVEMBER 2015

A heavy, early snowfall. Seven pristine inches blanketing the town, though it had melted on the black roads when I drove to the school with the other parents, once the crime scene had been processed. Over a hundred of us. I stood next to them in the parking lot, our breath smoking as if we'd come from the underworld, their children either already buried or home. Liam was still in the Neuro-ICU.

A walk through, to see where our children had been shot or killed. Some parents were angry because their children had been left lying on the floor for more than a day after they died, before funeral homes and coroners came to take them away. You always thought your pain was unbearable and often it was, but then you heard of others' pain that seemed worse. The narcissism of the present.

Inside, most of the lights were off—only sunlight through the windows—and, dazzled by the bright sun, I stood just over the threshold in the dim hallway to get my bearings as the other parents streamed past me like shadows and specters, like ghosts. They'd cleaned up most of the blood, though not all, the pools and big sprays of it, but here and there it speckled the spines of books or a chair leg. Strewn-about backpacks, some clothes, some books, a lot of SpongeBob and *Frozen* lunchboxes.

I entered each class. To imagine, I guess. Guns being cocked and shells clattering against the floor, screaming, crying, begging children, the smells of cordite and blood and fear. One teacher yelled NONONONONO before being killed; the school cameras recorded it, and most everything else, and some of the children had told reporters what they'd heard, so I had a pretty good idea. Liam told me a few things too. *RunIwanttogohomeWherearemyparents.* I was glad he'd then forgotten it.

Glasses and briefcases where teachers had died. One parent had been in to help with her special needs daughter; a sheaf of notes where she'd fallen. In the video, he came back into one room to shoot people again and wandered into empty rooms and shot up desks. Toward the end, he'd put a gun to one child's head but let him live. Later, I learned that boredom was common to spree shooters.

From Liam's classroom there'd been a long trail of blood, fairly wide, all the way to the bottom of the stairs. A ghost of it still existed, which I picked out as we walked, our footsteps echoing in the empty hallways. At first I avoided it and then I walked down the middle of it. The theory was that he'd been shot in the shoulder while standing beside Latrell, then hidden under a desk with part of his head sticking up and been hit by another shot. When he came to, he began to crawl, after the shooter had left the room but while he was still active. Through the classroom and down the hall to the stairs, dragging a yellow backpack behind him; not his. He'd fallen down the stairs, breaking his nose and cheek and orbital bone while the shooting was still going on.

One teacher had seen him sliding by and had wanted to run out to grab him, but she worried it might call attention to her classroom and that if she was shot trying to rescue Liam, all her children would die, so she watched him until he reached the stairs. She'd come to the hospital to check on him, to admit her guilt. To tell me she'd wanted him to have a witness.

Debbie Santo. *Pleasepleaseplease* she'd thought, over and over as she watched Liam sliding by, though she hadn't been sure what she was asking for. I walked by her classroom, following in the steps of the shooter, who'd gone that way before Liam did. The door was closed, the shade drawn; I couldn't blame Debbie. She'd lived and so had all her children, but already she'd said she couldn't come back.

Such a brave boy, Lamont said as we stood at the top of the stairs. He was really the only parent I knew. He put his hand on my arm to steady me. Latrell had been among the first to die, and one the shooter had returned for; no one knew why. The bottom of the stairs seemed a long way off.

You okay? Lamont asked.

No. None of us are or ever will be. I didn't say it. Since the shooting, most of my social inhibitions were slipping away, but the dim hallways spooked me.

When we were done, we streamed back into the light. Over the course of the walk-through the parents had sorted themselves into two rough groups, the parents of the surviving children in one, ahead of me, and those of the children who'd died behind me. I looked back at them. Still in the school, they were specters again, shadows lingering in the scene of blood and horror, and the image filled me with dread. They didn't want to leave the last place their children had been alive.

Why on earth did you look back, you idiot? I asked myself as I drove back to the hospital. Slowly at first, and, once out of sight of the others, as fast as I could.

The Price Is Right

What? I said. No, it's not for sale. I hung up, my heart beating. Three a.m., most of the world asleep; I'd stumbled through the darkened living room from the couch, thinking the ringing phone was the hospital to say Liam was fading.

Why would you think that? May said, after I told her it was someone who wanted to buy my car. It could have been a turn for the better, she said, and clicked off her light and yanked the covers up and rolled over to get back to sleep.

I stood looking at her. The room smelled damp in the dark and the woman on the phone and May had voices so similar they might have been sharing a voice box. Impossible, right? I couldn't make sense of it and went to the kitchen for some banana bread. May's co-worker Zhao had made it and though it was inedible it was also comfort food so I cut a slice to keep on a plate next to me and stumbled back to the couch and turned on the TV and muted it. When Liam was four he came into the kitchen and asked May for a slice of warm banana bread just from the oven.

Okay, she said, but just the one. She gave him two.

I knew you would, he said. I know how to arrange these things.

When she told me later we were both glad because the night before he'd been inconsolable. At the store he'd wanted a Playmobil model and we wouldn't buy it, telling him Christmas was coming, and he said, But last year I asked Santa sixty days in advance and the elf who helps him won't have time to make it this year! Santa's note said, *Made it myself!* and Liam tucked it into the first wallet he got.

Letters

Why aren't you interested in the police feed showing two nuns and a guy in a ski mask? It was a public school. Nuns would have been out of place. How come they never looked into that?

How come you never looked into that?

Must be because you're exhausted, keeping all the lies straight.

A Beginning

He'd been bullied, three of his friends talked about it, though his parents never knew. Lots of times, by lots of kids. But one event stood out for them, one he'd brought up again and again. Nash took notes on it and the story was almost always the same, down to the last details.

Slammed up against the lockers by four or five older boys when he was new to middle school and made to smell a girl's dropped used tampon, their big hands holding his head against the metal and forcing it to his nose and mouth.

He kicked their legs until they stomped on his feet, his wide brown eyes staring at them over the bloodstained tampon until they overflowed with tears.

That's it, that's it, they said in the softest voices, once he stopped struggling, as if they were helping him. *Breathe it in. Breathe it deep.*

Jazz

NOVEMBER 2018

Lamont showed up uninvited and unannounced and as usual with bourbon. It never bothered me. His coat carried with it the scent of the cold, of coming snow.

Let's eat, I said, leading him through the stacked boxes he'd helped me move.

Here, he said. He stopped and handed me a book, Steinbeck's *Grapes of Wrath*.

Should I keep it? I asked. You giving away your books?

All the rest to my church. He kicked a box. You should unpack some. Make the place homey. Get some Seabreeze candles too. Smell the place up nice.

Seabreeze?

Yeah. White people smells.

Wait, we have different smells?

You don't pay attention much, do you?

What's a Black smell?

Honeysuckle. He shrugged. Lavender and cinnamon. In the kitchen he blew dust from two glasses though there was none and poured us generous bourbons.

You cook, I'll watch, then eat, he said. Fair trade. He synced his iPhone with my speaker and thumbed through his music; he was always the aux. Jimmy Garrison on "Crescent," he said, and raised the volume. Smiling, like he'd just gifted me.

Patient and persistent, he was trying to teach me about jazz, and I was trying to learn. Every time he played something, I heard what he was getting at, but it all leaked out of my brain by the next session; I had to learn the same things over and over again. That was okay. I knew I was getting the band-me-down education intended for Latrell. Lamont said, Listen how Garrison only comes in at the beginning and end. Dude really brings the ruckus.

The scent of prosciutto sautéing in butter as Lamont drank.

Prosciutto? he said. American hams aren't good enough for you? Use a city ham. Wet-cured, brined. Moister, not smoked. Just like prosciutto.

I kept stirring, and Lamont switched back to talking about music. I sipped and listened. The album was *Live in Japan*. Coltrane, I said.

You got it! Such a smile. Dude was always in his first heaven with music.

That warmed me. I had the dutiful-schoolboy gene, which I'd passed on to Liam. There was never enough praise. May never understood that.

For a while we were quiet. But, perhaps because the song was recorded in Japan, before long Lamont began talking about his new wife, Akane.

I never knew my house had so much wrong. Drapes, he said.

You have to change them?

I *need* them. Don't you remember? I don't have any.

That's right, I said, adding a bit of fresh-cracked pepper. The clean look.

He said, The clean look is history. But you know what's good? She's not one of those women who eat so little and then brag about it like they're eating Bible pages.

He fell quiet and I hummed along with the melody as I stirred in the cream and the orange zest. Then I added the freshly squeezed orange juice.

I have to tell you something, he said, sliding his glass back and forth over the counter between his cupped hands like a puck, bourbon sloshing up the sides.

You trying to embroil me with another date?

Ha, no, he said. Learned my lesson with the first one. He drained the glass and refilled it. Though you should have given Palmer a chance. That woman's for real. Won the top salesperson award this year. Trip to Hawaii.

I gave her a chance, I said. I didn't say how in my dream of kissing her at the beach, her lips had tasted as sweet as carrots. The pasta was bubbling and nearly done; I scooped out some cooking water with a coffee mug to thin the sauce.

You remember DC? How I was gone for some of that first night, with Latrell? It was because you were going to read The Hardy Boys to Liam. I'd read some to Latrell earlier that year and he liked it okay, despite the prejudice, but after the second one he said he knew the way it would go, so I didn't want to be rude.

Rude how? Off the heat, I added pecorino cheese to the pasta. Over all the moves I'd lost some kitchen tools, so I used a vegetable peeler.

As if maybe I thought my boy was smarter than yours. Anyway. I felt bad about that so the second night we stayed in and you read more of it. The Mystery of Cabin Island. You were on your bed and Liam climbed down to sit next to you. When Chet saw the ghost on the island, Latrell climbed down to my bed to do the same. We listened. All the chapters you read. Then we turned the lights out and kept quiet just like that, each of us holding our boys until we fell asleep.

His voice had thickened. He drank some bourbon to clear it and said, I just wanted to thank you for that. I remember that night a lot. Before we left DC the next day, I went back to the bookstore and bought The Mystery of Cabin Island so I could read it aloud to him. But you know what? The rest of that book sucked!

I loved his rare bubbling laugh. I poured olive oil on the pasta to make it glisten and handed him his bowl. Eat.

He thanked me. I raised my glass and said, To our boys.

He clinked my glass and said, To our boys, and sat turning the pasta bowl, as if in a different position, it might look more appetizing. He could never eat when lost in thoughts about his dead son.

You talk to Liam today? he asked.

Every day.

He nodded and stared at his food, no doubt thinking he couldn't talk to Latrell. All the parents have an abiding sadness, combined with a seething anger, usually masked by a passionate commitment. Lamont's is the antiabortion crusade; May's the treatment of mental illness, but I didn't really have one, at least not that I admit, though really it's Kate. Every morning when I wake, she's one of the first things I think of. I'd never told Lamont any of that; Kate was mine.

I'd also decided in the aftermath not to waste anything, so, after I finished my bowl of pasta, I refilled Lamont's glass and patted his back and asked if it was okay if I ate his serving too. Part of my plan to become the world's fattest human, I said. He didn't like it if I took a bite of his food without asking.

You know, he said, pushing his plate over to me, three years in? Latrell's bones now. And if I ever find where the shooter's buried? His grave? I'm going to go piss on it. Every day until the Second Coming.

Call me, I said. I'll join you, and ate his dinner in addition to mine.

Mist World

NOVEMBER 2015

The Neuro-ICU ward had fifteen or twenty beds arcing around the floor, with thin sliding curtains between them, and in every one a bad case: strokes, car accidents, victims of beatings, all with neurological trauma, all constantly monitored and frequently tended, many of whom would die. It looked like Liam would be there awhile. They'd missed a single shotgun pellet that had entered just under his hairline and penetrated deep into his brain. Easy enough to do, with all his other injuries, but once you saw it on the X-ray, it was obvious. One day he'd talk, the next he wouldn't, the one after that he might be comatose or alert. Some days he walked.

The official diagnosis was damage to the frontal lobes and subarachnoid hemorrhages, bleeding between the brain and skull, which can cause a coma, paralysis, or death. A single subarachnoid hemorrhage increases your risk of death by 50 percent; he had three. Somehow, despite X-rays and CAT scans and an MRI, they'd missed them all at first. When I came across that 50 percent number as I did quick research on my phone, I stopped reading, not wanting to know any more.

Other people thought I should. A month into his stay on the Neuro-ICU, one of the residents called me into a cramped office behind the nurses' station. Trece. Short, with an afro and thick black glasses that magnified his eyes. He'd sat in on many of the meetings we'd had with surgeons and neurologists, pain management and pulmonary care doctors, never saying a thing, always wearing bright blue socks. Now he thought it was time I learned how serious this was.

I'm guessing you're taking in all this information and trying

116

to process it and probably not really knowing what's the most important part, he said.

I nodded. It was hard to understand all the jargon and they moved so fast I never had time to ask them to explain. Sometimes I looked up things on my phone, and now I could follow most of it, but a fair amount was meaningless, other than it seemed bad.

He put one foot up on a garbage can and called up an X-ray of Liam's head on the computer. The gray brain, the white skull. On the left side, between brain and skull, was a sea of black. With the point of his pen he outlined its vast, undulating circumference. That's the blood, he said. It shouldn't be there. Those are from the hemorrhages.

Will they have to operate to drain it? I asked.

No. It might drain itself or it might stay there forever or it might go away over time. It's only if it gets bigger that they worry.

How will they know?

Mapping technology. They have this one as a baseline and others they can overlay, to see any changes.

Lamont probably knew about that. That was the kind of thing he might be involved in. Not for the first time, I wished I was something other than an artist.

Trece ran the pen along the corpus callosum, the bundle of nerves that divides the brain into its two hemispheres. I thought he was tracking the route of the shotgun pellet.

Normally, he said, it runs in a straight line from the front of the brain to the back. That's off-center by about four degrees. His brain shifted that much from the impact of the bullet and from falling down the stairs. Maybe a blow to the head.

It was certainly new information, but I didn't really know what to do with that, either, so I thanked him and went back out to stand by Liam's bed, to listen to him breathe. It wasn't a bullet in his brain, it was a shotgun pellet, and the difference mattered, I told myself. I wasn't sure I believed it, but I wanted to. Why couldn't doctors be precise?

Two nurses were attending Liam so I stood aside and watched. They both had strong forearms and short fingernails. This might hurt a little, honey, the bigger one said, and rolled him onto one side and pulled the sheet out from beneath him.

And this too, the smaller one said, as they rolled him back.

Liam's eyelids fluttered but he didn't open them when he spoke. He said, Who paid your way through nursing school, Einstein?

Both nurses smiled at that one.

The numbers on his monitors were good. The O_2 saturation was above 90 percent. The gauze over the exit wound on his shoulder was blood-free, but he had a small red patch on the back of his good shoulder.

We'll have to watch that, the bigger nurse said. That can lead to bed sores. She spoke very quietly, not wanting to upset him.

She salved the spot and applied a bandage, and when they lowered Liam onto his back, he spoke without opening his eyes. Stop using your whisper voices, he said. I hate that.

Eternal Mysteries beyond the Grave

He left labeled discs behind, and a journal, about what he was going to do, the people he planned to shoot, and why. Nash thought it was fairly standard stuff: the world to blame for his troubles, how the shooting would make people recognize him.

But he'd torn random pages from his journal, one here, two there, twenty-four near the middle; all had vanished. And the discs: *Nixon, Bonaparte, Wee Willie Keeler.* Why? *Bonaparte* wasn't about grandiosity, *Wee Willie* didn't mention baseball, *Nixon* didn't deal with criminals or eighteen minutes of shooting. He'd planned for fifteen minutes before police arrived; he'd had eleven. Smart that way.

Nash spent a lot of time staring out his office window at rain and snow, at sunshine, at wind bending the pin oaks and pines, making anagrams from the letters, writing the names on index cards and placing them in different orders as the room dimmed and grew brighter from passing clouds, but nothing clicked. Nothing.

He wondered if the point wasn't to waste his time, one more *Fuck you* to the world. The shooter was practicing homicidal art, he wrote, and he had admirers, as sick as that sounded. Nash didn't let anger distract him, and he didn't stop trying, because he'd promised the parents of all those children he would. He owed them that, especially May.

There was something about her, and he hadn't told her the complete truth, though she'd asked. So, a touch of guilt, and a bigger portion of attraction, two-thirds of the pie maybe. You weren't supposed to get involved with victims or survivors, but sometimes these things just happened. Some pies you just wanted to inhale.

Last Will and Testament

In the Neuro-ICU, you got to know the other occupants if you had someone there for a while. Beyond the shot Uruguayan was a white-haired Ukrainian lady, a stroke victim who took up only a small portion of her bed. The attempted suicide, the man who'd been hit by a hammer after leaving a bar, and the two teen girls in successive bays who'd been driving too fast and flipped their cars.

The Ukrainian had come to America in her thirties as a nanny; her charges seemed to love her. Day after day people streamed in to see her, and gradually I began to recognize them. She'd lived in apartments all over Manhattan and she must have been given bonuses, because it turned out she'd bought property back in the Ukraine. A lot, it seemed. And she had no children. Sarah was the woman there the most. Early thirties with round, sad green eyes. At night before she had to leave, she sang Ukrainian lullabies to Galina.

One I especially liked. What's the name of that one? I asked. The ward was quiet. Dark outside already and the shift halfway through, most of the visitors gone. Beeping machines, fluorescent lights, I might have been imagining it, but I thought Liam's heart rate slowed whenever she sang.

Sarah said, I don't know. I don't know the names of any of them. I just remember her singing them to me all the time. I don't even know if I'm pronouncing them right or mixing up words from different ones. They're all rattling about my head, but I may have them wrong.

A week later she was back with a lawyer, who spoke Ukrainian.

Sarah came to get me where I sat sketching beside Liam. I was supposed to be working on CVS, but I was sketching him instead.

Hi, she said, sliding the curtain aside on its clicking runner. Sorry. Could I borrow you for a minute?

I looked at Liam's monitors. His O$_2$ levels were fine, his breathing. He'd talked to me a bit before drifting back into sleep, stray, unrelated comments, something about a ginger on TV and why I should turn it off, a couple of lines from *Goodnight Moon* in French. But he knew who I was. Sure, I said, and stood.

Can you be a witness? she asked. To Galina's will?

Oh. Okay. But whatever it says I can't read it. I don't know any Ukrainian.

That's the thing, Sarah said. She doesn't have one. We're making it for her.

She woke up? I was surprised. Since her stroke, she'd been unconscious, twenty-five days and counting; waking up would be a great sign.

No, Sarah said. But under Ukrainian law, this is legal.

We crowded around Galina's bed, Sarah and me and the lawyer, whose name I didn't catch. Short and stout and with the glossiest black hair and beard. I wondered if the hair was a wig. He shook my hand and said to Sarah, Ready? His voice so deep it sounded like it came from a well.

He began reading a document in Ukrainian. Now and then he'd look up at Sarah over his reading glasses and she would nod, so when he looked at me I nodded too.

Three dense pages; I must have nodded fifteen or twenty times, wondering each time what I was agreeing to, if they were fleecing this woman or making sure she'd always be taken care of, and whether Ukrainian law held any sway in an American ICU, and how on earth my life had come to this.

Okay, the lawyer said, when he was done. You just need to sign several copies. He put his broad thumb to the bottom of the page where an X had been typed, and I started to sign but paused.

What does all this say? I asked.

That she's of sound mind and body.

But she isn't, I said. Is that legal?

He shrugged and pocketed his phone. We'll find out.

What happens to all her property?

It goes into a trust.

For her?

He nodded. Once it's sold.

Who runs it? I asked.

A board. Fifteen of the children she cared for.

She doesn't have any of her own?

No. Nor living relatives. And after she dies, if she dies, the money is disbursed to a fund for indigent Ukrainian immigrants.

The flowers on her bedside table had wilted, their orange petals like crepe paper. I signed all seven copies even though I had no idea if what he said was true or whether to laugh or cry.

AIDS Cures Fags

DECEMBER 2018

In the video, Dexter Fenchwood peacocks behind the altar in a powder blue suit. Gaudy fits; he wants to be noticed. I'd realized that when I'd first picked him out in the waiting room. I've watched this two dozen times—a bad workday like today sends me back to it every time; sometimes it feels so good to smolder.

It *seems* like innocent blood, Fenchwood says, gesturing theatrically. It's *natural* for us to become incensed. Forty-three children killed! Forty-three!

Some of their faces flash on a screen behind him.

And twenty-seven wounded! he says, with Liam's face behind him now.

He stops, squats, pauses, says it again, his voice lower this time, barely a whisper, his palm moving over the floor like over a field of grain, the heads of children. Forty, three, children, killed, and, twenty, seven, wounded, he says, the dramatic pauses filled with silence. When he bows his head, his thin blond hair covers his face like a curtain and parishioners lean forward to take in his words.

But what about the adults? he says, bounding up to pace again, vibrating with emotion. Nine selfless brave men and women who stood in the path of bullets so that the young might live! Yet God has given us a brain. He has asked us to *think*! He stops, and here his voice trembles. Think about those children! Think about how two of their teachers were fags, inculcating them with their evil, possibly *molesting* them. And as you think, he says, his red face distorted with disgust, remember the Psalms. *The foolish shall not stand in thy sight: thou hatest all workers of iniquity.*

At the edge of the stage, he reaches toward the crowd. And

remember Leviticus when you give thought to our nation, our nation that argues we need to respect sodomy. He stares out at the crowd. And what did God say about that, generations before? *And ye shall not walk in the manners of the nation, which I cast out before you: for they committed all these things, and therefore I abhorred them.*

That's what God said about it. God *abhorred* them. Think on that word, take it to heart. God *abhorred* them! And recall Malachi. *I have laid his mountains and his heritage waste for the dragons of the wilderness.*

Now he's really rolling, his thin blond hair flying as he darts in front of the altar. In 1898 BC, he says, God destroyed Sodom and Gomorrah for their sins, yet now we have funerals for impenitent sodomites like the teachers of those children. In response to which I say, Our gospel message is the world's last best hope.

To which I say, Do not believe the hell-bound prophets with their Arminian lies that Jesus died for everyone. They are messengers of Satan, and accursed of God.

To which I say, If you *care* about your never-dying soul, if you *care* about total depravity: God killed those forty-three children and nine adults because FAGS BURN IN HELL, because GOD IS NOT MOCKED, because FAGS DOOM NATIONS.

He pauses, breathing heavily, and says, And remember that because of that, *we* say—he raises his arm—Can I have a chorus?

And as he brings his arm down again and again, the parishioners erupt, their voices drowning out his.

THANK GOD FOR AIDS! THANK GOD FOR DEAD SOLDIERS! THANK GOD FOR DEAD AND WOUNDED CHILDREN!

Wild One

DECEMBER 2015

A neurosurgeon who was also a neurologist sat looking through Liam's file, Victoria Wild; she went by Vic. It sounded like a porn name, which I didn't say, though I couldn't help notice her head of beautiful brunette hair and short skirt and her long, smooth shapely legs. Such calves! I wanted to draw them, to cup them in my palms. What a perv, noticing that while machines beeped, with damaged brains and ruined bodies and death death death all around. Then I wondered if it wasn't simply human, the urge toward life when enveloped by destruction, and took surreptitious glances until I made myself stop.

Her hands surprised me, though. Big as skillets with fingers. When she came to one X-ray, she told me she worried about shearing. I looked at her blankly.

She said, The brain is actually a series of very thin planes, connected by nerve fibers. Often in car accidents and sometimes in shootings and in falls down stairs, the brain is subjected to such force that the planes slide back and forth violently, shearing those neural connections. Brains can look relatively fine on X-rays or MRIs, she said, holding Liam's up to the light for me, as if I might know what I was looking at, but the damage is there.

How long does it take for those connections to regenerate? I asked.

Oh, she said. They never regenerate. The result is usually death. Occasionally the patient doesn't die, but remains in a vegetative state. For years, even.

She tucked the X-ray back in like bedding a tulip bulb and closed the file and stood up and smoothed her skirt, ready to move on to her next case. I was appalled by the casual nature of her comment, even as I understood she was simply doing her job. My stomach felt hollow, my chest. I had the odd sensation that I was levitating, that I no longer had lungs. Then she said, I wish you'd had a chance to talk to him, after the shooting. Then we'd know. She gathered her long hair in her hand and turned the bunched ends up like an umbrella handle and sniffed it.

I did, Dr. Wild, I said, and told her about how when Liam woke up in recovery after his first surgery he said, Happy Birthday, Otto! and we'd talked about what he wanted to get me as a present. I didn't say anything about the whole *benbow* thing, because I didn't think it mattered, and because it might.

Oh, good, she said, and slipped the file back in its place at the nurses' station and flipped her hair back over shoulder. I thought it must be quite a procedure to get it all under a cap when she operated.

She said, If he can talk like that, he doesn't have shearing, and walked off. The gold chains wrapped around her low tan boots winked as she walked.

I called May right away, wanting to share this victory, but it didn't seem to impress her as much as it had me. I sat beside Liam and fiddled with my phone and wondered if she'd detected my undercurrent of desire.

Kate

In her most-viewed video, she sits behind a desk in a crisp blue-and-white-striped blouse and dark jacket, with diplomas visible behind her on the wall, though what schools they're from seems impossible to make out. Remember that *seems*.

A pen and pencil set on the leather blotter atop the massive mahogany desk, bookshelves filled with legal books, all the trappings of an accomplished lawyer. She leans toward the camera to speak. We are almost certainly dealing with government-funded, legal propaganda to achieve a supposed national-security objective, she says, which is a Deep-State priority, the disarming of the citizenry.

Images of East Germany and the Soviet Union in the '50s and Afghanistan in the '80s flash on the screen. She says, The United States Department of Defense has conducted information operations for years in foreign countries during wartime, and now it's doing so at home. Civilian participants are almost certainly convinced these operations involve a good and necessary objective.

Pictures of me and Lamont pop up. Furthermore, she says, they are likely paid large sums and have signed nondisclosure forms, which include serious penalties, possibly imprisonment for a very long time, if the terms are violated.

Lamont again, in handcuffs, after a DUI, though there's no way for anyone to know that. Kate sits back in her chair and says: Unless you understand those elements, it's hard to grasp how these things can be pulled off. I know, because I used to be a US attorney.

Slick and convincing, the visuals, her obviously educated diction, the US attorney claim. That it's all lies doesn't matter; the gullible are willing. She repeats her allegation that the school shooting was staged, that "Liam" is an actor, a boy from California, and adds,

Further proof that "Liam" wasn't real is that his picture showed up in images from a massacre in Pakistan years later, from an attack on a hospital that supposedly killed 147 people.

After which the screen shows Liam's picture, one I released, held up with pictures of boys killed in Pakistan by an apparently distraught father. Why a Pakistani parent held it up is something I've never been able to figure out, but it's the one piece of evidence that doubters always come back to.

Then she shows pictures of a child actor next to pictures of Liam, and the boys look alike. If you saw it once or twice or weren't paying attention, you could believe it; she's very convincing. But I'm paying attention, especially to her final words.

A lovely face, she says. But don't worry. Before long, he'll appear in the next government-staged crisis event, presented by complicit media to a gullible public. Call Otto Barnes. Tell him to stop lying. Tell him America deserves the truth.

Her face fades and my phone number appears, one I've changed often. Each time, I put $500 away. If it comes to it, I'll pay a private detective to track her down.

Sometimes I want to find her so I can convince her she's mistaken, so she can convince others, and sometimes I want to find her so I can shake her, scream at her to stop making these outlandish statements, stop making me hurt, stop inspiring other hoaxers, who harry and harass us, who hurt May. And sometimes I just wish that, for a few hours, I could exchange with her my tired heart.

LBTS So It's Not for Sale, I Swear to You

DECEMBER 2015

How did you get this number? I asked, wheedling, when I'd aimed for menace.

Craigslist, she said, and hung up.

Awake now, I checked the computer and my car was for sale, at a ridiculously low price, followed by my phone number. *Late night calls acceptable.* After two hours, I got them to pull the ad. *Can't guarantee it won't show up again, though.*

I went back to bed. The room smelled of apple and cinnamon, May's new perfume, changed in hopes of changing our luck. You did this, she said. Pissed someone off somehow. That's why they're after you.

May, I didn't do anything. That's foolish.

Foolish? Then why are they after you? *You.* You and nobody else?

I knew she was scared and tired; I was too. We'd been told this would happen by a hospital counselor, that we'd grow angry over time and perhaps take it out on each other, that we should watch for it. I'd watched and I knew and I didn't care.

I wanted to grab her chin so hard I'd leave marks. Listen, May, I said, keeping my voice level and low, bunching the sheets in one hand. You better get something straight. This happened to both of us. Liam being shot. It didn't just happen to you.

She refused to answer. I was about to say something more when her lips trembled. *Hold her,* I thought, but she was still giving off a prickly pear vibe, so instead I made her a pot of her favorite mint tea to help her sleep, and when I brought her the steaming mug she thanked me and apologized and smiled.

Christmas for Beginners

DECEMBER 2015

After sunset, heavy marbled clouds filled the sky and the rain exploded and the wind picked up and blew in a cold front, behind which the slashing rain changed to sleet that ticked against the windows and snow that muffled sound. I watched it all through the Neuro-ICU window. Liam slept in the narrow, railed bed, his eyes darting under his eyelids and his body still, a good sign, Dr. Wild said, touching her Christmas tree pin as if for luck. Restorative sleep. I wanted to believe her.

The snow picked up. After she left, a great yellow reef of light flashed through the black clouds and a long crack of thunder peeled across the sky, rattling the window; thunder snow. Miraculous, but I had no one to share it with, May still at work and none of the nurses aware of it and no one in the waiting room I recognized.

That I was the only one who'd seen it depressed me, so I left the Neuro-ICU and walked down the long quiet hallway to the elevators past the multicolored Christmas lights blinking below the ceiling and rode one down to the first floor to go outside, hoping to see it again, or at least to see something different than the ward with its curtained bays and beeping machines and still bodies under the thin sheets and thin blankets and people waiting—desperate and hopeful—in the nearby waiting room. The hours we'd spent there, days of them, weeks.

Outside, cars came and went or idled against the curb, smokers with their windows open despite the cold, and I counted a dozen sodden or shredded umbrellas stuffed into trashcans or flapping in the gutters. Snow gusted past in the cold wind, white and then yellow when it slanted across the streetlights and then white again on the far side. A bell rang for the Salvation Army drive and I dropped all my change in the big red kettle and all the bills in my wallet without counting them. Snow piled up on the parked cars and street signs banged in the wind and a blue light blinked on a cell tower.

A handcuffed prisoner in an orange jumpsuit accompanied by a beefy cop wearing a bulletproof vest went by, the two of them chuckling at the skunky smell of weed hanging in the wet air; I wanted some. A bald man sat in his car parked against the curb facing the wrong way, vaping, his fingertips green where they rested against the car radio. He asked to borrow my cell phone and I almost said I didn't have one, but I let him; we were in front of a hospital, for chrissake. Then I thought I should tell him about Liam so he wouldn't drive off and felt bad about thinking that after he made his call and gave my phone back and handed me his pen.

Not a noob, he said, as I ripped it, and I nodded. An open sky-blue umbrella cartwheeled down the street in the wind and we watched it tumble past us and past the hospital and past three glowing food trucks until it snagged on a bush. We smiled at that and I handed him his pen. The salt crunched under my boots as I walked back into the hospital, its powdery trail tapering off over the big rectangular gray mat and down the black terrazzo hallway, which grew shinier the farther I got from the sliding doors and the cold blowing in behind me.

In the Neuro-ICU, nothing had changed. Liam didn't seem to have moved at all, one thin arm still angled over the gray blanket, his closed eyelids glossy and still, and still so dark they looked bruised. I sat with him and held his hand, my thumb finding his strong pulse at his wrist; he smiled. Snowflakes melted as they struck the warm window and the strings of beads stretching down the glass looked like tinsel. Then it was May's turn to sit beside Liam and I realized I was humming carols on the way to my car and wished I'd hummed to him instead, or to her. To both of them.

I should go back in, I thought, but noticed that my right rear tire was flat, a nail. It seemed too much, finally, and I stood bereft looking at it, my chest a canyon, until three strangers came and changed the tire and would take no money, though I offered. My skin prickled with sweat and I grew hot under all my layered clothes when I realized I'd given it all away, but it didn't matter.

No, the youngest said, the fringe on her vintage leather jacket swaying as she stood, no money, and put her green wool gloves back on and touched my face and said, Merry Christmas, and left.

Letters

Why is there no record of any environmental company that cleaned up the bloody mess? Blood and bones and brain matter?

You say your son's blood spread all down the hallway, and the blood of all those other so-called victims, the dead ones. Small children but still filled with blood. And the adults—"teachers" and "Parents". 1.5 gallons per person. Exsanguination is the technical term, but it adds up to a lot of blood. As long as their hearts are beating, it just pumps out of them, every bullet hole a gusher.

If 75 gallons of blood was spread out over all those classrooms and hallways, along with bone and brain matter, why did no one ever clean it up?

Saffron and Saltpeter

DECEMBER 2015

Katrina's parents, blond and bland, lived in a gated community with a meetinghouse. A big stone fireplace and leather couches, vanilla-scented candles and leather-backed books. About sixty of us came to the meeting.

Allocating donated money was tricky. Parents whose children had died should get a larger share, but wounded kids needed medical care—some for life—so how much did the pain of death trump the needs of the living? Nothing in our lives had prepared us for it, and no one wanted to appear hard-hearted or greedy.

Shen's father proposed the best solution. Split it sixty-forty, he said, standing in front of the fire, his thin face tight and pale. Sixty to those whose children died, forty to the wounded. Shen's leg had been amputated, and Henry's proposal seemed fair; we left the meeting room for coffee and cookies and to let it stew.

I'd made chocolate chip cookies; Lamont brought a bottle of bourbon.

Good choice, I said, ribbing him to lighten the mood. A mistake, I saw, and switched my attention to the news on the muted large-screen TV. Afghanistan.

What a fucking disaster, I said. Our longest war, and for what?

What would you do? Lamont said. Pull our soldiers out, so all those others would have died in vain? The cords on his neck stood out.

Come on, Lamont, I said, surprised into getting louder. Sooner or later we have to leave. Why keep sacrificing kids when it plainly isn't working?

Oh, right. He put down his coffee. You want to leave so the

Taliban can bomb us in another three years and we have to go back in and kill them all again.

Jesus, Lamont! They're still killing us now, only it's over there instead of here. I don't see how that's better.

That's because you've got your head up your ass. Why don't you get your money and get up through?

I turned away from him, eyes stinging, shoulders and neck tight, hands trembling with adrenaline. All the other parents stood in a semicircle, watching. I pushed by Henry and stepped outside to calm down, and when the door opened behind me and noise spilled out into the darkness, I turned to tell Lamont to fuck off or to take it offline, but it was Shen's petite mother, Jia, a stalwart at the hospital.

Intense, she said, and understandable. She hugged herself against the cold night air. Our anger comes out at the slightest provocation. Just yesterday I snapped at a saleswoman who showed me a sale rack of dresses. *Do you think I can't afford full price?* I said. I felt crazy even as I said it, but I kept hectoring her.

I took a deep breath and let it out slowly. Yes, I said. It makes us all nuts.

And always will, Jia said, looking up at the brilliant stars. Forever.

You seem pretty calm, I said, saleswoman aside. What's your secret?

Oh, you know, she said, and waved her hand. Faith. And we basically have a Lexapro lick in the kitchen.

I laughed. An owl hooted.

She said, You know what really gives me strength? Seeing how Liam's fighting. And that we endure. Watch. Lamont will apologize. She rested her slim hand on my arm. And I just know Liam's going to make it.

Superstitious under those wheeling, long-dead stars, I didn't say a thing.

The Wondering

DECEMBER 2015

Grandmummy was dead, right? Liam said. Can you tell me how they did it?

Did what?

The burning thing.

I shivered. Did the astringent scent of cleaning fluid make him think of fire? Not wanting to get graphic, especially here, I said, It's a very complex process, Liam.

You mean it's hard for you to explain?

He sounded just like his mother. It was nice to laugh in the Neuro-ICU, and I was glad he was talking coherently; I charted his days and good ones were becoming more infrequent so this, like the others, gave me hope. When May saw the chart, she told me I was using an incorrect formula, though not where I'd gone wrong. Yes, I said, to Liam. It's hard to explain.

He fell silent. Monitors beeped, a curtain swished shut farther down the ward—an invasive procedure or last rites—rain drummed on the roof. In the next bay, a ventilator pumped away, a teenaged girl pulled from a ruined car.

But tell me this, he said at last, and put a small hand up in the air and spread his fingers, studied his pale palm. His gown shifted and the circular bullet wound on his shoulder shone like pewter in the light. He said, They burned her body, right?

Yes.

He let his hand drop at his wrist, like a wilted flower, and turned his bright blue eyes on mine. If she was already dead, why did they want to kill her again?

Words of Sorrow, to Which
Neither May nor I Replied

December 22, 2015

Dear May and Otto,

I hope my writing you will not cause more pain than you have already suffered. I would not presume to write, except that to not do so would be cowardly, and would make you think I did not care about the enormous grief my son has caused you.

I have prayed every day that your son Liam recovers swiftly from the shooting. I read that he has had three surgeries so far and that he may have one or two more to go, but that he is expected to fully recover. That is perhaps the one bright spot in all this darkness.

We have never met, but this tragedy has linked us, us and so many others in this town that I grew up in and have always loved. From reports, I understand you moved here less than a year ago. It must have seemed a perfect place then, and must now seem as if the move was a horrible mistake.

I want to apologize for the suffering my son has caused you and your family, for the wounding of your son, for making you worry night and day, for making this place seem less than the paradise I always found it to be, for making the world seem a less-safe place, a cruel place. My son did this, my son caused this unspeakable tragedy, which is something I will struggle for the rest of my days to understand.

No doubt you will too. I pray that that struggle will pale in comparison to the joy you will feel, as your son returns to health and comes to be always by your side. May each step toward his recovery, however small, bring you hope as well.

Sincerely, and with profound sorrow,

Letters

Ask your friend Lamont this question: If your child died, why did you not allow his organs to be harvested? Other children, real children, needed them. Two were on the registry THAT DAY at the hospital. Both those registry kids later died, so either his child didn't die, or he's an asshole. To which does he want to admit?

Send me his answer, when you have it. The prick won't respond to my letters.

Interim 4

Number of school shootings since: 145

Number of school children killed: 242

Wild Again

I sketched the nurses' six small umbrellas, open and upside down, drying in a corner, translucent in the light. Lilac and lime green and silver blue and a lacy red one flanked by two black ones like guards. When Dr. Wild walked by I wanted to reprimand her off-handed mention of shearing, to say that maybe that wasn't the best way to deliver potentially devastating news, but I worried that it might anger her, and, after all, she was responsible for my son's care. Superstitious and cowardly, I held my tongue, watching her write out notes in her surprisingly beautiful hand.

Superstition didn't matter, and cowardice didn't help. Liam stopped breathing again and after they revived him he got violent and had to be restrained. He got loud too, screaming and cursing, and they cleared out all visitors from the Neuro-ICU except May and me. His bay was too narrow for both of us to be with him so we took turns sitting beside him or in the waiting area, just outside.

Liam's yelling leaked through the heavy closed doors into the windowless room. Bellowing, really. Not words, just noises, the eviscerating sound of relentless pain. They were evaluating him so I squeezed May's hand and got up and walked the hallways to find a deserted office where I let go, not wanting May or other visitors to see me cry, but when I came back his screams thrilled me; if he was screaming that loudly, he was fighting, and I wanted more than anything for him to fight because his life depended on it. *Scream!*

The man in the bed next to Liam was forty-two, Dominican American; he'd had a stroke. His family, huge and close, rotated in and out of the waiting room hour by hour, taking up two entire rows of chairs facing one another. Liam was screaming still and the man's immaculately dressed father touched my knee and said, It breaks my heart to hear that. So young.

They were the only words I ever heard him speak in English. The rest of the time he was the voice of reason and reassurance for everyone in his family, always in Spanish. I understood about half of it.

At dusk, his wife brought stacked, overflowing Tupperware containers of fragrant home-cooked rice and beans, plantains, and chicken and offered me some, and at first I said no, but once I took a plateful I couldn't get enough; it must have looked as though I hadn't eaten in months. She refilled my plate three times. We never exchanged names, no one in the waiting room did, but huge smiles, all around. I don't know if I've ever eaten anything so good. May didn't want any. I took a picture of my plate and sent it to Liam. Spicy foods were his favorite.

Later, I went out and bought a big box of donuts and a container of coffee for the whole family because May said the Dominicans she worked with loved sweets. The snow was heavy and when cars took corners too fast sheets of it flew off their roofs. All the way back my boots stove dark ovals in the deep snow. In the waiting room, the father brushed snow from my shoulders and helped me off with my coat.

A small moment of communion in an unlikely place during an unholy moment; I wouldn't forget it. My fear and grief didn't lessen, but I did for a few minutes feel less alone.

To Do List:

Move.

Drink bourbon.

Move again.

Find Kate.

Drive across state to pick up mail.

Work.

Try to work more.

Try to work again.

Find more work.

Find Kate.

Check car for tails.

Drink bourbon with Lamont.

Watch TV.

Read.

Draw faces and their spheres: nose, cheek, chin and eye.

Buy paper, pencils, stumps and tortillons.

Find Kate.

Drive across state to pick up mail.

Draw.

Practice shading: cast shadow, shadow edge, halftone, reflected light, full light.

Work.

Go for walks.

Check the car for tails.

Find Kate.

Go on dates.

Talk to May.

Talk to Liam.

Talk to Lamont.

Work.

Mark the solstice.

Mark a day of good work with a bad movie.

Drive across state to pick up mail.

Move.

Find Kate.

Move again.

Don't forget Liam's clothes.

Jazz'd

Lamont sneezed again, allergic to something in my apartment, and then again, so loudly I missed the announcer's call of a touchdown, so I moved the bowl of chicken wing bones and the empty beer bottles ranked on the ottoman, the remotes covered in orange dust. Finally Lamont said, It's the poinsettia.

A gift from Palmer. She'd left it at the door with a note—*I understand. Want to try again? Call me if you'd like to go for coffee!* When Lamont saw the note he urged me to. Nice woman, he said. And she always smells good. That's underrated. Cocoa butter. Just has problems in love.

Then how come you didn't go out with her instead of getting remarried?

Never mix shit and cookies, he said.

Should have, I thought. He and Akane looked like they were getting divorced. He'd called me one night, plaintive. *Thought she was an afromantic.*

We both cheered a big hit. Then Lamont said, Got a good letter this week. *You're fictitious, so how can you file a lawsuit? I smell a wet pile of BS yet again.*

Wait, I said. You don't exist?

No. I'm a government creation.

With all their resources, they should've come up with someone better looking.

Fuck you, he said, and laughed. Then he said, Still waiting.

For what? An apology?

No, he said, and swirled his beer, studied it. The thing about time. For it to mellow it out. It's just an endless pit in my stomach, morning till night. He sipped the beer, then drained it and cracked another and chased it with bourbon.

At halftime, we switched to the news. Two American soldiers killed in Gabon. When I clicked to the other game, he said, Switch it back, and leaned forward to watch more intently. Any idea how many places our military is in? he asked, and didn't wait for me to answer. One hundred forty-three countries. Ninety percent of all the countries on earth. He sounded appalled. The military that we love, he said.

You've changed your mind about the war in Afghanistan?

He narrowed his eyes and said, I've changed my mind about a lot of things.

Kind of a forever war, I said.

Nah, he said, and slid forward on his seat. You ever notice that when armed whites get shot, the NRA speaks up, or when armed whites get shit from the cops? But when Blacks do, the NRA says nothing?

It's a racist country, Lamont. We know that.

Great, he said. You're woke, but that doesn't mean you've got a seat at the cookout. You need to get woke to this. When there's a mass shooting? Press is a-l-l over it. Seventy-five dead, twenty, even four or five, our screens light up for days. The real toll is quieter though, and a fuckton worse. About seven thousand dead in the two big wars, Afghanistan and Iraq, after twenty years. But right here? he said. In our country? Thirteen thousand killed each year by guns.

It's not just the numbers, I said. It's the cost. All that money, all those soldiers deployed, the civilians who die in those countries too.

That's right, he said and nodded. Drank. That's right. But let's be fair. Let's go back to what started it all. 9/11. They say we're fighting to

145

stop another one of those, three thousand dead. But with thirteen thousand murdered each year with guns, if there's a forever war, it's against our own.

I drank quietly, thinking that it was maybe more complex than that. What 9/11 did to the economy and to the lives of so many people—those firemen who died in the building collapse, those firemen who lived but grew sick and died in the years following, their families, the families of the victims, our forever-punctured communal sense of safety. But then I realized the same thing was true for all the families of the murdered. The sorrow and loss of safety, the shredded lives.

You support gun control then, I asked him.

Hell no. When those hoaxers come to punch my ticket, I want to be armed. The hoaxers, he said again, and sipped his drink. The government, he said, and sipped again. White people.

I laughed at the last one, but he didn't. Poured himself more bourbon and said, Cops and school shooters. You're doing us in.

Not all of us.

Doesn't have to be all. Just enough that have hate in their DNA.

You could be a hoaxer, I said. Believing in all these conspiracies.

He got up, left. When he came back in he was holding a bat and a surge of fear jolted my body. Was he really going to come at me?

Look, he said. He flipped the bat and held it out by the handle, a peace offering, one long finger under my name burned into the barrel. I've got an identical one, he said. We can use these to dissuade the hoaxers when they come around.

You think that's a good idea? I said.

He tapped the bat in the palm of his hand, looking at me. Listen, he said. You got to let that shit out at some point. It's eating you up. Was me too, but now I'm letting it loose. So should you. Never know how soon it'll be too late.

He rapped the barrel on the ground and stood it upright in the corner. You use that, he said. Let them know what you're made of. Otherwise, I'll change your name from Bismarck to Gandhi, and you know you don't want to be in the coward's union.

Because we'd approached something so raw, we didn't say anything else until the game returned. Then we cracked open new beers and watched a few plays until an ad came on for wedding cakes from a bakery, not Silver's.

Lamont said, I ever tell you Karlene and I eloped?

No wedding cake for you then, I said.

Nope. Disappointed Latrell. We were sitting around a table at my cousin's wedding. First one he went to. About four or five years old. He asked if his mama and I danced at our wedding and I said no. Then he asked if we cut the cake and Karlene said no. You could see disappointment building. Frustration. He had this idea of weddings and we weren't living up to it. Finally he said, Did you at least do the part where Daddy stuck his penis in your vagina?

Good Will to All

I feel bad, not sending Palmer anything, so I dash off a card and sign it.

    Time to Get the Christmas Spirit! I vote for Bourbon.

May Calls—Schism or Reform?

DECEMBER 2018

Sometimes she makes the late night calls, sometimes I do. We always pick up. Residual love, guilt. To show we're not sleeping with someone else, though, divorced, we're certainly allowed to and sometimes have.

I feel so guilty at times, she says, and I put her on speakerphone, readying for a long conversation, one I've had many times in different apartments, in person, on holidays and anniversaries and random days of the week.

Guilty about what? I say, though I suspect I know, my Nash radar buzzing.

She's silent so long I think she's fallen asleep and I'm about to hang up when she says, You want guilt, Otto? It's Nash. *Bingo*, I think, and she adds, I had the worst thought when we first met him. I thought he was *hot*.

Oh, I say, surprised. *Probably his shoes.* She always noticed shoes.

May says, What kind of person thinks about someone being hot when they hear that their son has been shot?

May. He looks like a young Idris Elba. If the detective had been a woman who looked like Margot Robbie, I'd have thought she was hot too.

Margot Robbie's a blonde, she says.

An exception, I say. Anyway, no one's rational in those situations.

Which is true. I'm not blaming her for that, though I'm also thinking of myself. How I'd noticed Dr. Wild's legs, her small chest and silver necklace, the kind of woman I've always gone for. That, I don't tell May about. Instead I repeat that she shouldn't feel bad. The mind reacts to stress in peculiar ways, I say.

Not that way, she says. I don't know anybody whose mind does that.

You should get out more, I say, or you two should get married.

Otto, she says, exasperated.

No, I mean it, I say, despite her tone, or perhaps because of it, to break her free. How many times has she done that for me? You could marry Nash and he could take your last name and then he'd be Nash Barnes. Sounds like an action figure.

She giggles. That's your last name.

Yours too, I say. In the following quiet, I wonder why she hasn't reverted to her maiden name. In stores, cashiers recognize it and want to talk about the shooting, where they were when they heard.

She says, He's taking me to lunch next week.

New updates in the case? I ask.

No. Just a lunch lunch.

Oh, I say. A date, and realize that must be the source of her guilt, that she's going out with someone else, and that that someone else is involved in Liam's case. After the slightest pause I say, Good! Good for you. You need to date.

I don't tell her anything about Palmer, waiting for her to ask, but she says in a quiet voice, Well, what about hooky?

Hooky? But I know she's referring to the day of the shooting. If we play hooky again, it'll become a pattern, she'd said, and not one we want to set up for him.

A tradition, I'd said, but she hadn't relented.

By saying no that day I ruined everything, she says now.

You didn't ruin everything, I say. I don't hold it against you.

But I do. All the therapists say: forgive, and they're right, only I can't. I don't tell her that and never will; she probably knows I nurse that grudge as if time won't put an end to it, though I don't want to. The grave clears everything up, even regrets.

If I hadn't said no, he wouldn't have been shot, May says. You know that.

We fall silent, listening to one another breathe six miles apart. Then she says, You know what he said to me that day? After I'd already said he had to go to school? After I said, No hooky today? You'd gone out to the car.

He hoped you got a loose tooth?

She laughs, and I hear her shift in the bed, wood creaking. Beside her bed is a picture of me holding Liam after his first bath, his skin glistening. She says, He gave me that drawing of the red tulip. After, he stood in the doorway looking at me and it was the last thing he said to me in our house that morning.

I hold my breath, waiting. This is new information. I've asked about it but she's never shared it, so I'm careful not to interrupt, even as I find myself sitting up.

What he said was, Mummy, you look so much like you today.

So I asked him, How so?

He said, That skirt, that blouse, those freckles, that lipstick, that toenail polish. When I close my eyes and think of you, that's what I see. You!

Must be what Nash sees, I think, and feel shitty. We're divorced, for fuck's sake. My claims on her are in the past, but I have the soul of an arsonist.

Say goodnight to Liam for me, I say.

She says, I always do.

More Texts from Strangers

So the FBI comes out and confirms that your "school shooting" was a hoax! Where's the outrage? What else are we being lied to about? Waco? JFK?

Letters

Your grief, which knows no bounds, will be absorbed in His love.
We pray, each and every one of the Carmelite Sisters, that it happens here
on earth, soon. We have faith that it will happen in the hereafter. We pray
you come to, too.

Another Beginning

DECEMBER 2002

Gretels, a monthly get-together with college friends. Vikings-Packers, dark wooden walls and high-backed booths, big-screen TVs, roars every time the Vikes score. My friends and I join in, even though I secretly like the Pack, and by halftime, my voice is scratchy. Flannel shirts and the smell of wet wool, New England staples, backslapping at jokes the more beers we have; the women hit the hardest.

I notice the brave lone woman cheering for the Pack, her beautiful Slavic face under her white cotton hat, then, as I'm heading to the bathroom, she elbows her glass and beer sloshes over her white mittens on the bar.

I wring them out and say, If you really want frozen hands, just dunk them in your water glass and step outside for a bit. Cheaper and faster.

Cheaper and faster? she says. That's your pick-up line?

Been waiting my whole life to use it.

I want to see that smile again, so we talk while friends say goodbye; five minutes, ten, fifteen. We've already exchanged names and learned where the other's apartment is, and she's already told me her one superstition, inherited from her Swedish grandmother— not to wash sheets between Christmas and New Year's, or the person who sleeps in them will die—when we have our first fight. Her ring tone is "Silent Night."

All year? I ask. Evidently, I make a face.

You don't like it? she asks. Everybody knows it's the best Christmas carol.

Nope, I say, and shake my head. "Good King Wenceslas."

You're crazy, she says.

Could be, I say. Can I see your hands? and hold out my own.

She leans forward, elbows on her crossed legs, and rests them in mine. You're not going to play that hand slapping game, are you?

Something better, but you have to close your eyes.

When she does, I take out a pen and begin drawing on them, a swift caricature of me on one, my phone number on the other, the letters O and M.

Okay, I say, and slip my hand back under hers. Take a look.

One foot beginning to bounce, she doesn't seem pleased, which surprises me. What's this? she asks.

I point them out with the pen. Me, my phone number, and our initials.

That M looks like an N. And if I mash my hands together, it reads NO.

She puts on her still-soaking mittens and leaves, and I guess I'll never see her again.

A week before Christmas, I open my door to a traveling band of carolers and recognize May's startling cheekbones among them. They all begin to sing.

Good King Wenceslas looked out
On the Feast of Stephen
When the snow lay round about
Deep and crisp and even.

Nine months later, we marry, her most impulsive decision ever. I discover later her aversion to tattoos, that I'd nearly ruined everything at the start.

Liam at Eight

JANUARY 2015

I was working on shading. Slow, steady work, work I loved. Cold calling was tough, even though I was getting more and more local clients, but to get paid to draw, to spend this much time with Liam and May? I tried not to forget my luck.

Liam pulled the bird book from the shelf and leafed through it while I worked. Fifteen minutes, page after page. He knew my process, my need for quiet, how even so I liked having him beside me. Patience had been an issue, younger, but he'd worked on it. At the woodpeckers, he went more slowly still.

He stopped a long time at one page, then went on, then came back. He propped the page open with a smooth rock and nudged me aside and found the black feather with the white polka dots in my top desk drawer, where I'd put it three years earlier, where it had stayed throughout the move. He held it against the page. Got it, he said. He was right.

May didn't look up from my phone when I tracked her down to tell her. I'd asked her to jailbreak it; she said she was almost done.

Well, good, I said. And you were right about Liam and the feather. I should have paid closer attention.

Thanks, Captain Obvious, she said, and handed me the phone. Get all the free apps you want, now. Share some with your son. And pay attention when you do, you might learn something.

Letters

Prove he was born.

Send me a copy of his birth certificate.

And not an unofficial one. Anyone can make one of those on their computer, especially you. You're a graphic artist. Do you think I'm stupid? I was stupid once because as soon as I heard about it all the hair on my arms stood up. Little children! I gave money to the fund and I want it back, now that I know it's not true.

$200.

That's a shitload less than they're paying you, isn't it?

You can remit the check to this address:

Silent Night, Holy Night

DECEMBER 25, 2015

Fat flakes of snow drifting by outside the hospital windows. May decided to go into work after sitting with me in the waiting room for an hour.

Christmas Day? I said. Carols played on the speakers.

Otto. She touched my arm. I've missed so many days. Nothing seems to be changing right now. I need to catch up.

I was neither angry nor surprised. May wasn't a particularly anxious person, but whatever anxieties she had she liked to distract herself from by working. And for the past couple of days, Liam had been stable.

Okay, I said. One favor only.

Of course, she said. What's that?

Will you sing for me? A Christmas carol? You know which one, I said. I didn't want to have to say it.

I'll sing it at home, she said, and slipped her laptop into her new case, my Christmas present to her. I'd had it for months, the only reason she got one.

It'll be my present, I said.

Not fair, Otto, she said. Not here. And certainly not now.

I was aware that as I asked again, pleaded, I sounded like a bully; I was also aware that, without admitting publicly how superstitious I'd become, I *needed* her to sing or at least hum a few bars, to insure Liam's continued survival. I had no other means of convincing her. And even for my broken son, I wasn't yet ready to do that.

So I kissed her warm cheek and told her to work well and looked through articles on my phone. TBI, the Rancho Los Amigos Levels of Cognitive Functioning, Baylor and the Mayo Clinic; websites I refreshed again and again, looking for comfort, for specialized vocabulary: intracranial pressure monitor, the Glasgow Coma Scale, and on and on. When the doctors and nurses talked about Liam now, I knew most of what they were referring to, though the knowledge wasn't necessarily helpful, and certainly not hopeful. Baylor's site said that even two years out from a TBI, Liam was likely to show decreased function; to what extent changed with Liam's days.

Sometimes he'd follow commands to lift his legs or squeeze fingers, and sometimes he slipped back into a coma; sometimes he was minimally conscious, sometimes he'd carry on a coherent conversation for hours. Once he bit a nurse so hard he broke the skin and had to be restrained, wrists and ankles. That was hard to see, and for an entire day I didn't go in to visit him.

Then for one miraculous three-day stretch his cognitive functioning was up to Level 9, 10 being the highest, the best: *purposeful/ appropriate*. His memory was working and he responded to the TV show above his bed—singing along to *A Charlie Brown Christmas*. Then he slipped all the way back to Level 4 for a week.

Go home, Dr. Wild said, at the end of it. You look awful.

Dark rings under my eyes, lank hair, she was right. The cycles of hope and despair were exhausting, but I stayed on anyway. One of us had to be there.

After reading a couple of articles, I thumbed through my phone. All my new clients had moved on. I didn't blame them. Most told me to get back in touch once I could work again and I said I would, but I didn't know when that would be. Several new texts. May's sister, Lamont, a number I didn't recognize.

It was a Christmas carol video, a children's choir, so I played it, the volume unintentionally loud, the words spilling into the room around me.

Silent night, awful night, You have no peace, you're full of fright, God's righteous anger is close and near, His hate for this nation is painfully clear, Behold the wrath of the lamb, Behold the wrath of the lamb.

My ears burned with shame. Everyone had heard me pleading with May to sing a carol. *This* carol, they'd think. So at first I didn't look up.

Who is this? I wrote back, thinking it was a hoaxer.

The reply was instantaneous. *When Liam dies—and he will die, God is striking down children for a reason, and this is NOT the Lord's birthday—don't have a grave or a tombstone. Neither worship of the dead nor pagan idolatry will save you.*

Not hoaxers then. Dexter Fenchwood.

You fucker, I said aloud, and everyone in the room looked at me. Sorry, I said holding up the phone. Someone's bad idea of a joke.

I breathed deeply. Sighed. Held my tongue and my thumb. I wanted to forward it to Lamont, with just a few words. *Take care of this for me?*

But it was Christmas, and Liam was still alive; it wouldn't do to opt for blood.

A Second Beginning, Folded and Doubled

Sawyer knew about this one too, the boy's love of guns, that his mother wouldn't let him have them. He was an exceptionally gifted photographer and artist. He asked for a camera and a sketchbook before his last Christmas, and his mother bought him the sketchbook, but his father, with whom he was now living, gave him money and bought him his first gun, a Glock G17 Gen4 MOS. Put those founding fathers to good use! he said.

He kept the gun at his house and warned the boy not to tell his mother. As a reward for his continuing silence, he took the boy shooting every weekend, and the boy began sketching the gun in his sketchbook.

The gun and his targets, people. One boy twice his size who'd pissed on him in the shower after gym class after rating everyone's pubic hair. Marty. All around the shower room, other boys had stopped talking or laughing and were looking at him, and at first he didn't know why. It was just another stream of warm water, splashing against his leg, and then he realized that all the other boys were waiting for him to respond, for a fight to break out. But he would have had his ass kicked; Marty's arms and chest looked like a boxer's; skinny calves but thighs like mailboxes, it would be impossible to move him. So he laughed like it didn't matter, even as his face reddened, and soaped his legs, and his heart swelled with murder.

Letters

Why does your town's tax assessor's office website show that you and all the other "victims"' parents got free houses this Christmas—the Christmas only months after "the shooting"—when all government offices are closed? How would that be possible? Is this part of your payoff? Do you sleep well at night, knowing that you're taking taxpayers money? Knowing that you're lying? Knowing that we're onto you?

And it's your lies that have undone you. All the news stories say it was rainy the day of the "shooting," but have you looked at any of the pictures that accompanied the news stories? Even a single one? None of "the parents" are wet in any of them, none of the "first responders," none of "the police." Even the National Weather Service says your town got almost ¾ of an inch of rain that day. But no wet clothes, no puddles, no dripping trees, no rainbow in the sky. You guys obviously had a lot of money to stage it, but you made mistakes. You always do. Thus begins the great unraveling.

That was one of the first letters, the first one I kept and the first I responded to; it reminded me of Liam at five. I told them the story of how he'd picked out a black backpack for school after trying on six different colors and ruling out others. How he took so long to make his choice it felt solemn.

It rained while we were in the store, the pavement smelled of it when we came out, and he stood on the curb looking down at the snaking oily sheen atop the long narrow puddle tucked into the stone gutter, the empty backpack on his back. He got in the car still wearing the backpack and wouldn't take it off.

You sure about that? I asked. Might be uncomfortable.

I'm sure, he said, and I buckled him in as he leaned forward and we drove, mist thrown up by the cars in front of us, a rainbow arcing across the half-cloudy sky.

You see that, buddy? I asked.

I do, Otto, he said. And I have a question. How come black doesn't live in the rainbow?

Roy G Biv, I said, and told him about colors as it started to rain again and I turned on the wipers and the rainbow disappeared from the sky. I don't think he fully understood, but it didn't matter.

That's all right, he said, sitting back. There are other rainbows. Black can live in one of those.

Carjinx

It didn't turn over, so I popped the hood. One battery clip undone, scratches around the post. Fixed it, started it up, drove; when I braked, a car horn sounded.

At Otto's Auto—Liam's favorite business in the city—the serviceman showed me: someone had connected an old car horn to my brakes. Fifty dollars to remove it.

I texted Nash and sorted through my pictures of Kate, feeding my anger. *Fucking hoaxers.* I passed a gun shop heading to Cora and Henry's farm and fantasized about buying one, a hoaxer following me as I did, what would happen after. A week later, when I hit the wiper fluid, blood red liquid spurted across the windshield. When I told Lamont, he laughed so hard he sounded like he was in his first heaven. Happy New Year, bruh.

It was you? I said. What the fuck for? You cost me money!

Practice, he said. For hoaxers. A couple of drops of red food coloring. He couldn't stop laughing. I'll pay you back, he said, his voice gravelly. A night of hard drinking, probably, one of many, though less and less often with me.

I could have had a gun, I said, wanting to ruffle him.

Nah, he said. Never gonna happen.

I'll get you back, I said.

Nope. He laughed. 'Cause I *got* a gun. After a pause, he said, Just joking.

I laughed too, but I wondered.

Fallow Fields

She was exercising Liam's arms when he told her to stop.

I know you're here to steal my lunch, he said.

Linh giggled, but didn't stop. A Vietnamese American PT, who always smelled of gardenias and came by three mornings a week, she was tender and rigorous.

Coherent, Liam coped by joking—*It's going tibia okay*—but his voice told me that wasn't the case today. He strained against her and said, You stupid bitch.

I blushed and apologized, but Linh shrugged it off with a rueful smile.

It's okay, she said, and kept moving his arm. Happens in the Neuro-ICU a lot.

I didn't tell May.

The next day, his breathing was shallower and when he saw me he said, Tell Latrell to stop using my Xbox.

We hadn't told him Latrell was dead yet. Sometimes, he knew he'd been shot, and sometimes his speech made sense. I said, Latrell's not using it, buddy.

You're lying. He's been in here all morning and won't let me have a turn.

When my phone buzzed, Liam said, Quit spying on me, and I went out to the waiting room to talk to May. We'd established a routine, her turn to sit with him. I was going to get groceries; she needed to eat. I'd even begun working again, with long-term clients. I told her about Latrell, and then about the swearing and paranoia.

Let's go talk to the nurse on duty, she said. They seem to know more.

I followed her back in. For a few minutes we both stood beside his bed, which wasn't easy; the bays were narrow and usually we weren't supposed to both be there at once, but the doctors said if we did it now and then, it might ease his anxiety. He moved his legs back and forth, as if he was swimming, and his O_2 seemed dangerously low. I felt panicky, but May fiddled with the monitor.

Trece came over when he saw that.

You shouldn't do that, he said. Red socks now; I guessed they were seasonal.

Yes, I should, she said. It'll work better. She finished what she'd been doing, turned the monitor off and on again, and after a few seconds his O_2 levels climbed back into the normal range. There, she said. Now, about Liam's paranoia.

It's not just paranoia, Trece said. Nightmares too. Have they told you that?

I said they hadn't.

He nodded. Understandable. You've got enough to worry about. He leaned over Liam and with his thumb lifted Liam's left eyelid, then his right.

What do the nightmares mean? May asked.

Another sign of ICU syndrome. The constant noise, their continual monitoring, the endless ambient light. It messes with sleep patterns.

I hadn't heard of it. Will it get worse? I asked, my go-to question.

It might. It's dangerous, but easily treatable. He needs to get off the ICU.

But his breathing is still shallow, May said. Shouldn't that be monitored?

It'll be monitored in any ward. He shrugged. Let me ask you something. Does Liam look smaller than when he first arrived here?

Well, sure. May said. He's not eating a lot.

It's not just that, Trece said. Every three days here, patients lose ten percent of their muscle mass. Normal and correctible, though it can have lingering effects. His breathing is shallow because of his brain injury, but also because of extended bed rest. Makes it harder to breathe. PT can only do so much.

So, what should we do?

Trece glanced over his shoulder, to be sure no doctors were coming. He didn't want to overstep his bounds, probably, though I guessed he already had.

Get him up, he said. If he can take just three steps, he can move to a trauma ward. And if he's on the trauma ward, he'll get out of bed more. And get stronger.

May asked, Why don't they just do that already?

Trece retreated a little. It's a judgment call, he said. Specialized equipment here. They want to keep an eye on him. But the psychosis won't go away on its own, and every day he deals with it means his brain and body have less energy to heal.

Push the PT when she's here next, he said. Have Linh get him up. His recovery will speed up. Think of the trauma ward as a fallow field in winter. Recovering.

Three steps. Linh helped him out of bed the next day and his first two steps were fine, but the third came as he fell toward her.

It's okay, she said, catching him under his arm. That'll do. Three steps. She winked at me. He can move to the trauma ward now.

I was thrilled; May was too, though later, she came to blame everything that happened after on that move. To blame me.

Swag

Lean Luke was bright pink, 7" long and convincingly veined; he cost $12.99. We could get him with a suction cup or balls or both; the website didn't say anything about volume discounts. He also comes in 6" and 8", I said. Why 7"?

Lamont shrugged. Odd numbers are better. He laughed, a rare event.

All right, I said, and scrolled through the order. We'd hatched the plan over dinner, after Lamont told me he'd begun discouraging hoaxers by stuffing their hubcaps with rocks so they'd think they had flats, or filling their cars with shredded paper. The hoaxers were rolling deep, but for me, Lamont beat any larger crew.

I got one more, he said. My favorite. Sitting in the back seat of their cars and saying Hey! when they return from town selectmen meetings.

You could get shot, doing that, I said.

I could. But I haven't. And I want them to think that maybe they could too.

When I got to quantity, I said, We're sure about three hundred? And, do you think those GoFundMe people contemplated paying for realistically veined dildos?

They contemplated letting us do what we thought was right.

Okay, I said, and began typing in the credit card number, but I had second thoughts about actually spending money on a huge order of pink dildos, so I said, Maybe we should wait until after Valentine's Day. They'll probably go on sale then.

No sense waiting, Otto. The hoaxers are coming around more

often. That's not something you breeze over. Don't make me get salty with you.

But what do we do with the extras, while we're waiting for more hoaxers to show? It's not as if thirty of them will have a convention.

Keep them at my place. If we kept them at yours, we'd pay to move them.

How come you don't move?

They know not to mess with me. Angry Black man with a gun.

It's not just that, I said.

I know, he said, and put his hand on my shoulder. Something about Liam's wounding, that he was a survivor of the shooting, seemed to set them off.

I typed my way through the order form, giving Lamont's address and hitting Proceed to Checkout. I was just about to purchase them when I stopped and said, They could turn this against us.

How? If they complain about it online, everyone will think they're pussies. Showing up at town meetings to demand answers, and all they get is a carful of pink dildos? People will laugh even more at these cousin-fuckers.

They might turn around and sell them on eBay to raise money. They already sell shooting memorabilia.

I hadn't thought of that, Lamont said. Not all of them are stupid, you might be right. Let me think about it, he said, and excused himself to go to the bathroom.

The session timed out while he was gone, so I refreshed the form, wondering as I did why Palmer hadn't responded to my Christmas card, then pushed thoughts of her aside.

It was a smart idea to make the hoaxers who came around uncomfortable. To watch them, confront them, make them know they were unwanted. To let them know we knew their vehicles, had found their registrations, where *they* lived. To make them wonder if we'd come after them in *their* homes.

It would feel good, though I suspected that contact high wouldn't last long. I'd written back some of the hoaxers at first, exhilarated as I sent off the replies, but the thrill never lasted, and none of them ever changed their minds. Maybe a bagful of dicks would be different, though.

I know what we can do, Lamont said, back from the bathroom. To make sure they can't sell the dildos. Piss on them.

What? The packaging?

No. Take them out and put them all in a bucket and piss on them. Make their cars smell of it. Make it impossible to sell them. We'll use gloves and tongs to pick them out and place them in their cars. Pickled dicks.

Jesus, Lamont. That's too much.

Fuck you, he said, only partially kidding. Nothing's too much for these people. Nothing. He reached over my shoulder and pressed the trackpad to buy them all. And if you thought it was going to end here, he said, you're a fool.

What else do you have planned? I said.

You'll be hearing about it soon enough. He smiled. You'll see. They had a chance to get some act right. Now they're going to get what's coming to them. Just keep that old line in mind. A friend will help you move.

That's you, I said.

That's right, he said, squeezing my shoulder. And a best friend will help you move a body. That's you.

Be Mine

FEBRUARY 2019

Palmer's valentine is attached to a bottle of Blanton's bourbon. Pink background, a picture of a sharpie. *To: Otto From: Palmer r u a sharpie? bc ur ultra fine.* Sweetly awful, but I figure it's a response to my Christmas card, which was a thank you for her poinsettia; I hadn't called or texted since and now that I have it, I wonder if I've been a fool. I'd feel mean throwing it out, so I tuck the card into the Steinbeck I'm reading like a bookmark, and draw her a valentine in return. Which makes me think that she's still trying because I want her to.

All of Liam's valentines are hand drawn; May and I parceled out his earliest ones. Every year until this year we've traded them back and forth, but I haven't heard from her in a couple of weeks. Work, probably, or Nash.

When Liam was eight, he and May were in the kitchen, Liam sitting on a stool at the kitchen counter. A loose storm window rattling in the wind, May warming my tomato soup, grilled cheese cooking on the griddle. I wanted to join them but I was behind on a couple of assignments and I didn't have the time; still, I could hear them.

Liam said, I didn't get anything from either you or Otto for Valentine's Day.

May said, Liam, you and I made that beautiful heart cake with the red frosting.

Food isn't part of love, Liam said.

Well, Liam, love is lots of things. Like food. I'm making this for you and him. I got these beautiful tulips from daddy, but I didn't give him anything.

Then he probably knows how I feel.

The Beginnings of Baggy Bronchi

FEBRUARY 2012

Fevered and fretful, sick with whooping cough, Liam slept between us. He woke coughing at two a.m. and kicked the covers off his superheated body and put his hands to his face.

His breathing was shallow so I'd lain awake, watching him. Willing the antibiotics to help clear his lungs, the ginger and raw honey, the peppermint oil I'd rubbed on the soles of his feet. Wondering when his sweat would change; it still smelled sweet.

Hey Otto, he whispered in the dark, his voice froggy, and pressed his hands more tightly against his skin. My face feels pale.

Opportunity Knocks

Two years after the shooting, a letter came from a man who claimed to have worked for the NRA. He'd left the NRA after helping produce videos about 9/11 and several of the school shootings, he said, including Liam's, false flag videos that claimed they were all staged to give the government reasons to take away guns.

It wasn't official NRA work that he did; he made that clear. Black bag stuff, off the books. But the NRA leadership knew about it, he wrote. And supported it.

I have immense guilt about my role in all of this, his letter said. *Will you agree to meet me so I can apologize?*

Unlike the other letters, which I kept, I threw that one away, in a momentary spasm of anger: *Find your absolution elsewhere.* Later, I regretted it, but by then the trash had already been collected.

His name was something peculiar, like Howaniac, but I don't remember it clearly, though I do remember that he'd helped produce those videos, perhaps even ones that Kate appeared in. And I think he might even have known her name.

None of my searches about him ever turn up *his* name, no matter how I spell it or what the parameters are, so I'll probably never know.

The Line Was Totally Worth It

FEBRUARY 2019

A packed signing, the long line weaving between aisles of books. Fiction, Nonfiction, Cooking and Religion; Lamont stood for ten minutes next to Travel and didn't glance at a single title; he was picking out passages from the book he held: *Never Surrender, Confessions of a Hitter*. Tanner Weeks.

Rare that a football player came around to sign his book, rarer still one so high profile—three times an All-Pro safety—rarest of all that he was white. He was amazingly comfortable, Lamont thought, watching him talk to each person who offered a book to be signed, a jersey, a hat. Even if only for a few seconds, he tried to connect beyond the perfunctory handshake. Admirable, really. Most athletes didn't like meeting fans. *Deebo alert!* he wanted to call out, but didn't. Surprise mattered.

Bit by bit the line shuffled forward. Some of the women asked if they could touch Weeks's arms, the blue-and-white striped shirtsleeves stretched tight over them. One man did too and others talked about their own days playing football; Lamont pitied them. Weeks's glamor wouldn't rub off on them, as desperately as they wanted it to. And besides, the guy was a piece of shit.

At last it was Lamont's turn. He stepped up to the table and handed over his copy of the book. I'm your biggest fan, he said,

Thanks, dawg! Weeks said. He shook Lamont's hand and flashed his famous smile. Lamont thought it impressive that he didn't try to outgrip him.

Well, Lamont said, me and everyone else in the line.

A genuine smile. White people problems! Weeks said.

Lamont thought, *About to have some Black people problems.*

After Weeks signed the book, he asked, Did you play, my G?

Yes, Lamont said, shamed that he liked being asked, angry that Weeks had dropped into pseudo-street lingo because he was Black. O-lineman, he said.

Look like you still got it, brother.

Lamont shrugged off the compliment and said, You got kids?

I do, Weeks said, and smiled again and pressed his hands together as if in prayer, gold bracelets flashing in the light. Two boys and a girl.

This is my son, Lamont said, and handed him a glossy picture of Latrell in his football uniform, helmet off, with a fresh fade. Can you sign that too? he asked

Sure. Who do I make it out to?

Latrell, he said, and waited until Weeks was done.

Good, Lamont said, and touched his boy's face, stared at it for a few quiet seconds. Behind him he felt others waiting and didn't care. He's handsome, don't you think? Lamont asked.

Very.

Lamont rubbed his thumb over the signature, smearing it. And dead, he said.

What? No, hey man, look. Sorry. Weeks pushed his seat back a little.

Shot in that school shooting you always say never happened. Three times in this book. Lamont tapped it. Page 17, page 257, and page 399. The very last one.

Weeks's face was tight, a vein pulsing in his muscled throat. He stood and nodded at someone behind Lamont. Security, Lamont guessed. Around them chatter died out and Lamont felt attention shifting their way. And why not? They'd stepped into the spottie, and everyone was about to get the answer to the age-old question, if a tiger fights a bear, who wins? Weeks had two or three inches on him, and the broadest shoulders; he looked like he'd have to go through every door sideways. But Lamont was stone-solid, with huge arms and legs, a thick neck. He wouldn't be half as fast as Weeks, but Weeks also wouldn't have time to leverage his speed before Lamont smothered him; who got there first mattered.

Lamont said, Latrell died, and I'm his father, and I want to hear you say to my face that it never happened so I can smack you. *Say it.* After all, you got to be stronger and wronger than everyone about this, with your tweets and Instagrams, and I don't fuck with that shit. He raised his voice and went on. That my boy not only never died, but never lived. He gripped the table with both hands, as if he was about to toss it aside like a stack of paper.

Weeks spread his feet apart and angled his hips and said, Bro, no need to get salty.

Salty? Lamont said. I'm beyond that. Here's your chance. Man up, *dawg.*

Behind him someone said, Hey, watch where you're going, and others murmured as someone else pushed through the crowd.

When Weeks said nothing, Lamont tore the book in half and tossed the halves at Weeks. Then he picked up the picture and said, I thought so. Don't ever write or tweet about the school shooting again, or I'll find you a second time. And I won't be carrying a picture when I do.

Half a Truth Is Often a Great Lie

FEBRUARY 2016

At first Liam didn't have a roommate on the trauma ward. The night nurses let me sleep clothed in the other bed and by day three he was sleeping through the night, the nightmares gone. When he woke he drank like a cat, rarely but copiously. I breathed on the window and wrote his name in the fog and watched three men standing facing each other down on the sidewalk with their hands to their mouths, wondering if they were some kind of harmonica band, but it turned out they were only smoking. After they left, I taped sketches on the wall, some of which I'd made while watching over Liam. Apple picking, fishing, Liam and Latrell asleep after a day spent gaming. Also the horse Liam had drawn years before.

Dr. Wild smoothed that one flat. This is beautiful, she said. Brightens up the room. That's good. That will help him. The flowers too.

A dozen bouquets, jammed on the bedside tables and windowsills; freesias, roses, tulips, fragrant camellias; I couldn't draw them all. Friends, relatives, strangers.

You think so? I rearranged violet tulips in a waisted glass vase. I wanted so much to help, to not be a passive observer, and I was scared that Liam wasn't getting better faster. Scared and angry at him, as if it was willful. *Fight!*

If she intuited my need, she skipped over it. His sleeping through the night is a good sign, she said. With more rest, his brain can heal faster. The swelling will decrease, the blood flow improve. Brain function usually does too.

I cleared my throat. Usually?

She nodded and put her hands in her pockets, which I knew meant bad news. He should begin to speak more now, she said

He was speaking on the ICU.

Inconsistently. Some days he would, others not. He should begin to remember things from day-to-day now. If he doesn't, that's a bad sign.

When will we know?

She touched my arm. It's a process. All of this can be disturbing, because he doesn't seem like your child. Try not to become anxious. Ups and downs are normal. He's already come a long way. We weren't sure at first that he would even survive.

I didn't like hearing that. I'd worried he might die and twice asked nurses and doctors directly. *Tell me*, I'd said. *I want to be prepared. Will he die?* Both times, they'd said no. Now I knew they'd merely been trying to comfort me. Was Dr. Wild doing the same thing again? I suspected she wouldn't tell me.

What can I tell him about the shooting when he wakes up?

She picked at loose finish on the bedside table with her red fingernail. You should tell him everything. Don't spare him. It'll only make him distrust you later, once he finds out.

I must have made a face.

She checked her phone before responding. I know that seems harsh, she said and pocketed it. But I've been through a lot of these recoveries. Even kids want the truth. And it's especially important that parents know what that is, and accept it.

A message for me, I was sure. But what was she saying?

Lies, Damn Lies, and Statistics

MID-FEBRUARY 2019

Lamont stood out in the street yelling my nickname. *Bismarck! Open up, Bismarck, or I'll start charging movers' rates for my help! I know you're in there!*

I hadn't answered his texts or calls or the buzzer. I was tired and needed to get work done and I didn't want to drink, but letting him in was better than angering my new neighbors. Shut up, you fool, I said. You'll wake the dead.

Lamont brushed by me in his *Elbow Benders* shirt, purple script raised like a scar. He said, A guy on the other team brought his dad. Sixties, in diapers, his mind gone. If I ever get like that? Pull the plug. He poured bourbons and we sat on the couch to watch the recap of the DA's news conference about the shooter. A mouth guard fell from his pocket; he blew dust off it and pocketed it again and I thought, *Who rolls with a mouth guard at the ready? That's not good.*

I said, You ever think we drink too much?

Fuck no, he said. I was raised in Kentucky. Breastfed on bourbon.

The DA said, We couldn't have prevented this. There's no record of us being called to his house. We just didn't know. She fiddled with her blonde locks.

Bullshit, Lamont said, and leaned toward the TV. Some of his anger was Akane; she'd moved out and filed for divorce, but there was more to it than that.

The DA went on, sallow and tired, uncomfortable in the glare of TV lights. The rumors were that the police *had* been called to the shooter's house, two years before it happened. Hence the news. How do you know it's bullshit? I said.

Venny Bosc. Like what you've done to the place, he added. Unpacked boxes are always a nice touch.

Who's Venny Bosh? I said, ignoring the jibe.

Venny Bosc. The shooter's neighbor. She called the cops.

The DA answered another question. No, she said. You'd have to ask Ms. Bosc. We have no record of any interactions with her, either.

Lamont was sitting on the couch with the afghan thrown over it, to hide the rips. The reporters have it right, he said. I told them about Bosc.

I didn't doubt it. Reporters went to him for juicy quotes; he never held anything back. He'd told me that whenever someone gave him the finger while driving now, he'd drag them out of their car and beat them. I believed it; I'd heard all about him and Tanner Weeks, and maybe that's what the mouth guard was for.

Venny tracked me down, Lamont said. She wanted the truth out there.

The DA stopped taking questions and turned away, Lamont said, Watch. Her lies will come back to haunt her. But it's all good. I prefer this shit to be out loud.

He drained his bourbon and poured another, and, to be sociable, to make up for making him yell to be let in, I joined him, while adding the DA to my mental list of people who'd pissed me off.

Later I dreamed that Lamont slid off the couch clutching a pillow and began to smother me. I slipped away from him, riding a wave to shore, and when it retreated, I was left on dry land, awake and unhappy, staring at the ceiling.

It was getting to be that time of year.

Letters

Why would a police officer by the name of Lt. Fox, who never appears on any paychecks in the town or state records enter room eleven (11) at 8:55:31, which was supposudly the grewsome crime scene with dead children and school staff with blood and etc. and bodies and tell a male boy kindergardner found in the bathroom, who's name is redacted, and tell them (so it must be more than one), to stay and they will bot be back when it is safe? Why?

Kate

Got her! Helen Nix, 39, Atlanta-born and still living there now, near the zoo.

For a while I just sat in front of my computer, studying her apartment on Google Earth, saying her name over and over, silently at first, then aloud, her name echoing from the walls of my apartment. Luxuriating in triumph, the months of hard work that finally paid off. Oddly, it made me think of Palmer, how her lips might taste as sweet as carrots if we kissed. I decided to figure that out later.

A listing on ZabaSearch had led to a name I entered on Pipl Search that led to an archived article with yet another name that, when punched into TruePeopleSearch, returned Possible Associates: roommates, co-workers, friends, a smorgasbord of possibilities, which I relentlessly tracked over hours and through days, each and every name, one of which turned out to be hers. To be Kate.

I wanted to call May, Lamont too, to tell them both all about her, I wanted to run around the apartment shouting with joy, but it was three a.m. and the people beneath me needed to sleep—jobs and a new baby—and neither May nor Lamont even knew she existed, so I decided to hold off on notifying anyone or on marching in my self-congratulatory parade until it was all over.

Instead, three small satisfying actions:

- Ordered online a red cake with vanilla cream frosting from Silver's, Liam's favorite.
- Texted Palmer, *Maybe we can try again?* and included the drawing I'd made of her after our date. Too much, maybe, but worth a shot.

- Rescheduled freelance meetings, pushed back project deadlines, and bought a plane ticket. The bat would have to be packed in my suitcase, since I couldn't bring it as a carry-on, but Atlanta was in its future.

Cattle and the Wild Beasts, All the Birds of the Air, Your Whales and All That Swim in the Waters

FEBRUARY 20, 2016

I was late for Liam's physical therapy session because I'd stopped to sketch. Small moments of concentration. May frowned as Liam pushed Linh away. I don't want to walk, he said. And you can't make me. He was lying down.

She'd been trying to stretch his legs but now his arms were flailing, striking the bedrails, though with little force. He was weaker than when we'd moved him.

Come on, I thought, overcome with a sense of dread. *Do it. Get better.*

Can you evaluate him? I asked. Do the animal thing? May looked at me. It's a dementia test, I said. But Linh had said it also worked sometimes for TBIs.

All right, Linh said, and told Liam she was going to check his memory. Will you tell me the names of as many animals as you can think of, as quickly as possible? She set the timer on her watch. He said nothing at first. May gripped the handrail. At fifteen seconds, Linh said, A dog. A dog is an animal. Can you tell me more?

Dog, he said. Puppy. Flies, he said. Flounders. Farts. Cats.

He paused for a few seconds, then Linh said, Any more animals?

Giraffes, he said. Elmer. May laughed and he looked at her for a long time and closed his eyes.

At sixty seconds, Linh stopped her watch and frowned. He only got four.

Five, May said. Dog, puppy, flies, flounders, giraffes.

Puppies are just another developmental stage of dogs, she said.

Well, May said, I distracted him. By laughing.

Perhaps, Linh said. I'll tell Dr. Wild about this. Ask her to follow up.

What number do you look for before deciding there's a problem? May asked.

In sixty seconds? Anything above fourteen is good. Below that is concerning.

She left. May made animal noises, asking Liam to name the animals; he seemed to sleep. Why'd you ask her to do that test? she said.

I thought it might give us some good news.

Well, it didn't. And you shouldn't have been late just to sketch.

No, it didn't, I said, and pocketed my hands. Too late; the silver sheen of lead.

She didn't pick up on my tone. Or if she did, she decided to strike back. I don't think this ward has been any good for him, she said.

Of course it has, I said. He's sleeping better. He's not violent anymore. I think he's getting stronger.

You *wish* he was stronger. And you sort of have to believe it, don't you?

What? I said, surprised she'd turned on me.

It was your idea to move him here, she said. Out of the Neuro-ICU.

That wasn't how I remembered it, but I didn't want to fight over conflicting memories. What was the thing with Elmer? I asked, switching the conversation.

She waved her hand dismissively. Elmer the giraffe. It's a game we play. He wants a giraffe as a pet and I say he can get one if we name it Elmer.

When did you play that? I asked. I'd never heard about it.

It's okay, May said, trying to soothe me. I'm only trying to protect my son.

Our son, I said. She didn't say anything, but at least she nodded.

If Only

If Detective Sawyer *had* checked the computer during his visit to the boy's house, he'd have found a recently downloaded article about patron injuries at theme parks. Also a list of school shooters and their body counts. More and more and more.

Other missed signs included that the boy had been disciplined twice at school, once for cursing on the school bus and once for losing his temper over a failed math test, when he'd punched a thermostat hard enough to break it, then formed a gun with his index finger and thumb and pointed it at the teacher who confronted him and said, Rat-a-tat-tat, you're dead. The school sent letters home, but his parents claimed never to have received them. He might have intercepted them; he was home sick on the days when the letters would have arrived. He was capable of that.

The last clue was the boy's handwriting. It deteriorated badly in the months before the shooting. But in the journal two years earlier it looked fine, and most of his work for school had to be typed. One teacher noticed, that last week. An in-class composition about future plans that was illegible and, oddly, in the shape of an hourglass, as if time were running out. That handwriting, the teacher joked. Planning on becoming a doctor?

No, the boy said. He sat back and laced his fingers together and put them behind his head, elbows out, and pushed his legs out and crossed them at the ankles. Like a man in his recliner. No, he said again, and smiled. I'm planning something else.

In Sawyer's notes about it, from an interview after the shooting, the teacher shivered when he told him. *I knew then something was wrong. Why didn't I say so?*

Liam at Four

2011

On his birthday, sunlight streaming through the windows onto his bed, he woke up and said, How come I'm four and I'm still the same size?

Later in the day I overheard him singing to himself.

Happy Birthday dear to Me.

Later still, while playing with pots in the kitchen, blue balloons tied to one wrist, he kept grabbing his crotch, like a dancer in a rap video.

Exasperated, May stopped frosting the chocolate cake and said, Can you just let go of your penis?

May, he said, and stood. The pots clattered together when he dropped them. That's bathroom talk.

Well, what would you like me to say?

You could try wiener.

Letters

I was a U.S. Customs Inspector and Virginia State Trooper and an elementary school Vice Principal at two different school. I would have been a principal but they had a quota. Turn America brown!

Anyway, that's how I know this is all lies. I do this for a living. I'm a school safety consultant. If this was true, I would know about it in order to help other schools.

You must have been in on the planning. My guess is that it took at least three years to write the scripts for all of you. Did you call it an exercise or a drill? I've talked to the school board twice. They wouldn't answer my questions either. Why? BECAUSE IT NEVER HAPPENED.

I posted the video of you on your porch. Your street address. Don't think we don't know where you live. Don't think we can't find you. Don't think that in due time, your foot won't slip. Your day of disaster is near and your doom rushes upon you.

Fails

Helen turned out not to be Kate; a little more sleuthing uncovered the truth.

Palmer was furious when I didn't follow up, anger that built up over days and weeks and ended with a three a.m. text, the exact same time I'd sent her mine. *I'm glad you ghosted me. Know why? My middle finger gets a boner when I think of you.*

I understood, but I couldn't explain without revealing my obsession. I'd listened to the voice telling me that I should contact Palmer, when I should have listened to the smaller one warning against it. The cake I made myself eat without milk, in punishment, without even water. Hard, by the end of it, but I choked it down.

The plane ticket I couldn't get a refund on, only a credit, but I comforted myself with the thought that I'd use it at some undetermined time in the future, when I at last had the location I wanted to go. Kate was out there, and I was still after her. And she was still after me.

I pulled the window shade down and rolled it back up again a half dozen times, then drank some hot water and lemon before climbing into bed. Liam's favorite drink, even in summer.

Incident on 7th

MARCH 15, 2019

I was on my way to see Silver with the next series of illustrations. A warm spring afternoon, a day it felt good to be alive. So rare! A woman about my age walked up next to me, slim and tall, her spicy vanilla-scented perfume familiar. The same as Palmer's, I realized, and took a quick glance. Dramatically asymmetric black hair, the sleeves of her white blouse rolled halfway up her thin forearms.

For an entire block she walked beside me, loose black pants flowing. She smiled when I glanced over, and I had to keep from staring at the way her smile shifted her cheekbones, making her look Slavic. I tracked our reflected progress in the hardware store, restaurant, hair salon, consignment shop and bookstore windows, and fantasized about sketching her after languid sex in this same afternoon light, a vase of pink tulips behind her. Springtime, the warming earth, a touch to break the long loneliness.

She smiled at me in our reflections. Was she coming on to me? Foolish, I decided. For two stores I looked straight ahead, but at the liquor store I glanced again and, between posters advertising French wines and a coming play, her reflection was looking too.

I wondered if there might be something about me that attracted women who wore that perfume, some pheromone I was unaware of but that woman picked up on. Then I felt silly; May never would have liked it. Too floral, she'd have said, almost soapy, and with far too much sillage.

A skateboarder wove through pedestrians and swerved, blonde dreads flying, and when the woman sidestepped she bumped into me.

Sorry! she said, and gave a nervous laugh. Her shoe had fallen off, a black wedge worn at the toe.

It's fine, I said, and knelt to help her back into it. I listened to the skateboard disappear behind us, wheels clacking over the curb. You okay?

Fine, she said, and steadied herself with a hand on my shoulder. Just spooked. I thought she was going to run me down. You never know what's coming for you!

No, I said, and retied my shoe, to linger beside her.

And on such a beautiful day, she said.

Being gallant, I said, It is. And it seems as if it just got better.

Really? she asked, and smiled again, and her face changed again too; it almost seemed like a trick, it was so dramatic, not just the shapes but the shadows. That's so good to hear, she said. That makes me happy. You like brunettes, don't you?

·That threw me, but before I could answer she asked how far I was going and I forgot about it, temporarily.

Just a couple blocks, I said. To a bakery. What's your name?

What's in a name, Otto? My name in her mouth startled me, and kept me from realizing at first that she was holding something in her hand, pressing it into mine. Have a good day, she said, and turned and left.

How did you know my name? I said to her retreating back. And that I liked brunettes? She didn't stop or answer, and when I unfolded the flyer she'd given me, my ears burned with shame. WANTED! OTTO BARNES!

My picture, and my new address and phone number, and my email too. *Let him know we're onto him. Let him know the hoax has been exposed.*

I yelled *Hey!* and she looked back over her shoulder, allowing me to snap her picture, but she darted into the liquor store, and inside there was a dense crowd in its narrow aisles, gathered around tall tables with open bottles of wine—a tasting. I made my slow way sideways through the buzzing customers toward the coolers along the rear wall, awkwardly because of my portfolio, and by the time I figured out she wasn't in the store any longer and followed her out the back door, she'd vanished, down the alley past the trashcans or up another street.

Back inside, I clanked down a bottle of gin on the tin counter, paid, and made my way through the assembled crowd to the street, where I turned toward my apartment after texting Silver that I had to cancel. *Something sudden*, I wrote. *Nothing terrible, but important to attend to, I'm afraid.*

Okay, she replied. *But this is time sensitive. Let's meet soon.*

In my apartment, I cracked the bottle and poured a drink and went to the front windows, standing just back from them to watch the street. Passing cars, parked cars, an old man with a dog, two school-girls, three men in overalls and yellow hardhats. A waste of time, I decided, and took a picture of the flyer and texted it and the picture of the woman to Nash, along with a quick description of our inter-action. Then, depressed I'd have to move again, I tried to find her.

Nothing, when I loaded her picture into Social Catfish, and Google Images drew a blank too, as did TinEye. Fuck her, I said, and still half wished I could.

Conflict Resolution

Liam lay in bed, getting worse, Dr. Wild said. Struggling to breathe.

May gripped the bedrail, her knuckles white. She asked if taking the shotgun pellet out of his brain would help. You missed it at first, she said.

We did miss it, Dr. Wild said. We shouldn't have. And perhaps that makes you doubt our later decisions. But even if we'd seen it, we wouldn't have taken it out.

Why on earth not? May's hand cut the air like a blade.

Bullets are hot. They cauterize wounds, so the risk of infection is small. Then the question is, is it an immediate problem? In the heart, say, or adjacent to blood vessels, or causing an abscess? I'd go after it then. But most often we don't, because surgery can create complications. Further injuries, or infection. Or death.

So you're just going to let him die slowly now? Is that the plan? Because you're a doctor, you want to understand *why* something happens? Not to fix it?

If it was going to lead to his death, I'd operate right now. I'm a surgeon.

And you don't think it is, May said. A capitulation, not a question. Her clothes were baggy; she seemed to have shrunk two sizes. He's not getting better, is he?

I'm afraid not, Dr. Wild said, rubbing her wrist. Nor do we know why.

He's fighting, though, May said, standing taller. He hasn't given up.

Neither will we, Dr. Wild said.

Home, I unwrapped a new fruit basket and put it with the half dozen others on the counter as May flipped through the stacked mail. Bills, mailers, one personal letter. She tore them all up and said, I recognize the handwriting. Another fucking hoaxer. We were getting notes of anger or mock concern daily, and, most often, of moral outrage that we played along with a government conspiracy. Usually I found them first, sparing her. Nash couldn't do much unless they specifically threatened us.

I got out Zhao's lasagna and cut two slices to warm.

Just for yourself, May said. I'm not hungry. She turned a pear in her hands.

Come on, May. You have to eat something. It won't help him to waste away.

And you, putting on pounds? That's really transformed him, hasn't it? He's so much better now, after moving him to the other ward. Up and around all the time!

Come on, May, I said. That's not fair, turning on me.

What isn't fair is that our son is dying in a hospital and no one wants to do anything and you somehow can think only of food. She dropped the pear in the trash.

May, I have to do something.

Really? I've got news for you. The only thing you're doing is *acquiescing*. But it doesn't matter. Nothing you *could* do would help. So why don't you just go draw?

I wanted to throw the lasagna at her, but I put it in the microwave and reheated it while she showered, because it was better that I should eat than that we should continue devouring one another. I felt guilty that I liked Zhao's lasagna so much, had been looking forward to it. I wanted to protect her and couldn't.

A long shower, as if she was washing each strand of hair individually.

As I ate, I pieced together the letter she'd torn up. A few words, in a crabbed hand. *Fuck you and your fake child.*

Interim 5

Number of school shootings since: 146
Number of school children killed: 242

Saudade

Liam had to be sedated for his MRI; the clanking buzzing noises spooked him. And me. After looking at the results, Dr. Wild said he should go back to the Neuro-ICU.

This time we walked beside him as he was wheeled to the elevator, taken up three floors, and down the long empty hallway to the Neuro wing. May held one of his hands, as small as an infant's. He titled his chin up and glanced back over his head at the ceiling. You all right, Liam? I asked.

Yes. The lights, he said. I like their pattern, how they come and go.

When he was settled, I rounded the ward, checking all the bays. The only two I recognized were the Dominican who'd had the stroke and the old Ukrainian nanny, both smaller now. The nurse on duty said both were stable.

That must make her visitors happy, I said.

She hasn't had visitors for a couple of weeks, she said.

I stood by her bed for a bit. Had they taken her money? Had I helped them to?

Please God, I thought. *Don't let me be the agent of her disaster.*

When Trece saw me, he smiled. Liam all better? The trauma ward helped?

He must have thought I was there to provide good news. No, I said, looking down. He had on green socks. You didn't hear? I said. He's back here now, Dr. Wild thought it best for him.

I don't think I've ever seen a doctor look so sad.

The 10 Questions Cowards Like You *Never* Answer

1. Why on "shooting day" did FEMA offer an already-scheduled course in Planning for the Needs of Children in Disasters?
2. Why were the entire school grounds demolished and rebuilt?
3. Why did everyone who worked on the demolition of the school have to sign confidentiality agreements?
4. Why did they post guards at the site throughout the demolition when that's not standard industry practice?
5. Why did the state bar any information about where the demolition rubble was buried?
6. Why did the demolition company have to provide the state with proof that metal from the site that couldn't be crushed was hauled away and melted down?
7. What are they so worried about getting out?
8. What are they trying to hide?
9. What are *you* trying to hide?
10. Does this remind you of how the metal scraps from 9/11 were immediately shipped to China so they couldn't be examined for evidence? It should. I heard you investigated that. Tables turned, now.

Birthday Fungo
MARCH 30, 2019

Houses grew visible in the blue light of dawn and the high clouds flocked east, turning pink. I was waiting for hoaxers, a bat across my lap. Liam's birthday and Kate out with a new video, quoting a friend of Palmer's: *Otto Barnes told her he'd never had kids! They can't lie forever!* I hadn't seen it, but references to it were all over the hoaxer websites, so I knew they'd show. I should have been home working, since I had a deadline for Silver and I wasn't close to done, but I'd had enough.

The front porch light snapped on and May pushed open the storm door with her green coffee mug in her robe and slippers—Liam's alligators—and stood on the porch looking toward the fading darkness in the west, trembling. Perhaps the cold.

She looked good; she'd put some weight back on. She walked down the steps to pick up the paper and went back inside without glancing at it, and she'd make his birthday breakfast next, pancakes and hash browns and maple syrup, a glass of fresh squeezed orange juice, then eat it when he didn't. That was tradition too. He never liked breakfast and his birthday breakfast became hers.

The porch light turned off and the cab light came on in a dark green pickup with Wyoming plates on the opposite side of the street; I should have picked it out beforehand. The door creaked as he closed it. He stretched, hands to his back, a long drive behind him; I planned to make the drive home even longer. *Gandhi, my ass.*

He tucked his hands into his parka and walked by the house to the end of the block, where I watched in my rearview mirror as he crossed to my side and started back. Boots and a white cowboy hat, he really took this western thing seriously. I almost gave him points for that; it wasn't as if he fit in to his new surroundings. When he was at the car behind me, I stepped out and stood sideways in case he rushed me and his eyes flicked to the bat. He wasn't going to get by me, but he had nowhere else to go; boots made him slow and wherever he fled I could follow.

Hello, friend, he said, and smiled. Can I help you? He slid one foot forward and slipped his hands out of his pockets and shook his arms like a boxer.

No, but I can help you. I studied him before speaking again. About my size and age with skin darkened by a life spent outdoors; he could have been me but for twists of fate. Right now, I said, you're thinking about ringing May's doorbell.

Who?

I tapped the bat against my shoulder and said, No games. I know who you are and why you're here and what you're thinking of doing. You're one of Kate's spawn.

So, here's what we're going to do instead, I said. You and I? We're going to walk to your truck. I'm going to take a look through it when we get there, and then you're going to get in it and drive away and never come back.

Long, even breaths as he thought. He fisted and unfisted his hands, figuring his chances in a fight, but the morning was so quiet he must have decided that no reinforcements were coming, even in the shape of witnesses. At last he swallowed and cleared his throat and let his arms hang loose. All right, he said and sighed.

You think I'm a crisis actor, paid to do this, don't you? I said. How much do you think they're paying me to confront you?

No idea, but it must be plenty.

Nah, I said. Not a thing. I'd do this for free. I cocked the bat and swiveled and smashed it against his hip. The satisfying sound of wood on bone, of his shout of pain, is there anything like it on this earth? But I stood looking down at him, thinking: *Here's the pity.*

I couldn't tell him what I wanted, because I didn't know, and he couldn't tell me what he feared. I mean, what he feared other than me and my bat in that moment, the bruises it might inflict, the broken bones, the thing that had launched him cross-country from his life to interfere in mine. Neither of us knew. I wondered if we ever would.

I decided to let him go, as much as I wanted to hurt him, as much as hurting him seemed right. Deserved. If we could only exchange fatigued souls for a bit it might have fixed everything, but of course we couldn't, so I hit him again and helped him up and walked him to his car. It felt good to hit him, and to plan magnanimity. He didn't realize he was in the presence of grace. The bat, maybe. My wild eyes. He said, God is watching. Do you think He's on your side?

Give me your keys and lie down, I said, having forgotten to search him.

What? He looked terrified, convinced I was going to smash his head in once he did, which filled with me the gleeful desire to do just that. Instead I patted him down. No gun. I took his wallet and cell phone and asked for his password and once I had it thumbed through his contacts until I reached May's, which I showed to him, then erased.

Clouds streamed toward the east, turning pink, and my own red heart beat so loudly I heard it. I rested the palm of one hand against his stubbled cheek, scraped and bleeding from the pavement, patted his warm skin. *Do you feel that?* I thought. *In the presence of evil, I'm a good man.* You won't ever ask for her info again, I said, and sent all his contacts to my email. You have my email now. Write any time. Or invite me out. I'll come.

And as for God, I said and stood. I hope I'm on His side, and I sure as shit hope He's watching.

I tossed the phone and the wallet down a sewer drain and

opened his truck and searched it—checking now and then to be sure he hadn't moved—pocketing the registration and insurance cards. Hardy Starling; the name matched the one on the phone, so it was probably real. No guns, no knife either, which disappointed me, as I wanted to shred the leather seats, but flyers with May's picture, and mine, and with both of our addresses, though mine was out of date.

I said, I'm only going to chase this dog off the porch once. When you leave, don't come back. And be smart. Drive at the speed limit the whole way home.

You won't get away with this, he said.

I looked around. His car was in sunlight while he lay in shadow, trembling. I was trembling too. You see anyone coming to stop me?

I'll go to the police.

You do that, I said, and smashed one taillight with the bat, the sound shocking in the early morning quiet. I wanted to smash all his lights, his mirrors, to send his window glass flying, but I didn't want him pulled over, so I contented myself with humming. A dog barked in the distance. *Another stranger in another neighborhood,* I thought, and imagined an army of hoaxers, spreading out through our town, dispersing their poison, and had to contain myself. Ask for Nash, I said. He's a detective. The one in charge of all this crap. Crap like you.

I knelt over him and pressed the bat against his head. I felt large, giant, kind. He'll love your story, I said. He'll have all kinds of good things to say to you. Out back where he'll take you, near the dumpsters. No cameras there.

I stood again, and raised the bat. He was shaking; the end had come. My shadow stretched out before me as tall as a tree. I had that power, and it ached not to use it. Now go, I said and dropped the keys beside him. Before I change my mind.

He scrambled to his feet and limped to the truck and opened the creaking door and didn't put his seatbelt on and pulled out and drove away and gave me the finger through the empty gunrack on the rear windshield. I thought of chasing him, but decided against it; I might have missed a gun. Besides, why let him think he'd rattled me? At the stop sign he paused, before turning right toward downtown instead of left toward the interstate, but I knew he'd figure out his mistake sooner or later. I'd done what I needed; I wasn't going to help him straighten out his life any more than that.

When I got back in my car, I was shaking, so much I didn't trust myself to drive, so I put my hands under my armpits and squeezed my arms and rocked, trying to make it stop. No luck for minute after minute, and great heaving sobs built up inside me, until I was startled by someone rapping on my window, a man in a long yellow coat with his small brown dog on a leash beside him.

Sir, he said. Are you all right? What are you doing here? The dog's ears pointed in concern when he heard his tone.

I rolled down the window and said, I used to live here.

But you don't now, he said, and straightened. He had a birthmark on one cheek shaped like the state of Florida. So maybe you should move along. I don't know you, and we watch out for each other here.

Not well enough, I said. If you did your job better, I wouldn't have to.

His face reddened and he was about to respond, but I started up the car and drove off. I was already too much Lamont this morning and I didn't want to go full. The bat was still beside me, and his head had looked inviting.

Home, I found blood on the cuff of my shirt and stripped off my clothes, showered to scrub away my guilt and exhilaration, the evidence of a crime. It felt so good to hit him, so fulfilling, that it could become addictive. I would become large, gigantic, colossal. Was that what I wanted?

A transitory dizziness and I knelt in the tub, the water scalding my back, where I foresaw years and years down the road, when my vision would fade, my balance fail, my body falter. Would I be happy, beating strange men with bats, one after another after another, year after year after year? They would keep coming, I knew, as relentless as rust.

No, I thought, and bowed my head, water streaming from my eyes and chin, no. That wasn't my future. It wasn't the army I wanted; it was the head. The face of it.

Kate.

To Do List, Revised:

Refocus and get a handle on it, ffs.

Move.

Work.

Try to drink less bourbon.

Try to find Kate.

Talk to Liam.

Work.

Check car for tails.

Drink even less bourbon.

Talk to May.

Don't buy a gun.

Practice shading: cast shadow, shadow edge, halftone, reflected light, full light.

Check the car for tails.

Drink nothing at all.

Move again.

Don't forget Liam's clothes.

Try to find Kate.

Try to find Kate.

Still don't buy a gun.

Find Kate.

Letters

How could some autistic psyco with no military training shoot small frantic scurrying targets 3 to 11 times each with guns that hard to control? Maybe the adults, but the kids? They're not even big enough to shoot eleven times. In Iraq, I was lucky if I got two bullets in a single body. With the kids, it was hard to get even one.

Club Lucky

APRIL 1, 2019

Lamont bounces outside my door, without bourbon and with his dog. Winter is back; my balls clench in the cold. Yo, he says. Let's check out some music.

You look different, I say.

He holds his arms wide. Losing weight and living large, he says.

He is, getting back into shape, and happier too. Does he know about my run-in with Hardy Starling? Music and what? I say. Molly's a magnet for women.

Hey, if you only got wet when you should've drowned, would that be so bad?

Work isn't calling to me, and the contact high from roughing up Starling didn't last the morning hours; depression rolled in by noon. Maybe accompanied drinking will give me the clarity to face Silver's work in the morning. *Sure,* I think.

Molly stands by the passenger door, tail wagging. Sorry, girl, Lamont says. Otto cops shotgun. To me, he says, Just kick that aside and hop your ass in.

What is it? I ask, taking in its long, glinting brass length. An umbrella stand?

Spent artillery round, he says, fired in anger. Afghanistan.

That bassist is mustard, Lamont tells me. He ain't along for the ride.

We're sitting ten feet from the bassist on the dimly lit stage, his smooth copper face bobbing in time with the music while Lamont beats time on our table. What's that mean? I ask. I could write a bible with what I don't know about jazz.

It means his rhythm is the trio's pulse, and that he keeps the harmony going by sliding his notes in just under the piano. Three things, he says, ticking off his fingers. Rhythm, harmony, and melody. The bassist is responsible for the first two.

I nod, though I don't understand. Hookahs on some nearby tables; maybe smoking one would help. The bassist's purple-and-gold pants flash in the light.

Did you catch that one-finger tremolo? Lamont asks, after a solo. Timing and feel and a slow build, all that beautiful pain. It's like a middle finger you can dance to.

Lamont likes it so much that, during a break, he brings the bassist an Old Fo on the rocks. That was better than Paul Chambers in "Kind of Blue," he says. Crazy chops.

Andy Garland raises his glass to Lamont. You know your jazz.

Lamont asks Garland for his favorite bass players of all time and Garland says, Mingus, hands down, but Lamont holds out for Jaco Pastorius, Paul Chambers and Scott LaFaro.

Garland says, Mingus, Mingus, Mingus, Mingus, Mingus. Listen to him on "Mood Indigo" or "I Can't Get Started". He's places one through five. In sixth you can slot Ron Carter, for variety, maybe. Yeah, sure, why the hell not? "Alone Together."

Lamont says, C'mon, man, don't be like that, putting sugar in your grits. He keeps coming back to Pastorius and LaFaro, especially on Metheny's "Midwestern Night's Dream" and Bill Evans's "Sunday at the Village Vanguard."

Garland smiles wide, showing a missing fat molar. You're a romantic, he says.

Me? Lamont laughs. Not a chance.

Sure you are, Garland says. You just like them because they died young.

Lamont's face shifts. He leans forward and says, You take that back.

What? Garland says, and shrugs, sits back. Jazz is about the truth.

I like the truth all right. But you take back what you just fucking said.

Hey, Lamont. I put a hand on his massive arm. He didn't mean anything.

Garland is a lot smaller than Lamont; most human beings are. But he isn't going to back down. *Foolish*, I think. *You should Nope! the fuck out of here.*

I'm not taking back nothing, he says, his voice growing harder, and puts his drink on the table and his bass on its stand and himself in front of Lamont.

Around us, the room stills. Just the three of us under that blue light on the edge of the stage, and Molly at my side, standing now too. Let's go outside, Lamont says, so I can break your fingers. All ten. You're nothing but a big hunk of fuck.

It comes to me that Lamont hasn't just been teaching me about jazz all these months because he's passionate about it. No, it's because he's desperate. As if he's looking for something in it, something that might save him.

Garland doesn't pick up on all that, though he knows that he's opened the wrong door, then tries to shut it by taking a swing. But because Lamont is about three times the size of a normal man, he punches me instead of Lamont, which I guess makes sense, yet surprises the hell out of me and my cinderblock feet.

Lamont slaps my face with one hand and holds the bass in the other; Molly's snuffling my armpit. Bits of a smashed green hookah shimmer in the light. I think, *Men and violence, we are a sorry lot.* I'm lying on this sticky crappy floor with my head ringing because of him. But no, that's not fair. Garland is the one who hit me. But Lamont provoked him, threatened him. I close my eyes and want to sleep; it's too complex to figure out. I say, Did I get hit by a ham?

Lamont says. City or country?

I laugh. You said country hams were more dense, so I'm going with that. I notice his slip-on shoes. Has he worn lace-ups even once since Latrell died? I flash on him in the morning, looking forlornly at his closet floor, all those lace-ups he can no longer wear. I say, Where's Garland, and why do you have his bass? It's his life.

Don't worry about him. He ain't shit.

After another bad-idea bourbon, I convince Lamont to hide the bass instead of trashing it. The TV is on now and with the music gone we can hear it. A report on American soldiers killed in Mali. We have soldiers in Mali? I ask.

Down on all fours, Lamont ignores me. He slides the bass under a booth near the back. Sticky footsteps as we leave from all the beer, then piercing cold outside. We hug our coats closer and our boots punch wells through the crusty snow, which flashes red in an ambulance's whirling lights.

Bad night to get hurt outside, I say.

Lamont tucks his hands in his pockets and shrugs. Maybe the guy deserved it.

Wait, I say, and stop. A fog of exhaust turns red in the glow of taillights, the radio squawks, two EMS workers bend over a figure sprawled in the snow, whose pants look familiar. What are you saying? Did something happen to Garland?

Lamont keeps walking, shrugs again, says, He left the bar. After? Who knows?

He's so calm about it I decide he can't have done anything to Garland. Besides, he'd probably be happy if he had and would tell me, so I catch up to him.

Did you notice? Lamont asks. They have a sign in the window. *Apartment available.* Turns out it's right upstairs. Your next move is all set.

I wobble against him, pretend it's the uneven ground and not the drink. Molly bumps me upright. At last he says, You need to make friends other than me.

You're a good friend, Lamont.

The best. He slaps my back to prove it.

Aside from getting my nose broken, I say, pinching it for effect.

It's not broken. We're under a streetlight so he tilts his head back and looks down his long nose at mine. Well, maybe it is, but it's not leaking spinal fluid.

We get in the car and drive. The seats are cold, and he blasts the heat. I know that wasn't what we expected, he says, but in the end it was a win-win.

How's that?

You met someone, and I met someone to hate.

At first I think he's kidding and turn on the radio; jazz, what he always has it tuned to. How about I be the aux and pick something?

Fuck that, he says, and fuck jazz, and snaps it off, after which he decides not to go through a yellow light, causing the guy behind us to lean on his horn. In response, Lamont reaches down into the door compartment and pulls out a pistol.

Jesus, Lamont. We've had enough fucking death. The cops might come.

He says, I'll be ready when they do.

I'm glad when the guy behind us turns off a block later, gladder still when we make it all the way to my apartment without further incident. Guns and bourbon don't mix well, and his too-close-to-home craziness has me spooked, so, after I get out, I don't invite Lamont in for a drink. If he notices, he doesn't say. Instead he sets the pistol beside him and drives off, stopping at the cross street for a long time, head turning from side to side, waiting for something.

I don't want to know for what.

Gradually, and Then All at Once

APRIL 1, 2016

Liam had to be intubated, because once again he wasn't breathing on his own. They could only do it for a day, Dr. Wild told me, because they were worried about pneumonia. A pulmonary specialist stood next to her. Dr. Pradhep. He had the youngest face, like a ball boy. I thought he was a high school kid shadowing Dr. Wild.

She said, If we pull the tube out and he doesn't start breathing on his own, there isn't much we can do. His lungs were contused, and haven't fully healed, in addition to his other injuries.

Probably the fall down the stairs, Dr. Pradhep said. And whooping cough weakened his lungs when he was younger. He pushed his wire-rim glasses up on his nose and turned to me. Bronchiectasis, he said, and began to explain.

Yes, I know, I said, cutting him off, because I never liked doctors talking down to me. I said, In the aftermath of his whooping cough, his bronchi are big and baggy, so he gets infections more easily.

Dr. Pradhep nodded and clasped his hands in front of him and stood at his full 5'3" and said, Pneumonia would almost certainly follow reinsertion of the tube. And, given all Liam's other injuries, it would likely prove swiftly fatal.

I was glad May wasn't there. There wasn't much to Dr. Pradhep, and it would have taken a long time to put him back together.

Kate

I admire Kate, odd as that sounds, her ability to stay hidden, while I've had to move again and again. True, some of that is restlessness, the sense that each new place might finally feel like a home again, but some of it is that hoaxers keep posting my address on websites and forums and a Facebook hate group.

It takes a while for them to track me down, and longer every time because I've grown smarter, getting my mail across the state, but eventually I slip up. I shop at a familiar grocery store once too often, or speak to a reporter around an anniversary in an identifiable location, or confront a group of hoaxers at a town board meeting. Afterward, angry and adrenaline-filled, I usually forget to look for tails.

And it isn't only that I admire her, but that I learn from her, her ability to hide, to be private. To be safe.

The farther I go, the longer it takes me to discover who she is and where she lives and how to reach her, the more of that admiration she accrues. I grow heavier with desire, the needle on the scale continually climbing toward bigger numbers. I'll hunt her down, and I'll make her regret all her lies and all her skills, yet be glad she made the chase worthwhile.

Hemodynamic Stability

FEBRUARY 2019

Otto showed up at Palmer's unannounced and with his valentine, though he sat awhile in the car, because it was cold out and because he'd lost his nerve. Now and then he glanced at her curtained front windows, hoping to see her: no car in the driveway, no lights on, no movement; she'd probably already gone to work. He grabbed his sketchbook and colored pencils and drew the house, the stone path meandering beside it. Moonstone; he decided to investigate.

The leather seat creaked in the cold and the door moaned when he opened it and again when he shut it and his footsteps crunched over the moonstone. He knelt and sifted a handful of the cold stone through his fingers and had to admit it looked great there with the yellow house, which made him laugh. That's probably why he didn't hear her approach. He heard the revolver cock though, and when Palmer said, Don't move, he raised his hands above his head.

I said don't move, she said. I have a gun.

I heard you, he said. Sorry, reflex.

A car slowed before it sped up and away; he guessed the driver had seen a woman pointing a gun at kneeling man and wanted nothing to do with it.

You get guns pointed at you a lot?

No. Just twice. Well, three times now.

Really, she said.

A statement, not a question, but it seemed to contain both doubt and interest, so he breathed and took a chance and turned around slowly, his hands still raised.

Good Christ, she said, and lowered the gun with shaking hands.

Why didn't you say it was you? She wore a tailored suit. Dressed for work and now she'd be late.

With the sun behind her, he couldn't make out her expression, but relief made him jokey. Well, he said. That would have spoiled the surprise. A bad first date and a gun leveled at me for the second. Kind of memorable, don't you think?

She said, Well, come on in. At least let me get you some coffee.

In her bright chilly kitchen, a crazy cat clock with a crooked tail and dozens of postcards affixed to the wall above the marble counters. Impressionist landscapes, desert landscapes—Arizona!—a Thoreau quote about fishing. The more he absorbed of her the more he liked her. He was a fool. So, she said. The others.

Others? he asked. The sweat cooled down his back and legs.

Twice before. She nodded toward the counter where the gun lay in its lockbox beside red Lazzaroni Amaretti di Saronno tins and a collection of dog-eared cookbooks and a bottle of holy water that she explained was really gin. The wicker fishing creel surprised him.

Oh, guns. He sat back and broke off part of the scone she'd given him. Lemon with a lemon glaze, moist and crumbly, dense and tangy, it was like eating candied crusty bread. First, he said, did you make these yourself?

I did. My grandmother's recipe.

I would've liked to meet her, if she cooked like this.

Too late for that, I'm afraid. You'll have to do with me.

He nodded, ate some more, swallowed. I'd like that.

Don't get ahead of yourself, cowboy, she said, though she smiled. Wait till I hear about your gun run-ins.

One was over a girl.

You stalked her?

What? No. His face and ears grew hot. Another boy and I liked the same one. When I asked her out first, he pointed a rifle at me when I came over to tell him.

She shook her head. Boys. She didn't need to say more, so she didn't.

He was glad for the coffee, to warm his hands around the warm chunky mug. The second was random, he said. May and I were walking to a movie. A car pulled up beside me and the passenger rolled down his window and I bent down, thinking they needed directions. The car came to a stop and the passenger smiled at me and pointed a gun at my forehead and said, very helpfully, *Gun.* I didn't move.

What about May? Palmer asked.

Nothing, Otto said, and laughed, though as he did, he remembered the smile on the gunman's face, and how he'd felt, high up on his forehead, the exact spot he thought the bullet would enter his brain. Had Liam felt that? His stomach flipped.

Palmer said, May didn't say anything? Yell, run, anything?

She didn't notice. Not even that I'd stopped walking. She was explaining something about electricity and when she gets like that she can forget the world.

Electricity? Palmer asked. Lines crossed her forehead when she frowned. It was a genuine question, without sarcasm, which Otto liked; he still felt protective of May. And it was a mark in Palmer's favor that she hadn't judged her.

Otto nodded. That kind of stuff always fires her up, he said. Even when she was a kid. It was one of the first things I loved about her.

That made Palmer smile.

You have a nice smile, he said. I noticed that the first time we met. He didn't tell her about the dreams he'd had about her mouth; even so, she blushed.

Well, she said, and turned and began wiping off the cutting

board. He ate the last of his scone. It was so good he wanted to ask for another and wished briefly that he was a child, so he could. The crumbs cupped in his palm he tossed into his mouth.

Sorry about the gun, she said. I saw you outside.

Ah. And armed yourself against me. That first date was really bad, wasn't it?

He liked her laugh, but her face grew serious. No. I couldn't see who was in the car, just that someone was watching the house.

Sorry, he said. Didn't mean to make you nervous.

Not your fault. My ex. A nasty habit now, but for a while a necessary one.

Oh, Otto said. Then I'm really sorry.

She waved it off. It was okay in the end. He got especially mad about his comic book collection. Should have been a sign, right? A grown man collecting them.

Otto cleared his throat. I have to admit I do too.

Great, she said, and shook her head. I know how to pick 'em.

It's for my work. The graphic stuff can be bleeding edge. Need to keep up.

Okay. She nodded. That wasn't a line he ever used, so you get points for that.

Ha. So what, did you toss them?

He was in Mexico with his girlfriend. Needed money and told me to take them down to the dealer where he bought most of them and sell them all and I did.

And he got mad at you for doing what he asked?

She shrugged, put the last of the scones away in a tin and snapped the lid shut, which saddened Otto. He'd been hoping she'd give him one or two for the road. Nonspecific instructions, she said. I sold the collection for a dollar, put it in his account, and took a picture of the receipt. When he came back, he was pretty angry.

Otto laughed. Remind me never to piss you off.

She smiled and said, Thought the gun would have already given you that message. Her face fell as soon as she spoke. Oh, Otto, she said, and touched his shoulder. I'm so sorry. Liam.

It's all right, he said, though his heart clenched. It's okay.

She hadn't meant anything, he knew that, and it was impossible to always have things in the front of your mind. For others at least.

To make her feel better, he said, Tell you what. You can make it up to me.

She raised an eyebrow.

Not that, he said, and laughed, and was happy when that made her smile. How about you give me a few of those scones?

She did, and a kiss on the cheek after walking him to the front door. She held it open, the cold air streaming in, in no apparent hurry for him to leave. He liked that, and lingered as he zipped up his coat. It was cold out but, flooded with sunlight, the brown world just now appeared to be blooming. She took his hand and squeezed it.

This was nice, he said, and nodded while he looked out at a neighbor walking a Bernese mountain dog, who waved at them as if they were a couple. Thank you.

He didn't say it, but they both knew he would call her soon.

Traveling Through the Dark
APRIL 2, 2019

Yellow ribbons up all over the city, around trees, on school and stop signs, draped over lampposts, which hollowed out my stomach. I hadn't been watching the news but I didn't have to guess what had happened, and when I went to present Silver with the final product and my latest bill, she dropped the bread forms she was cleaning and stripped off her blue rubber gloves and filled me in. A school in New Mexico. The poor kids, she said, covering her eyes with her pale hands.

Home again, I looked it up. Twenty-seven dead, including teachers and one counselor, a far-off disaster that felt a little too close to home. And I wasn't the only raw one, all these years later; the ribbons showed that. I didn't want to see them. Cranky, my thoughts turned to Kate, but none of my recent emails about her had been answered, so I warmed chili and ate as I read others. The Vermont Fish & Wildlife office had written, to tell me that my sporting license was about to lapse. I had some money and it wasn't a good time to meet potential clients, given the black eye, so I thought I'd go fishing in Vermont for a few days; a week even, to let the local spasm of sadness pass while I endured my own.

Lamont's picture on my phone. Let's drink, he said. Also, why are you ghosting Palmer? She ditched the gun.

I'd expected the call; every school shooting set him off. How'd she know her gun bothered me? I said.

Woman's got a brain. Now. Let's drink.

Can't, buddy, I said. My vision is still messed up from my black eye.

What's that got to do with drinking?

I won't be sure which glass to pick up.

Aim for the middle one.

Unseasonably warm as I drove—low forties—and a huge orange full moon that rose over the stubbled fields an hour into my trip, which made me obscenely happy; every car I passed might hold a friend. I rolled down my windows and waved to them! A few waved back, but not enough, and the mood passed.

I drove faster, and by the time I reached southeast Vermont, the bright moon was smaller and whiter and high overhead, casting long black shadows over the pavement. So bright I could drive without my headlights, so I did, startling a half dozen deer who turned and leapt over the stone walls among the returning maples.

Ten minutes later, at the top of the far hill, a car headed my way. We drove down our hills into the valley, toward each other. About halfway across the valley he blinked his lights, to signal that mine were off. I ignored him and sped up and closed my eyes and pressed down on the accelerator and shot ahead. The wind was louder now, I heard it roaring through the open windows, though it might have been me, yelling into the void.

He began sounding his horn. Eyes closed, I held the wheel steady, thinking that if I drifted onto the shoulder I'd hear my tires crunching over the roadside gravel, even over his horn, and if I drifted the other way, I'd know it at the last.

The Song of the Three

APRIL 2, 2016

Before Dr. Pradhep pulled the tube, May and I bent over Liam, holding his soft, nonresponsive hands, stroking his slack face, telling him we loved him. He had been awake for a while with the tube down his throat. He'd arched his back and teared up and made noises with his eyes wide and tried to work his jaw; he wanted the tube out, we could see that. *Cyanosis*, another unwanted word I'd learned; his lips and fingertips were blue.

It's okay, sweetie, May said, and explained why it was in there, getting both scientific and abstract.

Only for a day, buddy, I said. When it comes out, you'll be fine.

With my phone I took a picture of him, thinking it might be the last I'd ever get. The oxygen tube, a scar on his beautiful face. Then I bent and kissed his warm forehead and walked out without looking back. It wasn't a Bible verse I clung to, but wisdom from a more secular wise man, Satchel Paige. *Don't look back. Whatever you're afraid of might be gaining on you.*

We sat in the waiting room holding hands while they removed the tube, hoping he'd breathe. At one point May said, That Dr. Pradhep has a kind face. Then nothing for the next few minutes as we waited. My throat clogged, I couldn't speak.

I don't know what May was thinking, but I began incoherently praying, even though I've never believed in God. The son of the man lying next to my son in the Neuro-ICU ward sat next to me, swinging his feet. Six, seven, mostly patient through the long hours of waiting, polite—twice, he'd thanked me for the donuts. Unlike the rest of his extended family, he spoke no Spanish, and whenever they wanted to discuss the state of his father without him knowing, they switched to it.

His mother was on the phone with an older daughter and handed him the phone. Say where you at, Santiago, she told him.

Santiago shouted into the phone. Where you at?

Take him, I thought. *If you need to take a boy? Take this one.* I was appalled, but I didn't take it back. Car accident or a fall down the stairs or a sudden inexplicable illness in the darkest watches of the night, it didn't matter. Just that it not be Liam.

And we waited. Waited and waited, to learn if he'd breathe with the tube out.

Liam at Seven
APRIL 2014

He was all dressed for his new school in his favorite jeans and chambray shirt, a couple of months after we moved. A late spring. Blue jays called and dropped from bare trees to peck at tufts of grass or mounded dirt showing around the patchy snow, and the scent of the warming earth floated on the warm breeze. He stopped on the porch, one hand on the white wooden rail, and said, I like the smell of this day.

He hopped down the stairs and skipped on the gravel driveway to the car and turned to face me before opening the door. Inside my nose, he said, it's mixed up with the smell of other days I like. It smells kind of like spring, and it's a happy smell.

Smart enough to realize it was a moment, as soon as I dropped Liam off at school, I called May to tell her.

Bycatch on the North Ship

APRIL 2, 2019

I bypassed Burlington for a motel on Lake Champlain, small A-frame cabins on the hills sloping down to the lake, mostly empty and completely dark; in another couple of months they'd smell of fishermen. Fox News on the TV, the bird-boned clerk dressed like he was trying out for a role as a Mormon in a high school play.

The school shooting, he said, tapping my license. The government did that.

The government shot the kids?

No, they're devious, but not that bad, he said. Crisis actors. No kids died.

Still drained from my moonlight ride, I contented myself with staring, hoping my black eye gave him pause, then paid cash and grabbed my key and parked on the brown grass in front of my cabin. I could go back in, confront him, but the odds were that would only escalate, and I didn't want to end up arrested. Time spent in court was time I didn't spend tracking Kate down; better to save my anger for her.

Full Gandhi, as Lamont would say. I sighed, grabbed my bag, let myself in. The pleasant woodsy scent of an unused lake cabin. The bed was fine, the bathroom small, but I'd be able to stand in the shower. I tossed my bag on the bureau and shut the light off and moonlight streamed across the wide pine floorboards, and when I closed my eyes I saw Hardy Starling's terrified face and wished it made me happy.

Morning fog, my shoes and ankles soaked during the short walk back to my car. The nearest bait shop had a big red door with a dog door cut into the bottom and a fat black dachshund poked its nose out, its front legs too, but then it got stuck and barked at me in a friendly way. It kept barking and struggling to get out until, with a last bark, it popped free. Right on its heels were two others, barking as they circled my legs, then two more, a clown car for dachshunds. Liam would love it.

My mood lifting, I imagined the GIF I'd send to his email and wondered if I could do something similar for the cheeses, convince Henry and Cora to name one after the dogs. Fat and creamy, a triple dachshund.

The counterman poured over maps, light shining off his bald head.

Planning to move? I asked, envious of the detailed pen-and-ink drawings of schooners behind him. The drawings themselves and the skill of the draftsman.

Ha, he said. No. Stuck behind the counter. With a pencil he pointed to a spot on the lake about three miles down. Was thinking that that would be the best place to fish this morning. Nice weed beds. Largers like the warmer water close to shore.

You have a website? I asked. Run it from your boat. Give advice that way.

Can't give it away, he said. I'll be broke.

The dogs had made it back in, all but the fat one, which was stuck coming in now, and barking again. Do a subscription service, I said.

Great! he said. You gave me the idea for free. Now if I can just get someone to design and market it, I'll be all set. In the meantime, what can I do for you?

Hire me, I said. To do the web design. That's what I do. Graphic arts.

His head went back. You see other customers here? he said. Let me guess. You pitched someone else the other day and they didn't like it either.

My bruised eye? No. A bar fight I stood too close to. You don't like my idea?

I like your idea fine. I don't like you coming in here pretending to be after fish knowledge when the only thing you were fishing for was money.

Hey, I said, hands up, palms out. It's not like that. I walked him through my thought process and said, I really am here to fish, and ordered a sandwich and wandered around the bait shop. Antique bamboo fishing rods, a cork-handled Kit Kast ice fishing rod, racks of fishing lures—Heddon, Creek Chub, Bagley, South Bend; a man who liked the present and the past.

He'd put on a straw hat and picked out lures for me and put together the sandwich—a local ham and cheese, which he cut on top of the map. I took a picture.

I can write down the name of the cheese makers, he said.

Pics are enough, I said. Visual clues work best for me.

Smart, he said. When you're fishing, look for the cormorants and gulls. They'll be near the baitfish. The bass will be after them. Anything beyond the clustered birds, the water will be too cold. On the knuckles of his left hand were tattooed the letters *FISH*. Name's Homer, he said, and reached across the counter. Brannock.

Otto, I said, and shook his hand. Thanks.

Sorry I was short with you. I get a lot of salesmen in here.

Hard to run a business, I said. I understand.

Tell you what, he said, and nudged the hat brim up with his forearm. If you meant that, about drawing up some stuff, let me know.

I said, I'll have it for you in under ten days, and, leaving, careful not to trip over the circling dogs, thought, *Work just might be the thing to save you.*

Almost the Same Beginning, Backwards

He was a bully, two of his friends said, though his parents never knew.

Fall of his sophomore year, weeks before the shooting, he picked out a new African American kid on Freshmen Friday, a kid even smaller than he was, and pushed him up against the lockers and made him smell a girl's used tampon, one hand at the boy's throat, the other forcing the tampon to the boy's nose and mouth. That boy's wide eyes staring at him over it until they overflowed with tears.

They hadn't been there to see it but he'd told them about it, everyone knew the story. They even knew the girl he'd paid twenty dollars to for her used tampon.

Nash spoke to them; embarrassed, the girl denied the story, but like the boys who told it to him, it didn't surprise her he'd shot African American kids. It surprised her he hadn't shot more. That was why she'd stopped being friends with him, long before.

Bound for Glory

SPRING 2005

South of Trieste, two other couples got on the train. The women reeked of perfume and the men each had on four button-down shirts, one over the other, the collars sticking up. They had enough bags of coffee to wake an army, bunches of bananas, and duffel bags, stuffed with other things we never saw.

We nodded and smiled at one another and fell silent, May and I now and then pointing out a passing sight as we made our way through Slovenia to Croatia. Laundry strung across an alleyway, red sheets translucent in the slanting sunlight, a line of women dressed in black holding bright blue plastic water jugs at a fountain, a farmer scraping the muddy flanks of a white cow with a hoe. By dark, in Croatia, the two couples had begun to talk. Through sign language and limited English, we discovered that they were heading back to Ogulin. They were surprised we were going all the way to Athens. Croatia was beautiful, they said, if broken.

Closer to Rijeka, they began chattering madly, gesturing at us. Three seemed to agree on something but the red-headed woman held out. Finally her husband, who spoke the most English, asked if I liked his shirts. They had enormous collars and were nothing I'd ever wear so I said, Yes.

Good, he said, and stood and unbuttoned the top one. You wear then.

He handed it to me, and indicated that I should put it on over my own, and the next one, and the next. Then the other man gave me his three extra shirts. Soon we were holding the coffee and bananas, and the bulging duffel bags were ours too.

Short-term rental, the first man said. Like holiday.

Okay, I said, unsure what he meant, already sweating under all that polyester.

I stood to open the window and they all burst out shouting. No no no!

So I sat and sweated.

The one with the unibrow looked at me a long time. American, he said at last. George Washington good John Kennedy good.

Yes, yes, I said, and nodded.

I wasn't up on current Croatian politics, knowing only that they were tricky, and that Serbs would be considered enemies, but Milošević was perhaps too raw a recent wound, so I asked, Tito?

Good! they nodded.

I decided to be venturesome. Putin, I said.

The man closest to the door looked both ways down the rocking hallway, then pulled his hairline back and said, in a low, low voice, Very very bad.

I nodded enthusiastically.

Bush? he said. Very bad. Is war.

Ten minutes later, the compartment slid open and two soldiers with automatic rifles asked for our passports. One flipped through them and handed them back and looked at me with my shirts and May with two coats on.

All this yours? he asked, and pointed.

In unison we said too loudly, All of it!

He stared at me for a long time, the train rocking. Your choice, he said, and left, sliding the door shut behind him. For another hour I wore the clothes, then returned them. They gave us each a banana and poured us some wine. As they were getting re-dressed the unibrow said something to the red-headed woman who'd not wanted to run the scam and she said something back and he slapped her, hard.

Decency, our implacable solidarity, all the pleasure in the compartment, they all drained away faster than the mark of his hand appeared on her pale skin. Her face hardened. May and I held our wine cups, not drinking them, though the four of them did. After a few silent minutes, the unibrow drank both of ours.

An hour after they left, the train stopped in the middle of the country. Dark trees close up against the tracks, just visible in the light spilling from the train.

Another guard appeared at the door and asked for our passports and when he saw we didn't have visas, said, Come, and I followed behind him, taking May's with me. He was huge, six eight at least; I jogged to keep up with him.

A long stream of people heading from the stopped train to the station, Perković, a name I'd never heard. We'd been told visas were a formality; you could get one in country with no problem, they would just stamp it on the train. Three a.m. and everyone sleepy, no lights on in the town except at the station, yellow against the dark. Taxis lined up outside, headlights on, though no one appeared to be leaving.

The guard said, American? John Kennedy, Bill Clinton.

Recognizing the game, I said, Good! Tito good! Putin bad, Bush is war. He nodded. I didn't want the game to end so, daringly, I put my fingers across my eyebrows, imitating thick ones, and said, Milošević, bad!

He glanced at me and said nothing but sped up and took me to the front of the line for passport stamps and gave them to the clerk who stamped each like he meant to break them. The guard took me back outside, pointed at the train and said, Run.

I thought he was going to shoot me in the back but a conductor blew his whistle and the train moved and I sprinted down the fifty yards of track while it picked up speed as other passengers tried to turn back and the soldiers yelled and prodded them forward. I flew past all of them, stumbling once on the gravel but remaining upright, and got to the last car before it gathered too much speed and gripped the rail and leapt onto the nubby iron platform, panting.

Later we learned that stopping the train in small towns and stranding the passengers was the only way towns made money, money they needed in the aftermath of war. A cheap trick, but the truth was they had to do it to stay alive; that's why I remember it. Contradictory truths are the ones that matter.

Liam loved the story; it made him giggle. Bush! he would say, forever after, Bush Is War! Milošević! he'd say, and put his fingers across his eyebrows like furry caterpillars, and roll over in bed laughing, then raise his hands as if he was holding a gun and point around the room and say, All this yours?

His shooting unmade me, and he loved a story where I might have been shot too.

May's Craigslist Missed Connections

MAY AT SUNSHINE DINER SUNDAY

You're a cute brunette and you were having breakfast with your friend around 9:30am I think you keep looking at me and smiled a couple of times. He seemed not to like it. You are beautiful and I'd love to get to know you better.

MAY AT THE COMEDY CONNECTION

Beautiful brunette computer lady that I sat with at the comedy show on Friday night. You're gorgeous and I'm sorry I didn't tell you that night. While you're still single, I would love the opportunity to take you out. Please reach out if you see this. You showed me a picture on your phone. What was it?

MAY ON HYBRID BIKE IN MONROE PARK

You were riding your bike in the park we spoke briefly if you find this tell me whose bike you were riding. I never thought about it, but I wanted to keep talking to you.

MAY AT MIDAS ON ELM STREET

You waited next to me and my son for our mufflers to be fixed. You gave him stickers and was so very sweet and absolutely the most beautiful lady i have seen in this town ever. I wanted to ask for your number but didnt think it was good to do so in front of my son. Hope you read this and i hear from you soon.

MAY OUTSIDE YANKEE CANDLE

You heard me and my friend discussing whether Vanilla candles were better than the cinnamon ones and came over to set me straight. You seemed nice and were cute, if you're single would you be interested in going out for dinner or drinks? I know you don't have kids.

MAY AT BARNYARD BUFFET

You're a very attractive brunette woman. I was sitting in the section next to yours but overheard you talking to the guy you were sitting with and you caught me looking at you and we made eye contact several times. You smiled more each time. I got your name but would have liked your phone number. Hopefully you'll check here while feeling we had a missed chance to talk.

MAY DID I SEE YOU AT STARBUCKS ON THURSDAY MORNING?

May I could've sworn I was right behind you in the drive-thru line at Starbucks on State Street Thursday morning around 8:00 AM. It looked like you looked at me through your rearview mirror. I know it was the car you usually drive. If it was you, contact me. I never got true closure with you and need to talk to you.

Stretched Out, Held Flat, Pinned Down

APRIL 3, 2019

I fished from the shore, the radio on. Homer Brannock had been right; gulls and cormorants clustered twenty yards out by the reed beds. The reeds bent toward me in the chilly wind and the birds faced into it and small waves pushed the green water onto the rocky shore. Cast after cast caught a fish. Liam always loved fishing and I told myself I felt his spirit, but it was only the wind and a few swift high clouds whose shadows raced over the water and passed over me and vanished.

A turtle paddled up, hoping I'd feed him, his back green with moss, and at the top of the hour the news came on, at the end of it a promo for an interview later in the day, the mother of Liam's school shooter.

I turned the radio off and ate the sandwich, squatting on the shore: tangy ham, sharp cheese. Lapping water, a chilly wind, vees of northbound geese strung across the blue sky, their calls muted; so much peace. But the NPR announcement had soured the day, so I packed up and drove to Joe Lay's, the local antique store whose familiarity was comforting. Dusty light shone through the stained-glass window over the heavy dark furniture and the piles of *Life* magazines, faded by time and darkened by dust. I snapped a picture of an old map and a voice startled me.

Can't you read the signs? Oh, Otto! Carol said, and hugged me. Some gray hair now, some extra weight, the same citrusy perfume. She fussed about my black eye.

It's so hard, she said. I wasn't there and I've never had a child shot and yet I can't ever stop thinking about Liam. I haven't slept a night through since then.

Me either, I said. Or May. Or any of the other parents, from what I can tell.

Listen to me, she said. Asking *you* to comfort *me*. I should be ashamed.

PTSD is odd, I said. Kids who were there and saw their friends killed, some of them are just fine now. Some of the teachers who were wounded. And then some of the teachers who were in the school and only heard the shooting had to quit. Two are gone, so don't feel bad. I didn't tell her that one was by suicide.

She squeezed my arm by way of thanks and said, Take as many of those maps as you want. Ruddy's idea. They were going to be big sellers. We haven't sold any.

I've always loved maps, imagining vanished worlds; Liam too. Once I pinned a large antique map to his floor while May had him at her parents'. When they came home, I said, Hey, buddy, how was your trip? I was thinking you might want to take another. Let's go up to your room and see where. May and I followed behind.

Cool! he yelled, and squatted and put his finger on it and said, This is where I want to go, right here! French West Africa!

Oh, good, May said. We're raising a little colonialist. She went to unpack while Liam crawled across the continent, sounding out the names.

Now, I selected a bunch of maps, thinking that I'd meant all I'd said to Carol, but thinking too that comforting her had drained me, so I paid for them once Carol disappeared through an old, thin four-panel door behind the wooden counter and left without saying good-bye. I got into the car and wished that when I'd sped across the valley floor with my eyes closed just a day before, the Mormony clerk had been the one heading toward me. That I hadn't swerved.

Letters

Your boy was declared dead in the first 11 minutes. By who? Why was that later overruled? How did he come back to life? Why did the entire country have an "accurate" death toll within 11 minutes? How could that even be possible in a scene that was supposed to be so chaotic and so gruesome? Who could count so many dead children so quickly?

And who decided it would be smart to have a "wounded child" that we could all root for? I think that's maybe the most devious and the cruelest thing you people did, all those news reports updating "Liam's" status. I had three neighbors who checked it every day, even though I told them it was a lie. Do you have any idea what your lies do to people? Do you even care?

April Is the Cruelest Month

I don't want to listen, but I do, Terry Gross, interviewing the shooter's mother. It shouldn't surprise me, but it does, Gross says. That you still love him.

Of course, the mother says. He's my son.

But a boy who did something horrific?

No silence before she speaks again, meaning she was ready for this question. Yes. He murdered other children and adults, including my ex-husband. Ruined many people's lives, including my family's. But that isn't *all* of my son.

It is to me, I say. Yell, my face distorted in the mirror.

He was a human being, she says, as if in answer. Later, she says that sympathetic neighbors sent her food in the aftermath. When she finally went home, when the media horde had given up and left her alone.

That must have made you feel welcome, Gross says. Glad for the kindness. You've talked about the outpouring of hatred. So, a ray of light must have mattered.

It did, but my lawyer said I had to throw it out, that it might be poisoned. I wanted to call the police to have it tested, to show him he was wrong, but of course I couldn't ask that they spend resources testing donated food, when so many were working so many hours to try and figure out what had happened.

Anyway, she says. It's part of why we buried him in an unmarked grave. To avoid having it vandalized. And to keep it from becoming a shrine. To a certain segment of the population, a twisted segment, it would be.

When she gets to her self-loathing, I'm glad I've listened. All the hatred I've harbored for years, the desire to confront her, to shove Liam's bloody clothes in her face. Terry asks, Could you have done more?

Yes. I'm not saying I did anything wrong, because he was raised in a loving household, an inclusive household. So he didn't learn his rage from us. But he was depressed. I realized that in the aftermath. And that I had missed certain signs. So now, I write everything down. Every memory. Every thought. And search it over and over for signs of what was to come. For places I could have intervened.

After that she switches to dreams, dreams I recognize, of her boy endangered and she unable to protect him. Falling from a ladder, a roof, a moving car. Each time she reaches for him, he slips from her hands at the last moment, which is when she usually wakes, to a split second of relief that it's only a dream, in turn overtaken by dread and anguish that the reality is even worse.

I don't like the familiar sound of that, so I snap off the radio, but ten miles later, realizing I'm furiously speeding past the glinting birches and somber pines, I turn it back on. Better to hear her perfidy than to turn a few small nuggets over and over in my mind. She's on to letters now. The hatred in some, the forgiveness in others, and the troubling nature of the rest. Again I recognize myself in her description, again it infuriates me. We are not the same, you and I, I want to tell her. Face to face.

She talks about the girls who wished they'd known him because they would have taken care of him, would have made sure he knew he was loved and desirable, so he'd never have had to kill to get the attention he deserved and was no doubt denied. Almost always with pictures, she says. Of their cleavage or their bottoms in bikinis and underwear, of them suggestively sucking popsicles.

All the broken people in the world, she says. They puzzle me. And they've persuaded me to do something about them, to help them.

Enough, I think, and snap it off again, and don't care that I'm speeding. I speed up more, and signs blur. I know Lamont will have heard all about it soon. Will probably have listened to it. Will, like me, want to do something about it, which is the one thing that scares me, so when traffic picks up and I slow down, I call him. Did you hear it?

Of course I heard it, he says.

Well, maybe we can call the bookstore, make sure they don't invite her.

They won't invite her, believe me, Lamont says. I took care of it. They won't have her in any bookstore within two hundred miles.

Lamont, did you call them up? The highway is crowded now, cars pinning me in on either side, making me panic.

You're damn straight I did.

Lamont. I drive with my eyes closed again, just for a second, trying to will it all away. You know the cops are going to come by. They have to.

Let 'em, he said. Going by that kid's house didn't do a damn thing either.

I open my eyes and slam on my brakes, just in time. You're older, Lamont. You're Black.

Yes I am, he says. And I have guns.

Interim 6

Number of school shootings since: 147
Number of school children killed: 247

Nash Calls Me In to Call Me Out

APRIL 5, 2019

For all our contact, this is the first time I'm at Nash's desk. Yellow
and blue paperwork, an old baseball, a coffee mug with devil and
angel emojis, a framed picture of his sons dangling strings of trout.
One looks like Nash himself, younger. As if accidently, he covers the
picture with some paperwork, a kindness that cuts.

Sorry, he says, but I thought it would be best if we did this here.

Sure, I say, and let out a deep breath through puffed cheeks. I
understand.

Have a seat, he says, and scratches the palm of one hand with
the fingers of the other. Listen. I know this time of year is really
hard for you.

I give him my stone face. Knowing he's trespassed, he gets right
to it. So, some background, this guy who was beaten. Turns out he
demanded proof that the children were real at a town meeting. Got
jumped after. Found lying on the ground, a pink dildo shoved in his
mouth. A wonder he didn't choke on it.

Maybe the balls weren't big enough.

Nash ignores my comment. His name is Hardy Starling. You
know him?

I shake my head no, but my poker face must slip, because Nash's
eyes narrow. Did you know the hoaxers were in town for the selectmen meeting? And did you have anything to do with his beating?

No. Nothing. How could I? Didn't know of the meeting. Is he
going to make it?

Yeah. He'll be okay. He was in the Neuro-ICU for a bit, but he's
talking now. Maybe some residual damage. He leafed through pages
of notes. There might have been two different attacks. The docs said

242

some bruising looked older, and he was found without a cell phone or wallet. John Doe, until a patrol noticed all the parking tickets, and that his car was filled with shredded paper.

His truck?

His eyes come up. I said car. We're trying to put the shredded paper together, see if it offers any clues. You sure none of it is yours?

Could be. I pick up his stress ball. Hoaxers steal my garbage all the time. For credit card numbers, my customers' names. Who knows what they do with the rest.

Anyway, he says. From the truck we got his registration, and from the registration we got his name. Then we got his cell phone number and followed its usage. Last place it picked up a signal was near your old house. May's place.

I know if they go through his records, they'll find the sent emails. The sent contacts. I shiver at the thought. Nash notices.

Yeah, your story's all wet, so here's what I think. Maybe you hit him and he fought back. That's how you got that shiner. It's about the right vintage. Purple still.

Polygraph me, if you want. This came from a bar fight with Lamont.

You two have a falling out? I thought you were friends.

Friends fight. You know that. I say nothing about the bassist.

I do, he says. But this guy was nobody's friend, and frankly I wouldn't blame anyone for jumping him. Especially not you. But let's say it wasn't you. Anyone else it might have been?

Lamont, of course, but I won't give him up. Yes, I say. I'm sure you have the list already. Any of the parents. All of them.

He ignores me. Happened about four Tuesday afternoon. Where were you?

You have witnesses? The thought makes my stomach tighten.

Would they have seen you?

If so, you wouldn't be asking me. But I was on my way up to Vermont, looking for freelance clients. Found one in fact. Homer Brannock. Ask him, if you need to.

If I need to?

I don't know, I say, and drop the stress ball on his desk. Maybe asking him isn't the best thing. If clients think I'm bashing in people's heads, it hurts my work.

He nods, taps the pen against the page. All right, for now I'll take your word on it. But if we don't develop any leads, I can't guarantee anything. Looks like someone used a bat on him. That doesn't give you any ideas?

Sure, lots of them, but you wouldn't like any.

I won't tell Lamont, because I'm his hope, his touchstone. That I haven't snapped means there's still good in the world. Only Hardy Starling and I know I have, and it seems likely he won't remember.

And if we search your car and apartment, we won't find a bloody bat?

Actually, you would.

He rubs his face with both hands, looks at me, sighs. Leans forward so our faces are only inches apart. *The good cop part,* I think. Otto, he says, his voice low, his breath minty. I know these people are relentless. Brazen. If I were in your shoes, I'd be doing the same thing. Hell. I'd want to kill him if I was you. But if you were in my shoes, you'd tell me to knock it off. These people are their own worst enemies.

I laugh. Not while I'm alive, I say.

He shakes his head and sits back. Listen. Once we catch a couple, charge them with stalking, get them into the system, jail them, it'll discourage others. They think they're heroes, waking up America to governmental false flag operations. But they don't want to pay the price to be real heroes. Eventually, they'll move on.

So they'll just be someone else's problem.

Yeah, he says. They will. But we're coordinating now, police departments in different cities. Different states even. Give us a chance.

I have, I say, my glance roving over his desk. Three years. On his calendar is a Thursday lunch date with May. So they're still seeing one another. Good for them.

They'll go away, Nash says. I promise you. They will. Just let us do our job. And give me something, if you can. Anything.

I nod, look to the side as if I'm thinking, then sit forward.

He sits forward again too, ready for my confidence, so I ask for paper and a pencil. He hands them to me and I begin to sketch, quickly, broad strokes, the forms of a body and a bat. As I work, I say, You still interested in drawing lessons? I wave the pencil. You asked about them once.

Oh, right. He laughs. Must have been a passing fancy.

Okay, I say, and draw on. Here, I say, turning it around once I'm done.

What's that?

A possum. Hit him with my car first, bat second. Hence the blood, if you test it.

For a minute he just stares at it. A ringing phone, which he ignores, a small plane passing overhead, radiators knocking, the sour smell of burnt coffee. Okay then, he says at last, and drops it on his desk. We're done here. I didn't order any bullshit for lunch and here you've gone and served me a four-course meal.

I feel a little bad and want to ask about his sons as a peace offering, but from his expression I don't think it'll go over well. As I stand, he says, May's right about you, you know. Your stubbornness.

She's right about a lot of things, I say. I hope one of them is you.

Was she right about you and the pink dildos?

Excuse me? I say.

Never mind, he says. I was hoping she was right on that one. So say I'm wrong. How about Lamont? he says. Think he could have done this?

You know Lamont, I say, smart enough not to pause or look away. He lives his life now like he's driving a stolen car. I don't think he has time for pink dildos. And you're wrong, by the way. I don't want to kill hoaxers.

That's good.

I want more.

Outside, the warming air smells of wild chives. I text Lamont.

Not asking, and don't want to know. But a hoaxer was beaten last week. Police just questioned me. Lose the bat, or douse it in Coke, and erase this text.

I'd seen the thing about Coke on a crime show, how it ruined blood evidence. I'm not sure if it's true, but it's worth a shot. Better than bleach, according to the show. On the way home, I pick up a six-pack to douse mine.

First Anniversary—Paper

APRIL 5, 2017

What's this? May said, and sat up in bed.

A fleeting smile, her taut skin shiny. I put the tray beside her, coffee steaming, and said, Wait, there's one more thing, and was back before she even took a sip. She adjusted the straps of her floral nightgown, a birthday gift from Liam, his most recent one. Here, I said, and handed it to her over the tray, careful not to whack the juice glass or the plate with the steaming eggs and sausage. Her Mother's Day meal.

You know I can't wait on presents. Her cheekbones looked like wooden knobs; she'd lost twenty pounds in the last year. A gust of wind blew against the house, rattling the windows and startling us; outside, the tall firs bent to the south.

Going to be cold, isn't it? she said. Maybe a storm. I nodded. But she was looking at the sky, at space, at nothing. Probably better, she said. I don't think I could stand a beautiful day. The paper crinkled as she unwrapped it.

She inspected the painting, the white church with its Egyptian-blue stained-glass window. So many times she'd said she wished she could paint it, hints, of course, that I should. But the hints had had an expiration date, which only became clear in that moment. We had each become our own galaxies, drifting slowly apart, and I'd thought the painting might forestall that, might call up the essential from memory. As stupid as trying to hold back a river with a spoon.

Oh, Otto, she said at last and ran her fingers over it. So beautiful. You've captured it exactly. But can you take it away? I don't think I can look at it ever again.

I didn't tell her about Liam's version, on the other side.

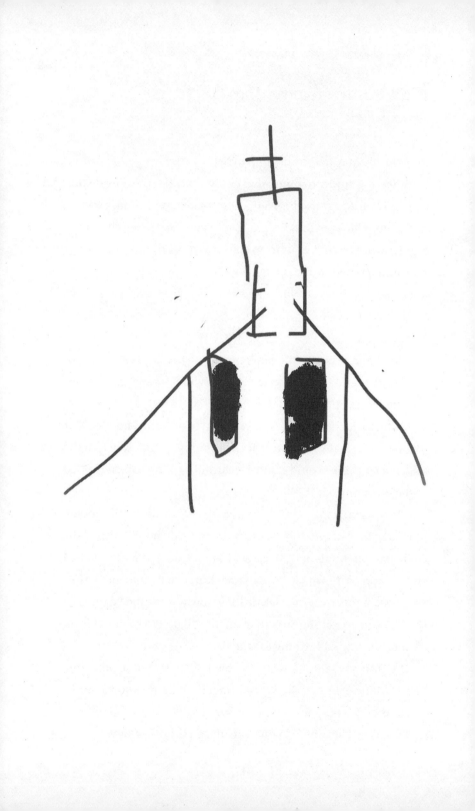

The War on Easter

The coffee in my mug rocks as a train rumbles past outside my apartment window and I push the mug aside and open the folded-over top of the cardboard box. Most of the case of liquor is gin; it's postequinox, after all. My phone rings and rings, then goes quiet and rings again. 193 unread emails, most of them probably junk, but some related to work. 194, 197. Unread texts and missed voicemails too; my phone buzzes with each arrival.

I've caught snippets here and there, and the voices sound angry, so why listen? And through the power of my current gincident, I know that a lot of the emails and texts are angry too, without even glancing at them. Who am I to ignore my new gin-induced superpowers?

That night, I dream someone puts me against a wall and holds a gun to my head. *Draw the cop's face!* No luck. My hands are encased in big Mickey Mouse gloves, and every cop I look at, in person or in pictures, has had their faces erased.

Followers Over Friends

HAHAHAHA THAT LITTLE LIAM HAS THE WORST LUCK, HE WAS KILLED AT SCHOOL REVIVED HIMSELF ELEVEN MINUTES LATER AND THEN MADE HIS WAY OVER TO PAKISTAN AND WAS KILLED BY THE TALIBAN HOW MANY TIMES IS LIAM BARNES (FAKE VICTIM) PLANNING TO DIE IN SHOOTINGS? IS THERE A CASINO WHERE WE CAN PLACE BETS ON WHERE HIS THIRD DEATH WILL HAPPEN? MY GUESS IS GERMANY. THEIR GOVERNMENT IS TAKING AWAY GUNS TOO!!!!!!!!!!!!!!!!!!!

Two Hearts Beat as One

APRIL 9, 2019

They had lunch at Rosie's Place, sitting in front of a wall-sized picture of sunflowers. Not wanting to appear paranoid, May waited until after they'd had salads and talked about their weeks to show Nash the Craigslist Missed Connections entries; she'd printed them out on a single blue sheet.

He smoothed the paper flat on the table and read it and shrugged and brushed off a few crouton crumbs with the blade of his hand. We were at the Sunshine, but those others? There are lots of Mays in this town.

She moved her coffee cup aside. I was at every one of those places. They showed up within days of me being there. Sometimes the next day.

Did you talk to them? He opened three sugar packets for his iced tea at once.

No. I didn't talk to anyone at any of them. So how did they get my name?

I don't know, May. The long spoon clinked against the glass as he stirred.

They're following me. You don't have to believe me, but I'm getting a gun.

Good, he said, patting her hand, which surprised her into silence. She had arguments and evidence ready, but now she didn't need them. Emails asking about her upcoming vacations, a box of camping gear someone had put in her garage, her social security number painted on the hood of her car with nail polish.

I've thought for a while you should have one, Nash said, shielding the lemon as he squeezed it into the tea. She liked that he did that; Otto had always done that too. A bittersweet memory now. Any ideas on what kind of gun you want? Nash said.

Fever Dream

Liam on the beach at nineteen, shirt off, hair tousled by the wind, the new tattoo on his chest visible from twenty yards. Four large lines of script, inked across one breast. Smiling as he walks toward us, feet and ankles sandy.

How could you? May says, marching toward him, in her anger dropping the pink conch shells she's collected. You *know* how I feel about them.

The script edged with red, as if highlighted; swelling, probably. It looks *awful*, May says.

By then we're close enough to read it. Four lines from "Good King Wenceslas."

It's the way you two met, Liam says, grinning. And it's my favorite carol.

May runs her fingers over the ink. Well, if you were going to defile yourself at all, she says, her voice losing its edge, you should at least have gone for "Silent Night."

Letters

A call came to the monastery, for prayers, after another mass shooting. I could not answer it, at first.

I had turned off the news when the headlines first broke, not wanting to see, to hear, to watch, as people ran for their lives, or collapsed when they heard the awful truth, or argued about the causes and solutions, or simply wept, overcome with despair.

I had already seen this before. And before. And before. And I knew I would see it again. In a day, a week, a month. That the places would vary, but that the news would not.

I wanted it to stop. You want it to stop. Nearly everyone does, and yet it doesn't.

Even as I tried to ignore the news, I knew that wouldn't help. That the pain and the hatred and the fear would go on, whether or not I allowed myself to watch and read, whether or not I grew angry or despairing, whether or not I prayed. And at that thought, at the realization that my prayers were as ineffectual as a lamb standing before lava, my heart misgave me.

Troubled, I took to my bed, my chest aching.

After a long period of silent contemplation, I came to realize why.

It was not my sympathy for those hurt that pained me, or rather, not just that, but rather that, buried in my doubt, small as a trembling mustard seed, was a reminder that prayer is at the center of the call to my way of life. Prayer that overflows into our service to God's people, people who are both beautiful and mortifying. I could not sleep, because, long ago, I had been called to serve, and service means work.

Work means I must write, must act, must intervene where and when I can to help change this world. It also means I must pray. If prayer is a weapon not of this world, it is nonetheless one of our most powerful, and one I must use. Again and again, as necessary. As God demands.

So I began to pray, first to change my own heart—to banish doubt—and then to change the hearts of others, to find some way to heal our wounds. God hears us. And if we know He hears us—whatever we ask—we know that we have what we asked of Him.

Pain Relief

The tattoo hurt, like a cat scratching me continuously for seventy minutes. Not a bad spot in terms of pain, the artist said, holding the needle in her steady hand as she swabbed my skin with disinfectant. Worse in the armpits and inner elbows or back of your knees, she said.

Silver's artist. I'd called for a recommendation, the tattoo parlor tucked between a hookah shop and an insurance agent, its plate glass windows cleaner than a bank's. Inside, patchouli candles and acid rock, my least favorite scent and sound. I said nothing, of course; she was the one who needed to concentrate, and the rub of extra discomforts kept my mind from fully focusing on the main one. She told me it wasn't a disorder that made her shift position so much, but a need to keep the sun from casting odd shadows on her work.

It was disorienting when her twin sister came and stood over me, watching wordlessly. They each had half a sun tattooed on one side of their faces, but she stood on the wrong side of her sister to make it whole and I wondered if that was intentional, if they'd come to regret it, or mere happenstance. The same questions I ask about so much of life.

Red around the edges now, and bruising. It looks funny in the mirror, four lines of reversed text on a shaved breast. I don't regret it, but it doesn't change my mood, so I crack open another bottle of Boodles, wondering what it would be like if May and I got half a son tattooed on each of our faces.

Jesus Nut

APRIL 7, 2016

Such a small coffin. Months after the other funerals, worried ours might reopen healing wounds, we didn't have a public one. Even so, the church was full, with police and first responders, with most of Liam's doctors and nurses, with many of his classmates and their parents. May's sisters, a couple of my distant cousins, and a single local reporter, who came and sat quietly at the back after nodding to me, and who never wrote a word about it. Later, I sent him a painting by way of thanks.

No Zhao though, at May's insistence.

I wore my black suit; May a skirt and jacket, lipstick and earrings. All that would attain significance, for some.

Pictures of Liam, and of Liam and May and me, flashed across large screens on the dais. His drawings too, and his flipbooks, a couple of his poems. The minister gave his sermon, about which I remember little, and there were prayers, about which I remember less, and finally a call for silence. After that, it was my turn.

I didn't think I could do it, but I made myself stand and walk across to the podium. For a long time I said nothing while the images repeated behind me. After a few minutes people begin to rustle, and after several more I heard some wondering if I was okay. Lamont checked on me. I told him I was fine and he sat back down and still I waited, and I made everyone else wait too.

I waited for May and for Liam, for Lamont and Latrell, for all the children and their teachers, their parents. Minute after minute. Eleven total, the length of time the shooter roamed the halls. And then I took out the pages I'd prepared and began.

I read the names of the children and adults who'd died, and I said, These forty-three children who were born in hospitals and homes, who had carefully chosen for them names and baby blankets and first day of school outfits, who took their first Communions, who were chauffeured to soccer games and swim lessons and play-dates, who had hugs and spankings, groundings and time-outs, who had their pets and friends and broken bones and July Fourths and seven or eight birthdays, who had their stories told on Instagram and Facebook and Tumblr, in tweets and letters and phone calls and emails, and these eight adults who told the stories of these children, who shaped and molded and scolded and comforted them, who died trying to protect them, all of them were sacrificed. They were sacrificed in a plague, and nothing will be done.

We debated the causes, briefly. Mental health and guns and absent parents, bullying. A surfeit of ease, the scandalous gluttony of souls harvested in violent video games, a lack of religion, a lack of cohesiveness, a lack of love. But history has already overtaken our history, and the plague will go on, with other children dying in other schools, and adults too, some of them trying to protect those children. So many of them gone, so many more still to go. So many passing, so many crossing over the river Jordan, the river Styx, so many at rest, so many at peace, so many beyond the veil, with their races run, so many dead and departed, destroyed, erased, expired, extinct, so many with their horses freed, their ghosts given up, so many gone to a better place, to their reward, so many gone the way of all flesh, so many gone west.

They've joined the choir invisible, met their maker, passed away, they've perished and begun to ride the pale horse, they'll ride those pale horses forever.

Murmurs in the crowd, which meant I'd timed it right, a pale horse galloping across the screens behind me as I spoke, until it disappeared into the invisible darkness that lurked beyond, darkness that none of them had been ready for but that had come for them nevertheless. Into eternity.

I went on.

Forty-three children and eight adults have already made that transition, my lovely little Liam the last of them. My boy is gone now, he has become those who love him. What have *we* become, I asked, that we will sacrifice our children and do nothing? I have meant to do something, but I have been too busy, and now it is too late. Thoughts and prayers and grief, they are not enough, not nearly enough, for what has been ransomed by the blood of children. We must do something more. Each of us, all of us. We must.

Done, I folded my pages and tucked them into my jacket pocket and crossed the dais again and sat. May squeezed my hand so hard I thought she'd break bones. Lamont said, You're a god now, like me. I must have looked puzzled because he said, We've sacrificed our sons, and for what?

I didn't feel better, or worse, I didn't feel anything at all, except an enormous absence.

Nearer My God to Thee

EARLY APRIL 2019

When the first victims were being buried, Dexter Fenchwood said that the shooting was God's plan, that it had to do with our nation allowing gay marriage. He called on Westboro Baptist to picket all the funerals, alongside his congregation.

Three-plus years later, I showered and drove to his church, remembering him watching me in the hospital waiting room with that feral and predatory intensity, and pushed past the picketers into the rundown brick church and took my seat in an uncomfortable wooden pew, wishing I'd brought my sketchbook. The long narrow central nave, its ceiling lost in darkness, the dirty, arched stained-glass windows, the expensive video screens glowing across the dais; Fenchwood knew what mattered. People filtered in, nodding solemn hellos, and then, just before the hour, the last congregants hurriedly took their seats. *You're in a church,* I thought. *Why are you noticing women's asses?* But I didn't stop.

Then the choir filed in in their black cassocks and began to sing.

Oh sisters, let's go down, down in the river to pray.

. *Who will wear that starry crown? Oh Lord, show me the way.*

Oh fathers, let's go down, down in the river to pray. As I went down in the river to pray, studying about that good old way, and who shall wear that robe and crown, good Lord, show me the way. Oh sinners, let's go down, let's go down, come on round, oh sinners, let's go down to the river to pray.

Startled, I shrank before those beautiful voices and soothing words; the power of song, of harmony, May and *her* choir, the beginnings of love. In my shrunken, inebriated state, I wasn't sure those around me even sensed my presence. I wanted them to.

Fortunately, the nasty words of "Jacob Have I Loved, and Esau

Have I Hated" restored me to full anger, and, just before Fenchwood strolled onto the stage, a video screen lit up, displaying in foot-high letters the message that, as of that morning, God had killed 6,959 soldiers in Iraq and Afghanistan, and that, since we'd sat down, God had cast 1,147 people into hell. As Fenchwood appeared stage left, the choir began a hallelujah chorus. They seemed to be singing his praises, not God's.

I didn't listen much as he began to speak, the fallen nature of the world, the 144,000 Jews God would save in the last days, and etc., because I was going by feel more than thought. It was something, though, those odd thin lips and the energy he gave to the parishioners, the energy he took back, so that he swelled and expanded.

Ten minutes into his stemwinder, which by that point had something to do with Jonah and the whale and drowning, I stood and apologized for the interruption.

I said, But sometimes I get loud when I've had a bit too much communion wine because I want to get really close to God. To commune with Him.

No one laughed at my joke. I turned to see if I raised even a smile but I hadn't. A lot of puzzled looks, a few concerned—some of the drab, dreary women—a few angry or annoyed, the bucket-headed men. So easy to piss off.

I wondered what Liam would think, if he could see me now, hull down on the path for glory, filled with righteous indignation. That I was fighting for him, or leading him astray? But I didn't want to waffle, not now. *Oh, shut up,* I said to that voice in my head, and evidently aloud as well.

I didn't say a word, Fenchwood said. But I will say this. When God speaks, you can't listen with your mouth.

He stood utterly still on the dais, with his peculiarly filament-thin blond hair glowing in a spotlight, and I remembered reading that he played the cello. The man of God who fulminated against gays and Muslims and protested at funerals loved Beethoven and Bach.

God's ways aren't mysterious, I said. They're moronic.

Calmly, he said, Brother. You seem to want to witness.

Oh yes, I said, swaying. I'd stood up too fast. I held on to the pew in front of me for balance or thought I did, but really it was a woman's shoulder, some ghastly yellow flower pinned to orange-and-white stripes, the fabric crinkling under my hand. I didn't want to hurt her, or not much, so after one last thrilling squeeze I let go and said, I hear you talk about God's plan a lot, how the shooting of small children was part of that, so I wanted to ask. If I shot you, would that be part of God's plan?

The devil's, he said, not skipping a beat.

Oh, yes, I said, making my way out of the pew past people pushing their knees aside so I wouldn't tread on their feet. They moved so fast I might have been molten, and perhaps I was. Thought so, I said. When I got to the aisle a couple of larger men were making their way hurriedly toward me from the back of the church but not running, not yet. I didn't have a gun. A few seconds, I figured.

I reached into my coat to make them nervous and said again, Thought so. Then added, Because you're a fucking coward.

Self-Medicating

EARLY APRIL 2019

My lips close around Palmer's nipple and she shivers, a dream
so real the bed vibrates. Not the bed, I realize, coming awake, my
phone, and squint to make it out.

Should have known you wouldn't come through, the message says.
Free? You get what you pay for.

At first I think it's one of Lamont's cryptic texts but the number
isn't his. Brain racking until I come up with a name: *Homer Brannock*,
the fishing store owner in Vermont.

You're fucking straight, you get what you pay for! I say aloud.
My voice startles me. I'll tell you what! I say. You'll get something,
all right! Just you wait!

At my drawing table, I sweep aside half-empty bags of Doritos
and a leaking carton of chicken fried rice to get started.

A Gift for Homer Brannock, to Assuage His Anger at HAVING BEEN LET DOWN

DEAR MR. SMELLFUNGUS,

~~I LIKE YOU. PEOPLE SAY I HAVE~~ ~~THIS, BUT I LIKE YOU.~~
~~I LOOKED YOU UP IN WHOS WHO. WHY ARE YOU LISTED~~
~~AS WHAT'S THIS? I KNEW YOU LOVE HIM, DESPITE~~
~~WHAT IT DID TO YOU.~~

FOR A SHORT WHILE I WORKED AS A SERVICE TECHNICIAN ON FEDEX PLANES. AFTER EVERY FLIGHT, PILOTS WOULD SUBMIT THEIR GRIPE SHEET, DETAILING ANYTHING WRONG ON THE PLANE. I WOULD FIX THE PROBLEM, AND REPLY TO THEIR REPORT. HERE'S ONE EXAMPLE OF A PILOT'S GRIPE AND OF MY RESPONSE!

```
        Pilot: Noise coming from under instrument panel.
               Sounds like a midget pounding something
               with a hammer.

Service Technician: Took hammer away from midget.
```

I LEARNED A VALUABLE LESSON AFTER THAT:
THINGS HAPPEN FOR A REASON, AND SOMETIMES THE
REASON IS YOU'RE STUPID AND MAKE BAD CHOICES.

SINCE
EVEN SO, TONIGHT'S BAD DECISION WON'T MAKE
ITSELF, I MUST TELL YOU, I WAS TOO BUSY TAKING
AWAY HAMMERS TO COMPLETE YOUR ~~FREE~~ DRAWINGS.
SORRY FOR BEING TWO DAYS LATE!

Two Cats Away from Insanity

Having discovered the company that makes Kate's videos, I type *Forward Solutions* into Snov.io, hoping she's a regular employee. No luck, so I search the company website until I find the head of Human Resources. Her I write directly, using my business email address, and say I'd like to cast her.

Half a bottle of gin later, I check my email to find that Alicia P. Hader has written back. *We don't give out the names of our actors. We take privacy concerns very seriously, and we hope you understand.*

I do, I write back. *But in one of them she claims that my child who was shot was never born and I want to know who told her to say that. The idea is offensive.*

I don't hear back from them after that, even though I send the same message eleven times and call a dozen more, and I wish I had more money from the Victims' Compensation Fund, so I could go down to Phoenix and camp in front of their offices until they tell me. I know exactly what Ms. Hader looks like, and I could accost her on the sidewalk. *Do you like causing pain?*

Even to me, that sounds creepy, so I won't. But I do have more gin, so I crack open another bottle of that Sapphire smoothness.

Extra Loudly Rumbling Engine Wakes Me at Dawn

Pink and red chevrons zigzagging the horizon, then the sky patch-worked with pastel blues and grays as the neighbor's boy arrives home after a long night out. Seventeen or eighteen, habitually anti-horological, his unmuffled Mazda a rip-roaring *Fuck you!* to the working world five straight weekdays at six a.m.

After a gin-fueled night of binge-watching Liam's favorite movies and shorts, then my new favorite *The Equalizer*, I want to yell *Fuck you!* back, but my head hurts too much for that kind of effort, so I press my face into the leather couch and clasp the pillow over my ears until the noise stops and drift back into a semblance of sleep, telling myself to dream of Kate.

She's invaded every facet of my waking life, after all; maybe chasing her in my dreams will help me catch her at last.

The Symbolic Will Have Its Say

In the midst of drink and food deliveries, I zip down to the bar to retrieve the bass and walk in front of the drunk throwing darts without incident, either invisible or invincible. At the booth in the back my knees and palms stick to the floor, but I persist, and recovering the bass earns a drink. At the bar a lumpy middle-aged man in a lumpier beige suit stoops over a broad, open Civil War atlas, looking at coastal Virginia. I think of fisherman Homer, awaiting my mock-ups. He will have received my drawing by now and I order a second bourbon in celebratory guilt. To Civil Wars, I say, and raise the glass.

Light flashes off his wire-rim glasses. How'd you know what I was thinking?

What were you thinking? I raise my empty glass, to signal I need a third.

Of the Civil War drowned, he says. How completely we've forgotten them.

Something stirs inside me. Are you a boatbuilder? I ask.

No, he says, and runs a loving hand over the expansive blue ocean. I'm a food executive. A job I was fated for since birth. He sips his drink, some pink affair, and carefully puts the glass down on the damp coaster. My name is Eugene Crumpacker.

That makes me laugh. I say, This must be fate.

Yes, he says. He turns his glass. Everything's fated. Especially us meeting.

I climb the narrow stairs to my rooms with one hand pressed against the bumpy plaster wall for balance, lugging the bass in my other, and open the unlocked door and stumble to my drawing table and fish out paper and pencils and draw.

Three straight days without a shower, ignoring my buzzing phone.

Well-Meaning but Stupid, One

APRIL 9, 2016

Cheer up. Liam wouldn't want you to be sad.

He wasn't a pet and yes, he would. He cried at every funeral he had to go to. Only one, but why should I tell that to this stranger in thigh-high black boots and a too-short dress?

He's in a better place.

No, he isn't. He was a boy, and he loved exactly where he was. Her heavily mascaraed eyes go wide in the ensuing silence.

Cherish all of the wonderful memories. They will bring you peace.

It was just his time to go.

So, how 'bout them Red Sox?

I can't imagine what you're going through right now.

Try.

Death is a gift.

One that takes more than it gives. He walks away without another word, his ill-fitting suit shiny with wear. *A cop,* I think.

Be strong, you'll get through this just fine!

When we die, we're met by our spirit guides, pass through a tunnel, and are greeted by loved ones on the other side with warmth and love and light.

He wasn't met by me or May.

I'm so glad to be here.

Everything happens for a reason.

To the first person who said that, one of his teachers with a kindly face, I replied, Really? What's the reason? What if it isn't for a good reason?

To the second person who said that, a stranger I suspected of being a hoaxer, I replied, If you say that again I'll punch you in the face. And there'll be a reason for that.

We're not having a funeral, we're having a celebration.

You shouldn't be attached to the body.

You know he was "saved," right?

All part of God's plan.

Could you tell me what that is?

God never burdens us with more than we can handle.

Liam's burden was a .45 bullet and some shotgun pellets and eventually they killed him. If I meant to silence her, it didn't work. *Well,* she said. *God needed another angel.*

God wants to make you stronger through this.

God.

God.

God.

At least you're young enough that you can have another child.

Belated Gift to Shooter's Mother in Response to Her Letter Years Before

Letters

Kate's back! She has proof!

You went on a date with one Palmer Sketchy and told her you didn't have kids. Couldn't keep the secret in the end, could you? A guilty conscience, or did you just fall for the honey pot?

Kate knows.

Kate knows everything.

That'll be it, I think, when I read this one. If she's back, I can track her down.

It's raining, but I go for a walk to calm myself, the only one without an umbrella. Black umbrellas, white umbrellas, black-and-white umbrellas, one bright umbrella colored like a beach ball. Soaked, I turn back.

Rain, puddles, birdsong, a bicycle bell, and the wind shaking water from the new green leaves of the pin oaks. The smell of wild onions, a ponytailed man rollerblading in the rain.

Track her down, track her down, track her down.

I will.

Well-Meaning but Stupid, Two

One or two of those were me, at other funerals, in earlier times. The
stupidest ones, really.

Judge not, lest ye be judged.

I try to remember that.

Bass Player Hunk Mail

MID-APRIL 2019

Dear Mr. Garland,

Yes, I got your emails and letters and phone calls.

And yes, you may have your instrument back. We never should have taken it. Of course, you never should have hit me. But I suppose you have sort of apologized for that, haven't you? I think somewhere in all those threats was an apology, but I could be wrong. Recently, my reading skills have regressed.

So, here's the map, which details where it is. I know you will find it useful. I certainly have. When I forgot where I put it recently (your bass, not my map), I used it to find it once again.

Good luck with it!

You strike me as someone who is always early but never prepared, but even with one arm in a cast, you should be able to follow it.

Your faithful servant,

Otto Barnes

Holy Spirits

MID-APRIL 2019

I woke in the light, I woke in the dark, I woke to snow blowing sideways, colored pink by the bar sign. At last, I woke in the dark to the dark ghost of May.

Behind her stood rank upon rank of other dark spirits with their dark eye sockets, a fellowship of the suffering, and their excruciating pain pierced my skin like needles and my own dark spirit left my body to stand among them. When at last I blinked and opened my eyes again, I heard a collective sigh—fifty souls leaving their bodies at the same time, and one to come—and there was only May.

I sat up and pinched her. Hey! she said, and let out a yelp.

Sorry. I thought you were an apparition.

She turned on lights and picked up food wrappers and take-out containers and dirty clothes, the former into one bag, the latter into another. It shamed me, but not so much that I got up to help her. I was glad I had on a shirt, rendering the tattoo invisible. Let me guess, she said. You felt like everything was falling apart.

No. I felt like everything was coming together. I'm not so sure now. But enough about me. You've put weight back on. It looks good. Healthy. I like your hair.

Riding the bike a lot, and eating regularly. Cooking. For myself, and for Nash. And I'm thinking about buying a gun. She knew how I felt about them. A hoaxer was here, she said. Someone jumped him after a meeting, beat him with a bat.

I wouldn't talk about it. I said, I'm eating too. Then I shrugged. Have been.

Disappointed, she toed the trash bag. I wouldn't really call this eating.

Sustenance, I said. Meanwhile, I've been attending to my spiritual needs.

I see, she said, and scooped up empty gin bottles. But, about the gun, she said. It's not just the hoaxer. It's Craigslist. She handed me a sheet of paper.

I read it over. What does Nash say about this?

Not much he can do. Lots of people have the same name. Besides, she said. You're the one who said we should do something.

I didn't mean buy a gun. I didn't tell her that I'd thought of buying one myself.

She shrugged and lifted the bass from the floor. Taking up music now?

In a manner of speaking.

She got on with her cleaning. The legs of my jeans stood open like stovepipes from continual wearing. She sniffed them and said, Were you fishing?

No, I lied, not wanting to discuss the trip.

When she came to the paintings she paused. The first was of two men looking at a three-masted schooner. She said, I thought you'd be this way.

And yet you came. Meant to be debonair but it sounded cutting.

You know, she said, her businesslike voice masking her pain, I don't understand how two people who came through so much ended up this way.

I said, Maybe we didn't come through it.

No, she said. I don't think you have. Me either, at times. Though we're still here, the two of us, together and apart. You're better than this, Otto, she said.

You want me to be better, I said, realizing she had been disappointed in this too, without losing belief in it. Not sure I am, I said.

Well, she said, is this your new work? She tilted it into the light. *We Remember Them As They Were Before Our Forever War.* There was another about hiding a bass. Around them were yellow legal pads and other scraps of paper I'd done the preliminary drawings on.

Morbid, she said. Who are these two? she asked. Kate and Fenchwood?

A minister. My version of what he might look like, if he lives to be older.

Which minister?

You didn't read about my little outing?

Oh, Otto. What did you get up to now? Was it something with Lamont?

I resent that, I said. I'm perfectly capable of getting up to trouble on my own. When she didn't even smile at my joke, I moved my tongue around in my cottony mouth and said, Nothing criminal. Just got tossed from a church.

Public drunkenness? Otto, your reversion to adultolescence is hard on us all.

Public anger.

And this Kate? And Mr. Crumpacker? Who's he?

His parents gave him his name, I said, ignoring her question about Kate. At least, I think so. And I think he's real, though I could have dreamt him.

Hallucinated, more likely, she said.

Semantics, I said, thinking of the spirits I'd seen behind her in the dark. Maybe he didn't happen. Maybe my unconscious mind pushed him to the surface.

Or maybe it was Liam, she said.

I nodded my agreement. Someone has shown me the way to the maps.

She had no idea what I was talking about, which was okay; that wasn't why she'd come. I didn't have to wait long. She cleared a chair of all its food wrappers and sat. Are you trying to kill yourself?

Music drifted up from the bar. The moon showed over her shoulder, and I remembered driving up and down those rolling Vermont hills, lights off, windows and sunroof open, how surprisingly *alive* I'd felt, and how much I'd wanted to die.

Finally, after a long bass line that Lamont would have appreciated, I decided to tell her both truths, that I wanted to live, and that I wanted to die. *Worst first,* I thought, and said, I've been trying to be brave enough to kill myself.

Stop it, she said. That's not courage. That's just cowardice about life.

Tough love, I said.

I don't believe in tough love, she said. Just love.

The quiet became embarrassing; I thought about getting dressed. Then she said, And you have to live for Liam.

I'm putting together a book for him, I said. The Book of Otto and Liam. An erasure book. An old text we found together. His drawings, mine, cutouts, stickers, letters, texts, lists, poems. The old into the new. If I die, you'll still have that.

Not if you don't complete it first. And the way you're going now, you don't stand a chance. You don't have to change the world, Otto. Just yourself. That's enough for me. And you have to stay in this world to do that.

Okay, I said, and sat up. I have to find her, I said. That's still my quest.

Find who? May asked.

I realized I shouldn't have spoken aloud, but also that, having done so, I couldn't go back. I sorted through my paintings and drawings, the work I was supposed to have done but hadn't completed, until I found my phone, where I ignored the piled-up text messages and called up one of Kate's bookmarked videos.

May watched it silently. She seemed to get bigger, like bread, rising in a hot oven. More music from the bar, and gusts of laughter. When she did speak, her voice alternated between flat and caustic and she'd grown still as a tombstone.

Why do you want to meet someone who lies about our son?

I put my pants on and said, I have slain the dragon of drink and the dragon of anger, thanks also to your help. But I have yet to meet the witch or the maiden. Once I do, and once I know which she is, I'll know how the book ends.

Will you kill her?

I suppose, I said, shocked equally by her question and by my answer. I fumbled with my belt and processed that. That or pardon her, I said, walking it back.

She fiddled with my phone.

What are you doing?

Sending myself these videos. Are there more?

Lots more. They're all on there. All the ones I have. A file with her name in the pictures, another file with her information in the notes. But why are you sending that to yourself?

The tip of her pink tongue poked out of her mouth while she concentrated. Done, she handed me the phone and said, Because some things in this world are beyond pardoning, Otto. I'm no longer a sad bitch in a bath. You keep that in mind if you ever meet her, or bring me along if you don't think you can.

Kate

An email came from Bob Williamson, a former classmate I'd never really been friends with, an invitation to a party after our upcoming high school reunion. *Go Barons!* He wanted me to RSVP.

It felt a little off, but I wrote back saying that I'd come. *Would love to relive some of those days. Remember the night we got drunk on pumpkin shots and filled a tree with construction cones and tried to toast frozen tortellini?*

Sure do! he replied within minutes.

Sounded like a good party, but it had never happened, so I knew it was a hoaxer, a follower of Kate.

That night I dreamed of sautéing onions and cooking pierogis for Bob and Randy Choate, another classmate I was never friends with. After we ate, we lay outside on the grass side by side, talking, until they rose up in unison and began beating me with their fists and elbows.

When they were done, they said, Stand up and cheer! and I tried to, but it was hard to catch my breath, and I couldn't lift my arms.

In the morning, I had a text from May, *Call me,* but I knew I wouldn't. And that I wouldn't tell her one more thing about Kate. She was mine, not May's.

Letters

Why did you send plainclothes detectives to my house who knew all about me to tell me to back off or something bad would happen when all I did was lawfully exercise my freedom of information act by asking questions? What kind of sicko are you?

I'm going to make sure you don't get to heaven, because you're not a benevolent person.

Stop Signs

After two weeks of obliteration, my brain returned to its socket. Among my texts and emails was an alert from Uber; the unlikely Mr. Brigadoon had given me a single star.

Picked Otto up at appointed place.

He asked to change his destination. From his apartment, to a certain bar.

I said, That's the same address.

At least he didn't throw up in my car.

Lamont hadn't come by, or if he had, I didn't remember the visit; perhaps he'd left some food, but no calls from him, which was unusual. Wondering if I'd said anything to piss him off, I sorted through my texts.

Hey can u pcke me up im to drnuk 2 driv

nvrmnd im home

His reply: *Yeah I knew that I dropped you off*

oh gud lest id idn drive

No, I drove. You steered a pie pan and made motor noises with your lips.

hahahahaha thought that wa a dream

Why did you say you wanted to go to Vermont?

I hadn't answered. The second was shorter and more cryptic:

1 time i aked my dad if he wuz virgin.

After that, Lamont sent a picture of him sitting on a couch reading to a young Latrell, Latrell tucked under his arm. *Life was simply wonderful with my boy.*

Then he asked a question.

You've got secrets, Gandhi. Who's Kate?

Had I told him, in my inebriated state? Shown him her videos? My palms tingled when I read that one, and the next.

It's okay that you don't answer. Got secrets of my own.

Eating Life, Drinking Time

APRIL 17, 2019

Was Crumpacker real? I wandered downstairs to the bar in the early slanting light. Sparrows pecked at cigarette butts in the empty gravel parking lot. Palmer's gravel, Palmer's gun. Did she really need it? Did anyone? Maybe I could borrow it.

The dim, empty bar smelled of spilled beer. The bartender poured boiling water from a teapot onto a long, thin silver tray in the sink and steam curled up around his handsome face where a spray of midnight blue stars arced under his left eye, like the constellation on the baker at Silver's. Had that become a thing?

Hey, I said, were you working any night this last couple of weeks?

Sure, Mr. Barnes. He put the teapot aside and wiped his hands.

I'm at a disadvantage here, I said. When we met, you were probably sober.

Darian, he said, and shook my hand. Bourbon mostly, but also gin.

Ha! I said, No. I was wondering if you saw me talking to anyone, especially one guy, beefy and broad and leafing through an atlas at the bar.

No, Darian said, playing with the black gauge in one of his ears. I don't recall him at all. I'd remember anyone who came in here with a book.

I sighed.

Want a drink to drown your disappointment?

He already had the Boodles ready, another bad sign. I declined and offered the bass instead, with instructions to hold it until Andy Garland arrived to pick it up. *Better here,* I thought, *than meeting a deranged musician in my apartment.* One of us might survive that, and the way I felt now, it wouldn't be him.

Phone Calls

APRIL 21, 2019

My phone lighted up and I pushed aside the penciled drawings for the cheese mock-ups, but I didn't answer. I was trying to reset before things spun apart again and I needed the freelance money. After running on hatred so long I was hollowed out and sluggish, my skin made of paper, my blood like tar, and Nash would never be about happiness, at least for me. Besides, he'd call May if he had information and I'd hear it from her anyway. The phone went dark.

Self-protection was a good thing, some of my therapists said, others that it was self-defeating. I'd listened to both and moved on. Years and years. But if I was going to get better, it wouldn't be sitting across a desk from them, though they were good people and tried to help, and perhaps they had. Work was the thing now.

I'd inked in half the lines before Nash called again. He didn't leave a message so when May called I picked up. She never mentioned Nash. Instead she talked about a note I'd written her years before.

This is what you said when I had my first presentation at Medtronics. When I was going for my job. You must have sent the email when I was on the road and knew my phone would ding while I was driving and that I wouldn't check it.

That sounds about right, I said. We'd had this conversation a few nights when she'd been drinking, so I knew my role, though I wondered about a call during daylight hours. I put my phone on speaker and resharpened pencils as I listened. That smell of pencil shavings never gets old. Maybe she was working up to the news Nash gave her by telling me this; that would be like her.

She said, You know, when I heard that ding, I got flustered

because I thought it was them canceling the meeting, because they were no longer interested in me or had hired someone else.

I didn't know that, I said.

A pause. I wish they had.

Ah, I thought, and knew where this was leading: if she hadn't gone back to work, we'd never have moved for her job, and Liam never would have been in that school. She rallied and said, But's that not why I called. I called because I wanted to read you that email.

You wrote: *I know the meeting is going to be a mess. You will walk into the room dressed in that blue and white dress and they will all forget everything they meant to ask and be prostrate at your feet. It's your brains they saw on the resume and no doubt they've already called all your references and know you are spectacularly good at your work, but it's everything else about you that will slay them upon first meeting. I almost feel sorry for them you should ask for a salary of a million dollars.*

She said, That mattered to me so much. But I still wish I could go back in time to change things.

May, Medtronics didn't lead to Liam's shooting.

No, she said, and cleared her throat. Back in time, before then. Before I ever met you. All the way to high school.

High school? Both of us had gone down many avenues of guilt over time but this was a different one we hadn't yet explored and I wondered where it would lead.

Yes, she said. I never told you this. In high school, my best friend Linda had a boyfriend who had a friend and the four of us drove out to Letchworth State Park, which was where we went to drink and get stoned and, if we were lucky, to have sex. I so wanted not to be a virgin.

A cop rolled up behind us and I dropped my beer and remembered my dad's dictum about putting a penny on my tongue if the cops wanted to give me a Breathalyzer, since it skewed the reading, but I didn't have any pennies and there wasn't time to ask and I didn't want to get in trouble since I was only seventeen, so I dipped three fingers in the ashtray and sucked off the ashes, just able not to gag.

One cop took me to the car while the other stayed with the other three and put me in the back seat. I must have looked the most likely to crack.

Here, he said, before he told me to sit down. Breathe on me.

What? I said. I was holding on to the open door, trying not to shake.

Breathe in my face, he said. I want to see if you've been drinking.

I just about asked if he was serious but thought it might lessen the ash so I did and his face paled.

You sure smoke a lot for a seventeen-year-old, he said.

I laughed because I thought the story was funny.

Don't laugh, she said. That was when it all started.

When what started? I asked, though I suspected I knew.

Our life. Us. You and me and Liam.

I said, You didn't get retroactively pregnant, May.

No, I didn't. But that's when I changed. A second chance, you know? Started doing better in school. Became a star in college, and got my first job and then the next and met you and got another job and then the interview at Medtronics. Maybe everything would have been better if I'd just been caught.

I tried to pick up where I left off with cheese but couldn't get back into the rhythm of work. Instead I found myself drawing maps of the world, like the one I'd stenciled on Liam's wrist his last day of school. That I'd wanted to draw on his wrist again after he'd died but didn't have the courage to ask. And I remembered Homer Brannock, how he'd put his phone on the map, how startled I was by seeing that, by imagining that the map continued on *through* the phone.

As always, I started with the Eastern Seaboard. Liam had asked why, once, standing beside my drawing table as I worked.

It's the one I'm most familiar with, I said. From my own childhood. So it helps me get the proportions right.

What will happen if you don't?

Everything will look strange.

Why don't you draw that? Liam said. The strange world? On here, he said, putting his hand on the part of the map I always left blank. I'd like to know about that, he said. To see it.

Lying in bed later, I wondered about May's call again, why she wanted me to know that about high school, what was about to happen. Her guilt was as ghostly as ink in water, spreading back through time. That was bound to lead to trouble.

Jonesing For My Groove

APRIL 2019

The curtains lifted into the room with the breeze and light spilled over the map. I straightened it on my drafting table with my thumb, admiring it. Not the work; its existence.

That map made me feel like I'd finally corralled blood that had been leaking from my veins and now had it running again in its proper channels. The painful surge of it down my arms and legs, the warmth as it radiated through my chest. If I could smell my blood, it would smell of iron. *This must be birth,* I thought, imagining leaves unfurling in the spring sun, and in my veins. New life. I wanted it to last, I wanted to be green again. Wasn't that the elixir I'd sought in the bottom of all those bottles?

Not a second chance, a third and fourth one. Sometimes they come in unexpected packages and sometimes they lead to good things and sometimes to Medtronics. But you had to try.

I had to try.

The curtains lifted again and I spread my palm on the map, on Liam's world, and closed my eyes and pictured him, humming as he picked apples. I hummed too, keeping up.

With Contrite Heart and Humbled Spirit

Dear Mr. Brannock,

This is a belated apology. By now perhaps you know something of my history. If not, allow me to say that I met you during a particularly difficult anniversary, and I was not at my best.

But my offer of creating work for you, work that I hoped would make your life a little more profitable, a little fuller, was genuine, and I am including a range of mock-ups here, so you can get an idea of what I'm thinking.

I worked for a long time on these, but did so happily rather than dutifully; large parts of this project remind me of my boy, Liam.

That's neither here nor there, of course. While I was in your shop, I noticed your love of old maps and sailing ships, and have incorporated those into the drawings. Your beloved dogs too. The idea is that these drawings, and the website you might create, will help promote your business, and that you will find the way I've taken the work pleasing, informative, and helpful.

If so, please let me know, and we'll figure out together how to make it work. If not, please do accept my apology, and know that I regret being so rude.

Sincerely,
Otto Barnes

Five Dachshunds
Fishing Guide

I spent most of my money on fishing.
The rest I wasted.

Filched

APRIL 2019

HOAXED.com posted a hacked excerpt of Detective Sawyer's redacted grand jury testimony. Once I saw it, my Homer high disappeared.

> *US Assistant District Attorney Claudia Pepper:*
>
> 1. Q *You never checked his computer?*
>
> *Detective Sawyer:*
>
> 2. A *Well, he hadn't yet posted a threat online. He was over-heard threatening to shoot people at his school. That's all.*
>
> 3. Q *A thorough investigation, then.*
>
> 4. A *Is that a question?*
>
> 5. Q *You wrote a report about your house visit in September of 2013?*
>
> 6. A *October. Yes ma'am.*
>
> 7. Q *And after the shooting, were you ordered by your DA not to tell the press, parents and investigators about that initial visit and report?*
>
> 8. A *Yes.*
>
> 9. Q *And were you asked to deny that the initial visit ever took place? Even to the FBI?*
>
> 10. A *Yes.*
>
> 11. Q **Redacted.**
>
> 12. A **Redacted.**
>
> 13. Q *And do you know what happened to that report?*
>
> 14. A *It's missing.*
>
> 15. Q *Was there ever more than one copy?*
>
> 16. A *There were four.*
>
> 17. Q *And all of them have gone missing?*

18.   A   *Yes, I believe so, ma'am.*

19.   Q   *Is that unusual?*

20.   A   *Yes ma'am.*

21.   Q   *How can you explain that?*

22.   A   *I can't.*

23.   Q   *And did you wonder why you'd been ordered to deny you'd ever made the visit or written a report?*

24.   A   *Of course.*

25.   Q   *And did you think that was wrong?*

26.   A   *Yes.*

27.   Q   *And yet you followed an order you clearly thought wrong?*

28.   A   *Well, it was an order.*

29.   Q   *Did you ever think it was an illegal one?*

30.   A   *From time to time, sure.*

31.   Q   *How do you live with yourself, detective?*

32.   A   **Redacted.**

33.   Q   **Redacted.**

34.   A   **Redacted.**

The Comforts of Home

APRIL 27, 2019

Tired from a day of cold calls, from driving across the state to get my mail, from realizing while driving that I'd forgotten to check the car for a GPS locator, I came home to find my apartment front door closed but unlocked.

I pushed it open and called, Hello? The rooms were filled with the lingering scent of bacon.

No one answered, which didn't surprise me; the stillness told me that no one was there, the creak of an old house settling, but nothing else. My newspaper had been brought in and put on the table, the chairs pushed in flush, not a way I ever left them, but it seemed nothing else was amiss, aside from three overripe bananas in the kitchen that hadn't been there when I'd gone out.

My landlord, I decided, bearing gifts as cover, allowing him to make sure I didn't have pets. Otto—rare to find someone with the same name—had been adamant about that, his allergies to cats, and was fussily neat, hence the chairs. Even so, I put a chair in front of the door after I locked it while I took my shower and was surprised that I had to clean Vaseline off the doorknob. Off all of them; someone hadn't wanted to leave fingerprints behind.

The next morning, beginning work, I discovered that one of my Homer Brannock mock-ups had been vandalized, a thick red cross sprayed across it.

A Gift for May

May texted me.

Stay away from Lamont. He was arrested again. Road rage.

Which didn't surprise me and explained why I hadn't seen him recently, though it was what she *didn't* mention that worried me: neither the filched grand jury testimony nor whether she was going to buy a gun. Nor Kate. She might not have seen the testimony—it was on the web, and not widely circulated—but Kate and the gun were telling. So I texted back.

It starts with vandalism, I wrote, to no response.

This kind of irrational response to slights or wrongs committed by others, this ongoing anger and rage. Still she was silent.

Then graduates to violence. We've seen the results in our own lives. Don't do it May. Just don't. Crickets.

I rarely ventured to her front door—*our* front door—because of pain, and because I might be followed by hoaxers, who somehow didn't seem to understand that May still lived there even though I'd moved out. Not a surprise, really; as a group, despite having the unbridled confidence of the truly ignorant, they're a few clowns short of a circus, but in general I tried not to leave them extra clues.

I leaned the *Forever War* collage against the screen, which was rusty, and needed replacing. The collage was a plea, a prayer, a warning, given in the hope that it might deter her. And maybe me.

I Do the Math

But pleas and prayers are never enough. Why did May want a gun? More guns meant more gun deaths, I *knew* that, but I needed to prove it to May, and to myself; I wanted one now too. I bullet-pointed the figures for visual impact.

Research is overwhelmingly clear: No matter how you look at the data, more guns mean more gun deaths.

- States with the lowest rate of gun ownership have the fewest gun deaths; states with the highest rate of gun ownership have the most deaths.

- A 1% increase in gun ownership correlates to a 1% rise in the firearm death rate. This is true for homicides, suicides, domestic violence, and violence against police.

- The US has 6 times the gun homicide rate of Canada, 7 times that of Sweden, and 16 times that of Germany. Canada: 1 gun for every 3 people; Sweden: 1 for every 4; Germany: 1 for every 5; the US: 2.0 per person.

- Across all industrialized nations, 6.3% of crimes are violent. The US clocks in at 5.5%. So, we are, in fact, *less* violent than Canada, the Netherlands, Sweden and the UK.

- Instead, the US has more *lethal* violence—due to the prevalence of guns.

- Every study shows that new legal restrictions on owning and purchasing guns is followed by a drop in gun violence.

- Opponents of gun control tend to point to other factors to explain America's unusual levels of gun violence, particularly mental illness.

- But people with mental illnesses are more likely to be *victims*, not *perpetrators*, of violence. 78% of mass shooters were *not* mentally ill.

I sent the email off and laid out my work for the next day—a continuation of the campaign for Silver, a name for a new triple-cream cheese for Henry and Cora, six cold calls (my weekly quota) for new business—and had one beer while watching *SportsCenter*, then rolled into bed without looking at my phone. If May had responded, I didn't really want to know.

Pistols kept me awake, GunBacker's review of the best 9 mm: the CZ 75 B. Such lovely pluses: a low bore for reduced muzzle flip and more rapid fire; ease of control for greater accuracy; a full-metal frame to reduce recoil. I drifted off to sleep imagining one in my hand and woke an hour later to someone banging on a door. Not mine, and I began to nod off again, to remember I'd been dreaming of Kate.

Awake still, brain hazily engaged, I thought, *Shoot her. Or yourself.*

I sat up. No, I wouldn't buy a gun, and I wouldn't kill myself. Or Kate. But it was time to cause her serious pain. Find Kate indeed. I'd been lying to myself that I was over it. Somebody had to pay for something. Maybe May's colleague Zhao could figure out some kind of algorithm to help me track her down.

Empty Barrel Birthday

Nash drove with her without speaking through the crowded rush-hour streets to get the gun, as if they were going to church. Some gun shop owners turned people away based on a gut feeling, which was both legal and smart. He doubted that would happen with May, but you never knew. She wouldn't seem angry, that was unlike her, but nerves could show; almost everyone buying their first gun had them: a jittery hand, a breaking voice. He noticed, as he drove, one pink fingernail tapping a thigh. His presence would overcome any nerves; having a detective with her was the gold standard. He laughed at his own self-importance and she smiled.

May had done her research. A pistol, she said to the clerk, palms flat on top of the glass display case, not a revolver. Her name was Aubrey and as she began a disquisition about her fifteen best sellers, May interrupted her, A Glock 19, she said. Aubrey nodded and went to fetch one. Nash gave a low whistle of appreciation.

I wouldn't have taken you for a sexist, May said.

What? No. He felt his face getting hot. That's not what I meant.

That I'm a woman and know guns?

No, that you're a civilian and know guns.

I'm a citizen, Nash. We're not at war. And I've been around guns most of my life. Yours is a Glock 19 too, for example. Not a wonder nine, but a great one.

Things I didn't know, he said. Your dad always had them? Then, seeing her look, he added, Or your mom?

My father was a cop.

He must be proud of you. An engineer.

She nodded. He was.

Oh, sorry, Nash said. He was still getting to know her and she was parsimonious with personal information. Private, he would have said, not secretive. It surprised and touched him that she'd asked him to go with her, but what did it mean that buying a gun was a kind of date? A recent passing? he asked.

Years ago, she said. Suicide. And yes, by gun.

Sweat prickled his armpits and groin and he studied her face. May, he said. Should we talk about this?

It's okay, she said. I'm not buying the gun to do myself in. Mental illness, she said, and touched his wrist. It's a terrible thing, but not what his life should be judged by. I'm not depressed like he was. Mine has to do with my son being shot, his was long-standing and formless, and I'm not buying the gun because of depression. I'm buying it because of the hoaxers. If they come to my house, I'll be ready.

The clerk returned. May handled the gun as she extolled its virtues, its compact size and light weight, its minimal recoil and consistent trigger pull, its best-sellerdom, which meant that May could buy ammunition for it almost anywhere. Accurate and extremely reliable, she added, and because it's popular, upgrades are common. This, for example, she said, and demonstrated the back straps, which allowed for a customized grip. Nash watched May's concentration approvingly.

Aubrey had paperwork and a few questions and a distracting mole on one eyelid. May showed her license and a recent utility bill; Aubrey bent her head to check that the address was the same on both. The hair around her part was thinning, which surprised May. Such a young woman.

She gave May federal form 4473 to fill out and went off to file the state background check. May made her way down the list, answering *No* every time.

- *Are you under indictment or information in any court for a felony?*
- *Have you ever been convicted in any court of a felony?*
- *Are you a fugitive from justice?*
- *Are you an unlawful user of, or addicted to, marijuana or any depressant, stimulant, narcotic drug, or any other controlled substance?*
- *Have you ever been adjudicated mentally defective or committed to a mental institution?*
- *Have you been discharged from the Armed Forces dishonorably?*
- *Are you subject to a court order restraining you from harassing, stalking, or threatening your child or an intimate partner or child of such partner?*
- *Have you ever been convicted of a misdemeanor crime of domestic violence?*
- *Have you ever renounced your United States citizenship?*
- *Are you an alien illegally in the United States?*

All of May's answers were pointlessly truthful. Some could be checked online, but if you wanted a gun, what would stop you from lying about being an illegal alien or addicted to drugs? She shook her head.

Aubrey came back. She wore her Glock in an OWB holster on her left hip; years ago May and Otto and Liam had been at lunch and seen a woman wearing one just like it. Otto had said it made him nervous. Not me, May had said. It's the concealed ones that concern me.

You passed the state check, Aubrey said and tucked her hair behind her ear.

The domestic violence case was taken care of out of court, May said, joking. From Aubrey's face she saw it was a mistake.

A joke, Nash said and put his hand on hers. Dumb one, but a joke.

Aubrey nodded as May blushed. Do you have IWB holsters for this too? she asked, to shift attention, and left her hand under Nash's. She liked its warmth.

Several models. I'll bring a few after I run the federal check.

How long will that take?

Thirty seconds, Nash said, and lifted his hand and Aubrey nodded again.

She had other paperwork for May, but there was no waiting period, and she didn't need to be fingerprinted, which surprised May. She had the odd thought that she could commit a crime with the gun and if she filed off the serial number no one would ever be able to connect it to her. The thrill of the dark side. She couldn't remember the last time she'd felt it, or if she ever had. Well, people changed.

What about a gun safety course? she asked Aubrey.

Not a requirement, but this flyer lists ones we recommend. They'll give you all of the information you need, and the asterisked ones have you fire and clean the gun. Good things to practice.

The last thing to buy was a locked carrying case. May had no real preference, so she opted for the least expensive hard-shelled one that had dense, Glock-specific foam, wondering as she did if it was a mental illness to want to kill someone.

While Aubrey rang up the purchases and May fitted the gun into the case Nash leaned toward her. One thing. Maybe your dad told you this, maybe not. Laws have become trickier over time. If you ever use the gun? Empty the clip. If you don't, judges and juries might think you didn't really fear for your life. Empty proves your fear.

Empty it is, then, May said. Every time. The thought made her shiver and she wondered: Fear or anticipation?

Letters

Why does the Social Security Death Index not list a single "victim" of the school shooting, and why do FBI crime statistics for that day, month, and year not list a single person murdered in your hometown?

Your story was pretty good, but if you lie, eventually you're found out. You didn't cover all the bases!

And the most delicious thing is that the FBI, which is part of the deep-state cover up, is the one that fucked up this time. Good thing they're not really competent, or we'd all be in trouble.

Liam at Five

May, with little patience, snapped at Liam for denting the front of our new dishwasher with his tricycle. He'd been riding it around the first floor because the temperature outside hadn't gone above ten degrees for a week. The sun was a crust in the sky, a distant memory, and he needed to *move*.

How could you think slamming into the dishwasher was a good idea?

He stood beside the wounded appliance, looking at the mark his handlebars had made. At last he turned to her.

You know what, May? It's not easy being a kid. It would be a lot easier if you came out as a big person, knowing all this stuff already.

This is how you learn it, she said, and took away his tricycle. Growing up means learning from decisions.

Nice, May, I said, when he walked away with his lip trembling. Maybe we should go with the less-brutal parenting option.

Not brutal, she said. Just realistic.

What was she being realistic about now? She hadn't written me back or said a thing about the painting I'd left as a gift.

River of January

MAY 12, 2019

Torso forward, Nash said, and pressed a penny to May's collarbone, once she had the stance down. He let it go and it dropped to the floor. Perfect, he said, kneeling to pick it up. It flashed in the light when he held it up to her.

Just remember that and you'll be fine. The natural tendency for beginning shooters is to hold their arms out front and their body back, to stay as far away from the gun as possible, but that leads to poor control.

His touch lingered through her blouse, like a burn. She wanted him to unbutton her blouse, kiss her nape, make her shiver. For the first time in a couple of years, she had put on a bit of blush.

Pocket that, he said, of the penny, as a reminder. Bring it with you every time you go to the range, it'll help you go through your checklist.

He packed for the range. Interior and exterior hearing protection for them both, safety glasses, the gun case. He'd chosen orange earmuffs for her, a color she hated, but for now she decided not to say so. Finally, he picked up the gun he'd taken the clip from. Three times, he'd walked her through the drill: insert clip, chamber bullet, empty clip, unload the single bullet. After she'd done it the third time, he'd done it once more. To be certain, he said. It was his gun and he was always responsible for it, even if she used it. The action was open now, the chamber empty. That's how you always transport it, he said. He held it up and asked, Is this unloaded?

Yes.

He laughed and said, No. Remember, a gun is *always* loaded.

That's the only way to think of it. Always loaded, always ready to save you, always possibly lethal.

May liked that he was a patient teacher. You must be a good father, she said.

He laughed again. I try, but my boys might have a different opinion.

Oh, sure, she said. They always do, growing up. Ask when they're in their twenties, though. It'll be different then.

She touched the urn with Liam's ashes on her way out.

She'd been to the industrial park a few times, mostly to pick up packages from the UPS store, once or twice with Liam to go indoor rock climbing. Another boy's birthday party, once on their own. He didn't much like it, but while she'd never been an athlete, she'd enjoyed the climbing and had meant to return; she wondered now why she hadn't. Inside, the shooting range looked like a cross between the waiting room at a large doctor's office and a bowling alley lounge, minus the beer signs. A right-angle bar with tall stools, a couple of seating areas with shooting magazines, large-screen TVs. The lack of beer signs was one tell, the sound-safe viewing area to watch the shooters another, the oversized *Range Rules* sign a third. And the gun shop. But still.

Because Nash was a member, she got a reduced rate on the ammo and targets. The boy behind the counter buzzed back and forth in his wheelchair. He had the tiniest hands; congenital, she guessed. He seemed barely old enough to drive, but he was comfortable walking her through the steps and had the most beautiful hair. She smiled as he handed her the paperwork she had to sign, and again when he helped her choose the ammo and the targets. The pink ones were all men.

Do you have any female silhouettes? May asked.

He did, and steered his wheelchair to the back room and came back with three. Blue, for some reason.

Even with the double hearing protection, the noise shocked her, and the recoil hurt her hand, but after Nash repositioned her supplemental hand, reminding her to press it firmly on the grip, it felt better. And she shot better when she mastered squaring up her sights. She was glad he'd had her dry fire it at her house; it would have been harder to learn the gun's nuances while actually shooting it.

She fired the entire clip at the first target, the paper shredding and dancing.

You can pause between shots, Nash said, when she was done.

Don't you remember what you taught me? His blank face meant she needed to remind him. Empty the entire clip, every time.

Oh, yes. Of course. But that's only if you're shooting at a person.

I was, she said.

He said, Finger off the trigger, and she flushed, embarrassed. He'd reminded her on the drive over, to prepare her, and she disliked making mistakes. Otto and Liam always said she was like a cat.

You did really well, Nash said right after. She wasn't sure if the praise was genuine or if he'd picked up on her quirks. Both, maybe.

Hard not to, she said. It's only five yards away.

When my dad first took me, Nash said, he put the target only three yards away. You want first-time shooters to enjoy themselves. Even so, I didn't do nearly as well as you.

Ha. Faulty memory, she said. Time does that.

Nope, he said. I have it at home still.

Your first target?

Yep. I'll show you sometime. You'll see.

———

On the ride home, she was mostly quiet, and he didn't try to get her to talk. She'd told him she enjoyed it and that was enough for him. She liked that about him, his security.

As they passed one fast-food place after another and a hotel—*Why was there a Marriot in the middle of all these small factories*, she wondered—she stretched her fingers to relieve the surprising soreness and went over the list he'd first impressed upon her:

- A gun is *always loaded*, so treat it as such.
- Keep your finger off the trigger until ready to shoot.
- Be sure of your target and what's behind it.
- Never point the weapon at anything you're not willing to destroy.

She lingered on that last one.

Home Alone

MAY 14, 2019

The apartment over Otto's Auto had a landline, leftover from a previous tenant; Otto had asked that I keep it. I hadn't given the number to anyone and it rarely rang and when it did most of the calls were marketers, though a few were for previous tenants. I always took down their forlorn messages.

One morning at three a.m. it rang, and a woman's voice asked, Are you home alone now? Is your door locked?

I checked that it was and looked out at the rain sheeting down so hard it blurred the streetlights and went back to bed and it rang again.

You're not alone. God is watching you. He's always watching you.

I disconnected it and was woken at five by a knock on the door but whoever it was was gone by the time I answered. The rain had stopped, the wind picked up, the old building creaked as it blew. They'd left a red Nike shoebox wrapped in a purple ribbon on the welcome mat, and a Valentine's card taped to the door. No trace of perfume, so I guessed it wasn't Palmer. The downstairs door opened and shut. I wasn't quick enough down the sloping hallway to the front windows to see them, but when I turned on the outside light, it was as if I'd turned on a hundred of them, it was reflected in so many puddles.

No way I'd get back to sleep, so I made coffee and opened the damp envelope while waiting for it to brew. Not a valentine, it turned out, but a mental health checklist.

Bipolar disorder, Anxiety, Depression, MPD, ADHD, Psychosis, Eating disorder, Mood disorder, Dissociative identity disorder, Somatic symptom disorder, Substance abuse disorder, Intellectual disability, Asperger's

*syndrome, Autism, Paranoia, Delusional disorder, Body dysmorphic disor-
der, Hypochondriasis* and *Disorganized schizophrenia.*

Which do you have? Check any or all. And below that, *Do You Not See
That GOD Has Afflicted You?*

Fenchwood or his followers, I guessed, payback for having
appeared at his church. *You fucked with the wrong Fenchwood!* Inside
the box was a tiny coffin with a hinged lid that, when opened,
revealed a picture of Liam's face.

For a while I sat on the sagging couch and tried to control my
breathing. I could move again, but I didn't want to, and I didn't
feel I should have to, though two groups were after me now, Kate's
followers and Fenchwoods, and I sensed I was running out of time.
I wanted to get at least one of them, before one or the other got me.
My hands shook with fear, with desperation and desire, with the
hope that I was the only one. *Not May, please. Not her.*

But knowing them, she was probably a target too. I pushed the
coffee table over with my foot and spent a long time on my knees
cleaning up the mess.

Interim 7

Number of school shootings since: 148
Number of school children killed: 257

Interim 8

Number of school shootings since: 149

Number of school children killed: 258

May in May, Twelve Years Before

MAY 2003

I woke thinking about a hot day May and I took a trolley to the beach, a day that seemed like a gift. A cooler, backpacks with books and sunscreen, towels to stretch out on. Lazy waves and an intermittent wind, both of us drowsy in the sun.

She lifted the hair off her neck and I pressed a cold beer to it, kissed the damp skin, making her shiver. I said, The day will end with oysters and great sex.

A week later, when she went off to work, I tucked a note into the lunch I'd made her. Cold carrot soup, a curried chicken salad sandwich.

May

I stroked your lips. You began to hum. By the shore, bees and flowers, sand-speckled thighs, beers sweating in a cooler. Pressed into the sand, we slept and shared a silver dream. You and I, we are an airplane, wings and everything, hovering above the earth. I whisper your name like a psalm.

Social Media Updates

A text message from Silver.

*FYI. Facebook post, supposedly from you, but I know you don't have a page.
Says:* I'm working with Silver's Bakery now. Me and a bunch of fallen
women. Perfect! Never could stay away from the whores.

Don't worry, she wrote. *We get this a lot. Creeps come in and want to talk
to the girls about what they used to do. Sometimes put money on counter
and ask if they'll do it again. Thought you'd want to know. Hope you're well.*

Ghosting

The bartender cut another twist from an orange peel and dropped it into the old-fashioned and rested the partially peeled orange on a shot glass. It looked like a miniature beach ball with its alternating orange and white wedges, and I pulled out a sketch pad to capture it, but before I could my phone buzzed and my heart sped up; I was hoping it was Palmer.

Not Palmer, but Lamont. I waited to read it until after the bartender rang up my drink, the reflection of the computer screen flashing white and blue on his glasses. Palmer hasn't answered my barrage of texts or calls, and even my emails went unread; I wasn't surprised, I'd sent her a drunken text during my bender. Well, dozens. And at least it worked, one way or another. This was the first I'd heard from Lamont in weeks.

Palmer says to stop.

She also says: I didn't post anything about you NOT having children, and certainly didn't tell anyone named Kate. I might have said something to one or two girlfriends about our date, and who they might have told, I couldn't say. I don't know anything about "Kate."

I texted back my thanks and drank, the ice clinking in the heavy glass.

No problem, he replied. *The hell's this about? Whoever Kate is? Shut her ass up.*

I didn't reply, because doing so would only cause trouble. Besides, I'd been trying, but if Kate was back, she was keeping a low profile. Not a single new video out of dozens on the hoaxer websites I tracked; I knew, I'd watched them all. I rubbed the orange peel around the rim of the glass and drank again.

Interim 9

Number of school shootings since: 150
Number of school children killed: 260

Interim 10

Number of school shootings since: 151
Number of school children killed: 275

Letters

If real children died, why was every casket closed?

If real children died, why, for the first time in US history, did the final report on the "criminal investigation" not include the names, ages, or sex of the alleged victims?

If real children died, why were none actually identified?

If a policeman had made the call to the dispatcher saying he had multiple weapons—a shotgun and a rifle and four handguns, which is NOT the number of guns other police give—why didn't he identify himself and why is there no record of those guns?

Stupid Things People Say
in the Months after Funerals

Focus on the blessings in your life.

Now that he's died, you shouldn't get money from the survivors' fund and *the victims' fund.*

If you believe, why not belong?

But I don't believe.

Then you'll never belong, anywhere.

Pull yourself together. You need to be there for your kids.

We don't have other kids.

Then it's time you get over it. It's been a while since he died.

Letters

Silence can be cruel, a type of violence, when it's the silent treatment, and yet for most of us the experience of God is silence too. Do not mistake that silence for absence.

We used to sit in silent contemplation from after Night Prayer until noon the following day, every day, when I first became a nun. Vatican II changed that, and while I believe most of Vatican II's changes were for the better, losing silence seems a real loss.

I still believe silence enables us to hear God, if only we can listen. To the wind in the trees, the gurgle of a flowing stream, the birds at dawn and dusk.

I imagine some silences in your life must be nearly unbearable, and for that I am truly sorrowful. But perhaps in some of those very silences, beyond the pain, lies some balm, a seed of understanding, of hope. I pray daily that this might be so.

Three Years After

Detective Sawyer testified about his visit to the shooter's house, years before, occasioned by Venny Bosc's phone call. Local news carried the trial; May didn't watch. The prosecutor asked Sawyer why he'd never said anything about that visit to the families, who wondered if somewhere along the line someone had missed warning signs.

Sawyer's clothes were put together—a peak-lapel corduroy jacket and a crisp white shirt—but his face looked pained. He smoothed his thin paisley tie every time he spoke. I wanted to say something about it, he said, for a long time. We couldn't have known, really, but we were warned, however obliquely. We weren't really guilty, but we weren't innocent either.

All the later writings in the journal, that revealed what was about to happen? That detailed it? Where he wrote about cutting down the stock of one of his shotguns and wrapping it in duct tape so it looked like the one Eric Harris used, and had named it Barb? Where he talked over and over about wanting to die, about suicide? None of that was there when I read it. He leaned forward. I swear to you.

Poor May, I thought, switching off the TV and going to the window to look at the evening sky. High pink clouds stood banked to the east and the wind moved through the bright green new leaves of the maples and carried the scent of freshly mown grass through the screen. She'd believed Sawyer all along. I had too, but I'd known it was stupid to do so. I hoped she had as well.

To Do List, Further Revised:

Find Kate

Fuck the Fenchwoods

Letters

You say you're being followed.

You're right.

Death is coming to you real soon and nothing you can do about it.

No sense looking back.

Have you made yourself ready? Death is behind you.

Tomorrow or tomorrow or tomorrow.

My face will be the last one you ever see, until you get to hell.

That one was persistent. When that didn't get a response, she found my email and phone number posted online and contacted me that way, my phone dinging half the night. I can't change either of them now because of my freelance work. She emailed me thirty-three times before she was arrested.

Interim 11

Number of school shootings in the three years since: 152
Number of school children killed: 275

Monday, or, America's Longest War

Ninety-six Americans will be killed with guns today, seven will be children or teens. Forty other children will be shot.

African Americans are eight times more likely than whites to be among the dead and wounded. Most of them males, most of them young, many of them unarmed.

The radio detailed another murder. School shootings get the news, but day-to-day shootings are where the numbers pile up; Lamont taught me that. He was angry about that, about a lot of things. About abortion, about hoaxers, about me.

I stood barefoot in my kitchen, my wrinkled shirt untucked, turning a ripe peach over and over in my hand. Not wanting to listen more, I turned off the radio and thought, *Scariest of all? I haven't heard from Lamont in a while.* He wasn't responding to texts, he didn't pick up my calls.

I tucked in my shirt and slipped on shoes and walked the three miles to Lamont's house and rang the bell and then again when he didn't answer. I pressed my face to the glass sidelight and cupped my hands around my eyes to see better; days of mail scattered on the floor, weeks of it, bills and circulars and glossy catalogs, some of my work among them. He'd need a shovel to sort through it.

I returned home down back alleys past a bakery and a print shop and a row of restaurants—Italian, Thai and Cajun—whose rear windows were always open, because I loved the smells of fresh bread and ink, of garlic sautéing in olive oil and lemongrass and paprika and cayenne pepper, but even those scents and the chalked bright yellow sun and green grass on one stretch of sidewalk didn't lift my mood.

Liam, Me and My Grandfather, All of Us at Eight

MAY 2015

Liam sat on a stool at the kitchen counter and swung his feet in their blue LeBron 17s and ate a chunk of Boar's Head liverwurst from a napkin on which he'd drawn a sinuous cat. I liked that, liked each sign that he was like me. As a child, I'd drawn on every surface I could, including two crows once on my grandfather's pale legs while he slept in a hammock with his faded red baseball cap pulled low over his closed eyes. Just the once; he hadn't liked it. I was eight.

He'd told me a story about shooting crows in the Indiana corn-fields as a boy my age in the '40s, earning twenty cents for each pair of crow legs he brought to the county agricultural board, and shown me the wooden crow call he still carried with him. It looked like a small clarinet and I'd worked it from his pocket as he slept, desperate to try it but afraid to wake him, and so contented myself with the drawing.

Liam could draw anywhere, as far as I was concerned. The more he was like May or me, the more I liked it. Like her, he pinned rulers to the page with his fist.

The kitchen smelled of liverwurst and of the limes I'd cut for the key lime pie. You know what I miss from Vermont, Otto? he said. Butcheroni. I must have looked puzzled because he swung his feet faster and said, You know. Our butcher? Mr. Steigerwald? That stuff he used to make and give some to us when we went in?

Oh. Bologna.

Yes. That's what I said. He looked right at me, daring me to correct him.

Sometimes in my memory I do, sometimes in my memory I don't. Both can't be true, but I don't know which one is. Time, swallowing us all.

Colonel Mustard Did It

MAY 22, 2019

Nash! May said, and pushed the door open to the scent of blooming lilacs, which made her drowsy. We have target shooting scheduled?

He shook his head. She was always glad to see him, especially when she was upset, like now. His calm presence throughout, she thought, her fingers on the cool doorknob. Not the flare of lust she'd had upon first meeting him in those terrible early hours, which had recently been rekindled, but his compassion, his fidelity to their sorrow. As if he was pledged to it.

And there was more, of course. Movies, dates, dinners. She'd gone with him to a fundraiser for a wounded colleague, met his sons. They'd made love once and it had been much better than she'd expected, his face pressed to her neck, his baritone voice in her ear, its pitch rising and falling with her desire. The thought of it now made her spine tingle.

Would you like to come in? she said. She offered her cheek for a kiss.

Nash glanced over his shoulder, as if someone was waiting for him in his empty car, parked askew on the street. He must have come in a hurry, she thought, after she'd called the station. He turned back and gave her a fleeting smile. Can't, he said. Just had to tell you in person.

Tell me? she said. You didn't come because of the hoaxer?

What hoaxer?

It was a man, she said, and he heard the fear in her voice. He'd heard it before, linked to this case. Venny Bosc, when she made her call about the neighbor boy all those years ago. And from May, that first morning. Then he decided that was wrong. May had felt terror that morning, that her son might die, not fear; this was different. He had something to tell her, but it would have to wait until this was sorted out.

She leaned forward and looked over his shoulder, both ways, but no one was on the street, walking or sitting in a car, watching. I'm sorry, I thought you knew. It's the first time I've been this scared in a long time. I was glad I had that gun.

Nash said, Did this hoaxer try to force his way in?

Oh no, he was respectful enough. It's just that he came here. To Liam's house. That's a first. And he said he'd be back. To answer any questions I might have.

Why would you have questions?

Because I'm an actress who's been stealing money from gullible people for years. Questions about how I might put things right with God. She shivered again when she said that, and he wanted to touch her arm, to calm her, but he couldn't.

Nash's face changed. It looked miserable. He always called before he came over, so that he hadn't this time when it *wasn't* because of her call was surprise. Another in this day of them. His tie was disorderly and his corduroy jacket crumpled and her heart misgave her. Something had gone wrong. She forgot all about the cruel hoaxer and began to worry that Otto had done something stupid with Lamont.

News is going to come out soon, Nash said. He looked down and scuffed his cap-toed shoe over the brick step, the same beautiful shoes she'd first noticed years before. More scuffed now, but still that beautiful buttery leather. Today, he said. Maybe it already has. He took a step back, as if she might hit him, and blinked twice.

News about what?

He cupped his right elbow with the palm of his left hand, a familiar gesture, and said, That there was a report. About the shooter.

There have been a lot of reports about him, Nash. She felt herself getting smaller, like an animal anticipating a blow.

No, he said, and shook his head, and his shoe rasped over the brick as he scraped it harder. As if he was trying to dig a hole he could drop into. Not like this one. At last he looked up. This one was from before. Two years before.

She felt interior supports collapsing. Ribs, hips. The cathedral was imploding, the delicate architecture that seemed so gaudily sturdy—groins and vaulted ceilings—failing. She wanted to sit down. People knew about him? They knew ahead of time?

Not everything, no. Nash shook his head again. He realized he was doing that a lot. But a warning, he said. A visit to his house because he'd been overheard talking about shooting up his school.

Oh, Nash, she said. She willed steel to form in her legs, to keep her standing, even as her spine turned to Jell-O. That's what her life had been these last months and years, after all, a sustained effort of will. You always told me there wasn't a visit, she said. No warnings.

I know, he said. He made himself hold her gaze. Made himself go on, since she deserved that. I was ordered to. And I'm sorry I listened to those orders.

He was going to tell her about all of it. Even the journal. The same journal he'd seen years before. True, there'd been nothing in it at the time, but the boy's hatred had begun to spill onto the pages in the months after Nash's visit. It had more drawings as well. Of the school, of his planned places of attack, of dead kids in pools of blood. The high school, it turned out, since that had been his initial plan, but still a school. He would tell her about that too, because if he didn't and it came out later—the way this had—he would look even worse. He said, It gets worse, May.

How could it get worse? May asked. Her voice quavered and tears were already rolling down her cheeks. He wondered if she already knew somehow, on some level. Had always known, but never admitted it to herself.

It was me who wrote up the report. Who visited the kid. Who missed the signs. It'll be out soon under my name. Nash Sawyer. Everyone will read about it in black and white. I wanted you to hear it from me first, ahead of time.

Oh, Nash, no. I asked you again and again.

She started to tremble and he wanted to reach out and touch her but he didn't think he should. Thought he'd probably lost that right forever.

I've been trying to right my initial mistake all these years, he said, but now I see I only compounded it.

That can't be true, May said. Now I know you're lying. When she shut the door on him, he couldn't see inside through the glass, only his own startled reflection, and he had the odd thought that it would stay there forever and be the first thing she saw each morning, or the last each night when she came home.

Interim 12

Number of school shootings in the three years since: 153

Number of school children killed: 281

Ghostbusted

MAY 25, 2019

I glimpsed Kate when I pulled into the parking space, pushing a cart through the grocery store sliding doors. *It couldn't be,* I thought, but it was, which made perfect sense. After all this time, Kate had grown impatient, had come for me so I didn't have to come for her; she too must have ached for a final confrontation. For three years she'd listened to me lie, and now my time was up.

In my lust to get her, I slammed the door on the seatbelt, though hurrying was foolish; she could only make her way through the store and back out. If I waited, she'd reappear and I could surprise her. Fewer witnesses, less likely to interfere. But I couldn't wait, not now, she was devious, after all, a master at staying hidden, and perhaps she'd sneak out the back, so I grabbed a cart to remind myself to remain calm and ducked under the hanging baskets of fragrant French strawberries and pushed past the stacked bags of charcoal to find her.

A small crowd in produce, blocking my way, mothers with fidgety children, gleeful at being released from school, trying to decide which quart of blackberries was best, or whether to go with the green grapes or the red. Couldn't they hear my pounding heart and slide aside, just enough for me to get through? At last one woman in a pink tennis outfit moved toward the apples.

And there stood Kate in black pants and a white blouse with an unbuttoned thin black cardigan, filling a quart bottle with freshly squeezed orange juice. I'd know that hair anywhere, though my certainty crumbled at the sight of her hands. Off somehow, her fingers too small, and when she turned and saw me staring and smiled, it sickened me. The same cheekbones, the same smile, even the same beautiful teeth, but miscolored eyes a little too close together and a turned-up nose. There must be a thousand women in the country who looked enough like her, I thought. Five thousand, or ten. Under the intimate intensity of my gaze, she pulled her sweater closed across her chest.

To make matters worse, she filled the juice bottle just like May, slowing, stopping, starting again, stopping once more, getting every ounce she'd be charged for; Kate as engineer manqué. I ditched my cart and hefted a bag of grapes and left.

Arrest me, I thought, put me in a cell with a blanket as thin as a Bible page, let the years pass over me like a steamroller, pressing me into the earth, but no one did, not even as I sat in my car eating grapes one after the other while they turned ashy in my mouth. I stared blankly at the tops of green trees visible above the store, at the blue sky crossed by a fattening jet contrail, at a pair of geese winging slowly across it, glossy in the sunlight. I wanted them to come for me, I wanted my obsession with Kate to be over, the view of the green trees to be enough. The green and blue and black and white, the world. *Please,* I thought. Prayed. *Let it be enough.* But I knew it wasn't. I wondered if it ever would be.

Not-Kate came out and popped open her trunk and stashed her groceries and pushed the cart into the cart corral and drove off, and I followed her out of the parking lot down streets I didn't really know, trying to rekindle my righteous anger, the bat rattling in the trunk on the sharpest corners. Maybe I'd been right about her, after all, I told myself, but my heart wasn't in it, and, eventually, I let her go.

Missing May

I waited fifteen minutes and ordered a drink, watched the chef and a line cook disagree about the size of the fire under the steaks. The line cook had three rolled dish towels strapped to her back under her black apron ties and kept insisting it was high enough, while the chef, who seemed to have chosen the red kerchief that held his hair in place to match his beard, insisted it wasn't. He won: it was his kitchen. When I saw the line cook's face after he left, I was glad I hadn't yet ordered; the next few steaks were going to be blackened. Idly, I hoped that soon I could get back to a place that whether or not steaks were done enough was all that mattered.

I ordered another old-fashioned and resisted looking at my watch. I was going to tell May about seeing Kate in the store, the not-Kate, as a warning. To her, and to me. Already, I felt it wearing off, and I knew how rarely, recently, I'd missed the right opportunity to make the wrong decision.

At last I called, but it went straight to voicemail, which worried me, since she'd never missed one of our dinners, even when she was sick, even at her most depressed. On a hunch, I called Nash, but he hadn't heard from her in a week.

I pulled up our texts and tapped her location and then stared at the phone while the waiter refilled my water from a sweating chased silver pitcher. What the hell was May doing in Oklahoma? I called a second time, hoping to find out, but it went to voicemail once again. *What are you up to, May?* I said. *Call me.*

Even after a roast turkey dinner, followed by a baked apple, she hadn't.

Double Indemnity

JUNE 12, 2019

Purple redbud blossoms blew against my boots. I stood looking at
them in the warm grass-scented breeze and at the broken glass on
my driveway and the smashed headlights and the four flat tires on
my car, the giant yellow Easter egg wedged into the back seat. It was
filled with pictures, dead American soldiers, gay weddings, endless
crosses in military cemeteries. I got a broom from a peg in the hallway and swept up the glass and some of the blossoms and threw
them all out, the egg and the pictures too, and, inside again, I called
to have the car towed and canceled the morning appointments and
put my hands under cold running water to force the adrenaline out.
I didn't know if it would work, but I had to try. I drew.

At the bus stop, a gangly carrottop in his twenties stood too close
to me. He smelled like the rankest weed yet had a cross shaved into
the hair above his ear. He didn't get on the bus and I forgot about
him when I noticed a striking blonde woman sitting two rows up,
with the smallest, most regular features. As we rode, I sketched
her face and her arms after she pushed up her sleeves to reveal a
series of black tattoos circling her wrist that at first I mistook for
cigarette burns.

She was on the bus on the way back with groceries as well, greens
jutting from the top of her bag. She didn't get off at my stop so I
chalked it up to coincidence, but when the gangly guy was there
again, now wearing a camo vest, and followed my route home, I
knew it wasn't. I sat up all night but no one came.

The next day she took the booth behind me for lunch. Tag-team
hoaxers, I thought, or Fenchwood aficionados, and when she

sat three rows down from me at the movies that evening I'd had enough. Miss, I said, and approached her.

She stood and said, The Lord is my witness, I've told you I don't want to see you anymore. If you don't leave right now, I'll call the police. She tugged at the silver cross around her throat in a convincing display of nerves and people looked up at us like a tableau. After a stunned few seconds, two men rose to stand between us.

Go ahead, I said, thinking to call her bluff as the bearded one pushed me back, stubby hands on my chest, but when she dialed her phone, I left, knowing how it would look. She'd say she'd been at the diner and on the bus first and now I'd followed her to the movies, and if they leafed through my sketchbook, they'd see her.

At the apartment, I called Nash, but when I told him I'd thrown away the Easter egg and its contents and the mental health checklist and the box with the coffin, he told me there wasn't much they could do. You didn't see what happened to your headlights, he said. No fingerprints, no proof, and it would be hard to track her down. Almost all of these come right up to the line but don't cross it.

I popped Bubble Wrap with my X-Acto knife. What about the damaged mock-up? I asked, and drew the knife across my wrist. A red line but no blood.

Sure. If you could prove someone else did it, and not you on a bender. When I didn't respond, he said, If something else shows up at your apartment, or in your car, or your car is damaged again, call me right away. And don't throw anything out.

I housed the blade and said, Heard from May? What's she doing in Oklahoma?

He hadn't heard from her. He didn't even know she was gone.

Letters

Why are you lying about a boy who'd never lived?

I didn't bring the letters back to my apartment anymore, a vague feeling about them and where I lived and karma. I read this one sitting on a wooden bench with a copper dedication plate in a small park across from the library, where the daffs were out and had been out for a while. Drooping now, the color of old butter.

My thighs grew hot in my paint-splotched khakis. The jays in the serviceberries and the cardinals in the redbuds squawked about territories until a jay dropped from a branch and swooped at the cardinals before tilting his wings and swerving back to his own, where he called and preened on the trembling branch.

This letter included a picture of Liam's grave in Vermont. The daffs were up in front of it too. Farther north, they were a fresher color, the color of daisies.

The library doors slid open and an old couple walked out, holding hands. The man held a DVD and they seemed in no hurry to get home. *What might have been,* I thought, and breathed in the scent of skunk cabbage down by the brook and looked at the picture that came with the letter. Scrawled across it in red ink were the words: *Empty Grave!!!* It was, though no hoaxers knew that. We'd figured that, sooner or later, they'd move on from attacking us to attacking him, and had set up a false target for them. At least it hadn't yet been vandalized. Latrell's had, and for a week Lamont had kept watch among the resiny poplars behind a nearby crypt, waiting for the vandals to return. I never asked, but I assumed he'd brought his gun. Perhaps I would too, if they knocked down Liam's gravestone. I studied my pale hand, imagined my fingers curling around the grip of one.

The Valley of the Sun

JUNE 13, 2019

May had crossed Oklahoma to get to Phoenix, though I had no idea why. She broke her leg in the accident and had a gun and was in such a state when they arrested her that she was in the hospital for a few days. I used the voucher from the canceled Atlanta trip to buy a plane ticket and finished up work in the intervening hours.

My morning doodling had splotches of color and shade, a seated figure, the barest outlines of someone walking, a circle for the head and four small ovals for hands and feet, slashing lines to connect them and indicate movement. But mostly circles, nearly all the same size, one after the other after the other, next to one another and ranked one behind the other in rows, as if they were sitting in an auditorium. I counted fifty-three; it couldn't be accidental.

I put my pencil down and listened, to passing cars and a pedestrian, to the tapping of her shoes on the pavement, to her low murmuring voice as she talked on her phone, to the distant buzz of a lawnmower. The smell of manure drifted through the window, the smell of renewal.

It was time, long past time really, so I pulled out a calligraphy pen and began to write.

Dear Mrs. Letts,

I hope this letter will be neither too painful nor too much of an affront. Years ago, in the aftermath of the shooting, you wrote May and I a heartfelt letter, expressing profound sorrow and shock. I never asked, but I imagine it was one of over fifty such letters you felt you had to write in the midst of your own loss, which was no less considerable, and compounded by what must have been horror. Horror and guilt and misery, because your son was gone too and yet had been the cause of horror for so many others, so many of us.

I could not bring myself to write you then, and only recently sent you a cruel painting by way of recompense. The reasons for that are immaterial. As a mother who lost a son, as a person who expressed remorse, as someone in pain who reached out to others in pain and did so with grace and honesty, you deserved better. I am profoundly sorry I added to your pain and hope that, someday, you will find your way to forgive me, and to forgive so much of the world that has shunned you.

I read it over and put it aside and got back to the work at hand, the logos for Cora and Henry's latest gourmet offering, a triple-cream cheese, young and full of moisture. Three hours of solid work, penciling in the underdrawing, gestural lines, blocks, cylinders, wedges, my fingers tired from the overhand grip, then a dip pen with black India ink.

When I was done, I fixed myself a ham and Swiss sandwich, sawing off the stale first few inches of a baguette from Silver's, and read the letter again as I ate. Imperfect, but passable. I pressed my thumb to the breadcrumbs sprinkling the paper and told myself I'd done enough edits and rewrites. Of Cora and Henry's presentation, of the letter. There were other things I had to attend to, so I packed.

Letters

I found Otto's "birth certificate" online. Note how it doesn't match other state forms, here, here, and here. You say your kid died? Prove it. Exhume him. Let me film the entire process. If it's real, let us see his rotting corpse. The world will listen to me, because, unlike you, I'm not a fucking liar.

Interim 13

Number of school shootings in the three years since: & etc.
Number of school children killed: & etc.

Phoenix

JUNE 14, 2019

I walked into the hospital through the yellow light and blue shade cast by the late-blooming palo verde trees and tucked my book under my arm as the cool air rushed out of the automatic doors and blew bunches of the dropped yellow flowers toward me. The plate glass windows were dusty from the wind.

Nash sat in the waiting room, yellow petals stuck to the sole of one boot. I thought of telling him but I liked the splash of color and thought May might too. I was glad he was there for her, though jealous he'd been called first. Across the street a swing hung from the big sign advertising a country-and-western bar and a woman sat on it, waving to passing traffic as she swung back and forth. It was 104 degrees, but she was dressed in an old-fashioned frock and a bonnet, big petticoats under the full-length black skirt showing every time she swung her legs up. Nash watched her.

I ignored my ringing phone and stood over him and said, No, don't get up.

I wasn't going to, Nash said. He looked up and didn't smile. He had one ankle over the other knee and his polished boot began to bounce.

I thought, *Irritated, are we?* but said, Yeah, I figured. You talk to her yet?

No. That's why I still have these. He held up a bouquet of pink tulips.

I didn't tell him he had the wrong color; better he learn firsthand. I got a question for you, I said. You're teaching May about guns, right? I thought you were supposed to travel with them unloaded.

His boot stilled but he didn't answer, which I liked. He'd have had to denigrate her if he did, which was why I'd asked him, to see if he'd protect her. He'd lied to her, after all, and I wanted to see if he'd come through. He had, so my tone for the next question was a little softer. She didn't get to Kate, did she?

Not even close. The address she had was all wrong. He tapped his phone with three fingers. But I talked to the locals. Kate's real. She was only in it for the money. Not a true hoaxer. She doesn't know any of the people who came after you guys.

You believe her?

Nash shrugged. Didn't see the evidence myself, but they're pretty sure of it. Phone records, computers. For what it's worth, she feels bad about it. That's why she stopped, she said. A couple years ago. She's going back to school for something else.

For what? I said, my desire to confront her flaring.

He lowered his boot to the floor and shifted forward on the squeaky vinyl seat. You don't need to know, Otto. Just let it go. If not for you, then at least for May.

I stood nodding. He was right. I hoped he believed me when I said I would. I asked, Are they saying it's just family? Who can go see May?

Yeah. He switched the flowers from one hand to the other. I liked that his shirt looked freshly pressed. They don't want her upset.

I'll tell them you're my brother.

Ha. I'm a little too dark for them to believe it. Plus, the different last name.

I shrugged and turned away, toward May's room. She'd like the pressed shirt too. Over my shoulder, I said, How do they know what my mother ever got up to?

My phone rang again as I headed down the bright hallway through squares of warm sunlight past framed pictures of blooming cactuses. I put it on vibrate.

Letters

This morning I woke in fear, to bells tolling the hour. Dark still, and for a few seconds I had no idea where I was, and the bells seemed to toll for me, alerting the world to my passing. I felt a bitter solitude.

Later, parsing my hubris—as if the world waited hourly to learn of my fate!—I realized that, in the midst of my fear and loneliness, I'd thought of you. How, as your dear Liam's journey neared its end, you must have been afraid. For him and his approaching death, for your coming desolation.

After his death, perhaps other emotions took over. Anger, doubt, fear of other losses, the desire for revenge. Since in all your interviews, I've been struck by your kindness, probably a surge of compassion for the parents of other children at Liam's school. No doubt those emotions still swirl through your mind, through your days and life.

Two years ago, several sisters and I traveled to China. Often we were served tea, in the smallest cups. In truth my hands are so large they looked like thimbles. Embarrassing, at first, until I passed through my vanity. Then I was able to note that the cups were never allowed to be empty. Whoever served us, served us attentively. Every few sips, the cups were quietly but assiduously refilled.

An apt metaphor for God's love and compassion. Always present, always being refilled, but often unnoticed, distracted as we are by other emotions— vanity, grief, anger. Few of us have felt most of them as deeply as you. But even in the face of that, I maintain that God is there. Even when it seems He's vanished, He hasn't.

As my own journey nears an end, and as I wake some days in darkness and fear, I remind myself of that, and, newly calmed, awaiting the coming of the light, I am able to fully hear the beauty of the bells, to bask in it. No matter for whom, or what, they toll.

My Only Swerving

My phone vibrated again and I took it from my pocket. The fifth call from Lamont in an hour; this one I answered. High school graduation today! he said, his voice crackling with anger. Know what high school valedictorian Jayden Boone did?

I stopped by a window and held the phone away from my ear. Outside in a schoolyard kids were playing and yelling behind a brick wall, with joyous, indistinct voices. Springtime, green things growing. I breathed on the glass to fog it over.

Jayden read the names of every member of the class who graduated, Lamont said. And the names of every member of the class who didn't. Three suicides, two car accidents, one late-night illness. And the shooter! He said his name! *Tracy Letts.*

Everybody processes trauma differently, I said. He's a kid.

I don't care if he's a kid. Someone's got to cancel this.

I wiped the glass clean. Three black cats sat poised on the brick wall, as still as owls. I didn't remember them being there. I said, Brother. You have to let it go.

Oh no I don't, he said. I'm not tapping out on this one.

I knew he wouldn't. Lamont, I said. He's just a boy. Let him take his path.

A boy all lined up for a lesson. His voice trembled with anguish.

I thought long and hard. I was in a hospital, for fuck's sake. I could go back to the waiting room and tell Nash, who would make some calls, someone to stop Lamont, however briefly. But Nash was here for May, and she needed that. And however long a stay Nash might arrange for Lamont, once he was done with it, he'd start up again. Anger and revenge were bound around his neck and written on the tablet of his heart. I could alter his trajectory, but I couldn't stop it.

I closed my eyes and rested my forehead on the warm glass and listened to Lamont's breathing. He was waiting for me to guide him in somehow from the dark, only he wouldn't be guided home anymore; I could hang out all the lanterns I wanted but he was too far gone, all his navigating in the past. He'd found true north.

I'd been close to that. May too, it seemed. An armed torpedo that needed a new target for its tender mercies. The high school kid couldn't be it, even Lamont knew that, which was why he called me. But what? Or where? Or really, who?

I could think of only one name. Was it a gift I was giving Lamont, or a prison sentence? Maybe I was fooling myself and I only wanted him to do what I couldn't do myself, just another white guy getting a Black man to do his dirty work. Well, if it saved a kid, I could live with that, and I suspected Lamont could too. Our twined paths; that was why he'd called. He was probably thinking Kate, but Kate was off the table, so I'd give him something better, and then it was his choice to become the hawk-god or not. Perhaps steering his path to an adult was the path that I was being shown. I opened my eyes and said the name Dexter Fenchwood and my skin tingled.

Who's that? Lamont asked.

Hold on, I said, and thumbed through my contacts. I'll send you the link.

Good, he said. No peace for the wicked.

After, I felt like a god, the god Lamont had told me long ago I'd become, deciding who someone might go after, and wondered if that had once driven Kate. But my deceitful heart wasn't happy with its new power, even if it meant Lamont might now emerge a free man from the sea into which he'd passed a slave.

Fevered and Fretful, Lord Knows
I'd Like to Smile

May's pale face against the sheets, haggard and remote, heartsick with hope deferred; there's a reason we all hate hospitals. I rapped the pure white cast on her leg with my knuckles. How'd you know Kate was in Phoenix? I asked.

Wasn't me, May said, and tried to scratch her cheek, but the wrist shackle stopped her short. I scratched it for her. Zhao did it, she said. Much better with computers than me. Some program that clarifies pictures. And he owed me.

For what?

Doesn't matter. She waved her fingers dismissively, the shackle clacking. Remember the video where she's supposed to be a US attorney? He lifted a name from the diploma and captured a jewelry store receipt for a necklace. With those two things, I tracked her down. I didn't get to see her yet, but I will. After I get out.

I thought of Liam, long ago, violent and restrained, and bent and kissed her warm forehead, smoothed back her tangled hair. Don't you realize? I said. The person we wanted to get? The person we wanted to kill? It was never Kate.

If it wasn't, I drove all the way out here for nothing.

You got charged, I said. Transporting a loaded weapon across state lines, bringing a firearm to within one hundred yards of a government building. The person we were after died long before our son did. The day Liam was shot. Tracy Letts.

She turned her face to the window, to the woman on her swing. Back and forth in the blistering heat, skirt lifting and petticoats flying. Don't, May said. His name should never be spoken. He should be erased from the world, a blank space.

I'd stood outside near the swinging woman, smelling BBQ cooked on mesquite, appalled at the heat. *I'd rent out Arizona and live in hell*, I'd thought. But it felt good to be alive, to breathe the heat and scent of BBQ into my lungs, to study light and shadow on the adobe, to watch the yellow palo verde flowers tumble in the wind, looking like gleeful children released from school as they swirled past me.

May, I said. He set things in motion that no one can control now. Kate wasn't the head of some group, just a figurehead for a belief. You'll never kill that.

A belief in what? That we're evil, fake-mourning a son who never existed?

A belief that the government lies. And it did, again, about that first visit. Little nuggets like that are all the hoaxers need. She didn't respond, and I understood; I'd just hung Nash out to dry. Hey, I said. Nash was just following orders. And he's here. Ready to take his lumps. That's something, May. Not a lot of people face up to things.

We fell quiet. A plane flew overhead, two doctors were called on the hospital intercom, an ambulance drew closer, siren wailing. I hadn't pierced her armor.

Enough with the killing and the death, I said. What's it given you? Given us?

Something to look forward to, she said. Revenge.

You can come back from this, May. And I'm not the only one who thinks that.

Liam's not here, she said, turning her gaze back on me. Those same beautiful blue eyes as his. He's gone, she said.

Yes. Three years now. But not Nash. He's here. He's right outside.

Her eyes were still flat; Nash wouldn't be enough, so I turned manipulative. What would Liam think of you driving cross-country to kill someone?

Don't say that, she said. You can't even be in the same house with him. You don't get to use him against me.

I can't be in the same house with his ashes, May. You should let those go too.

She didn't say anything, but tears rolled down her cheeks, and I knew I'd hit home. I felt her anger beginning to slip, a turning tide. Love was left, and a little hope, but those probably wouldn't be enough, since she'd always warmed to a tangible goal. I'd given Lamont one, and I needed to give her one too, something with a bit of astringency. I said, If you can't forgive Kate, you can at least give her food and water.

Why would I do that?

I held up Evelyn's ragged green New Testament and quoted Proverbs 25.

If your enemy is hungry, give him food to eat; if he is thirsty, give him water. In doing this, you will heap burning coals on his head, and the LORD will reward you.

It might work, it might be just the thing, I said. Or get Zhao to start a listserv. People to write the hoaxers. Over and over. Give out their addresses, make them afraid too. See how they like feeling the waters rise around them.

I saw a flicker of determination. It was enough, I knew, and opened my book and pulled out the letter I'd written, unsure I'd be able to control my voice, that I could say what I needed to. I gave both to her and waited while she read the letter.

Dear May,

Our boy died, that's the main thing, but it's not the only thing. No, Liam lived too and that's what gives meaning to his life; not death. And this is his book. Our book, his and mine. And now ours.

In the end, it's a love story, as all ghost stories are.

May ran her hand over the book cover; it was no longer just an erasure book.

I love this drawing, she said, Liam's red tulip visible beneath her spread fingers. Goosebumps rose on my arms as her fingertips traced the flower.

Departures and Arrivals

Back in the waiting room, Nash peeled flowers from his boot and dropped them in a yellow pile on the blue chair beside him and asked where I was headed.

To the airport, I guess. You'll be more help navigating what's to come than I am. But you've got my number. Call if you need anything.

I caught his look. I'm not abandoning her, I said. I've already arranged for a good lawyer, and from what she says, May'll be out within twenty-four hours of arraignment. Then she'll want to go home. You should take her. You're the one she called.

Okay, he said, and nodded. And what about you? Back home? Work?

Work in a bit, I shrugged. There's someone I want to see.

Not the hoaxers, I hope. Wasn't tuning up one enough for you?

It had been, I saw, and that he'd known all along. I thought of how, on the plane ride out, something had shifted in me, a pinprick in the balloon of my hatred, how it had drained away mile by mile, though really it had begun to leak out after following not-Kate in the grocery store. Earlier, even, post-Vermont, and even earlier than that, with Hardy Starling. There was no real satisfaction in hurting others. Balm for the soul came from other sources, at least for me. Perhaps for Lamont it would be different.

I was the cop in the post office parking lot now on the anniversary, looking at me in my car as I hoarded my anger, swollen with it, understanding it would do me no good, understanding too that I'd have to learn that on my own. He'd been so much wiser than me, or perhaps simply farther down the long sorrowful road we all have to travel, toward some sort of final understanding or conflagration.

Lamont was headed toward the latter, but I realized I no longer was; you see yourself more clearly sometimes because of what happens to others. Kate was out there and always would be, her or someone like her who would take her place. I could find her and all who followed her and it wouldn't change a thing. Hoping to stop the hoaxers by getting Kate would be useless, like trying to strangle ink.

No, not the hoaxers, I said to Nash. I'm done with that. Someone else. Someone good.

You got someone special? He slapped his boot. That's good. I hadn't heard.

I don't know, I said. Maybe. She told me her middle finger got a boner every time she thought of me.

Ouch, he said, but smiled. That smile. No wonder May fell for him.

Yeah, I said. But I deserved it. Maybe I can make it up to her.

I stuck out my hand and he held his up, sticky from the flowers, and stood and hugged me wordlessly until I turned and left. I would go see Palmer and I would tell her the truth, all of it, let her review my past, and then I'd listen, for however long she wanted to talk or yell or give me the silent treatment, and in that way we would argue the past together. Even a small chance was worth it. If nothing else, I might find out about that malfunctioning middle finger in person. Better to do these things face to face, to do everything face to face, than to communicate online.

That's part of Liam's gift too.

Liam chose Yes no Yes no Yes no
Yes no Yes and Yes and Yes

The Lazarus Taxon

JUNE 21, 2019

In the end, I stand on Palmer's doorstep, hands loaded with flowers and a bag of dusty stones and a container of potato garlic soup I've made for her, sunlight and shadow streaming down her hallway as she holds the door open, my long shadow and all I carry with me, Liam and those who pursued me, the name I'd given Lamont, all of it. She has to know. She will.

And about the beautiful names of the streets I'd seen in Arizona, the ones I liked because they recorded its history, a history I didn't know but found myself curious about. Pecan Road and La Brezza and Alhambra Square, Peters View and Fruitland Acres. *You could live here,* I'd thought. The new New World. They had guns there too but they had them everywhere, and so I would make my way forward as I could. If moving around hadn't helped with moving on, maybe moving away would.

And after I tell her? We'll see what happens, if I'll be allowed to rest a little, or a little longer, and by myself or in company. It's worth a chance. She has postcards from Arizona on her fridge: *I love the desert most of all,* and the Thoreau quote about fishing stuck to her toaster, and tucked in my pocket is the brochure I picked up at the airport. *Fish Arizona!* Perhaps we would. That fishing creel on her wall.

Come in, she says, and stands aside. She touches my arm as I brush past, striding toward my shadow stretching down her hallway, until I stop so fast she bumps into me. That scent? I say. From the kitchen? Lemon scones?

Yes, she says, and as I walk again she steps beside me and slips her small warm hand into mine.

ACKNOWLEDGMENTS

Jeff Skinner read an early draft of *Otto and Liam* and made wise, crucial and transformational suggestions. Nicole Aragi read it next, and once again showed that her peerless agenting skills are matched by her keen editorial eye. Once I'd thoroughly revised it yet again, Ryan Ridge and Chris Fox told me it wasn't yet done and pointed out ways to sharpen it. Sometimes, small changes bring big results.

Cassidy Meurer's art was a source of wonder and pleasure, shimmering work that captured the story at decisive points and inspired it at others; I can't thank or compliment her enough. Laura Hill's art arrived at the perfect time, and sent me back to create and revise.

The people at Sarabande are uniformly superb. Sarah Gorham, whose unflagging enthusiasm and support were paired with precise, insightful and illuminating editorial suggestions—at every turn, she was right; Danika Isdahl, who has overseen its incredibly smooth production (even in these peculiar times); Joanna Englert, ready to advocate for the book from the start, and her thoughtful, necessarily improvisational approach to doing so in the midst of a pandemic; and Kristen Miller, who helps keep the ship together. Near the end, Emma Aprile provided her usual meticulous exactitude as a copy editor, and Alban Fischer came along with his powerful cover. To all of you, many, many thanks.

I have been lucky throughout this process; I wish all writers could have the same experience. Along those lines, I'd like to thank Aspen Words and the Catto Shaw Foundation. Their generosity and hospitality were unparalleled, and I wrote part of this manuscript while an Aspen Words Writer in Residence.

PAUL GRINER is the author of the novels *Collectors*, *The German Woman*, and *Second Life*, and the story collections *Follow Me* (a Barnes & Noble Discover Great New Writers choice) and *Hurry Please I Want to Know* (winner of the Kentucky Literary Award). He teaches writing and literature at the University of Louisville.

SARABANDE BOOKS is a nonprofit literary press located in Louisville, KY. Founded in 1994 to champion poetry, short fiction, and essay, we are committed to creating lasting editions that honor exceptional writing. For more information, please visit sarabandebooks.org.